A Dangerous Dance

Other Five Star Titles
by Pauline Baird Jones:

Byte Me
The Last Enemy
Missing You
The Spy Who Kissed Me

A Dangerous Dance

Pauline Baird Jones

Five Star • Waterville, Maine

First Edition
First Printing: August 2004

Set in 11 pt. Plantin by Carleen Stearns.

Printed in the United States on permanent paper.

Library of Congress Cataloging-in-Publication Data

Jones, Pauline Baird.
    A dangerous dance / by Pauline Baird Jones.—1st ed.
        p. cm.
    "Five Star first edition titles"—T.p. verso.
    ISBN 1-59414-098-7 (hc : alk. paper)
    1. Governors—Election—Fiction.   2. Politicians' spouses—Fiction.   3. Fathers—Death—Fiction.
    4. Assassination—Fiction.   5. Politicians—Fiction.
    6. Louisiana—Fiction.   I. Title.
    PS3560.O52415D36 2004
    813'.54—dc22   2003065571

To my girls
Elizabeth, for her wonderful cover art
Jessica, for being my first reader

And to Nathan, a wonderful son and a great cook

And a special thank-you to Marilyn and David Taylor for support above and beyond

And always to my husband, Greg, who sticks with me through thick and thin

... ...

Chapter One

Remy Mistral was watching for the opening and still he almost missed it. Out of the corner of his eye he caught the impression of a break in the dense foliage on his left and hit the brakes. There was no one behind—and hadn't been for the past half-hour of driving—so he backed the sleek gray Mercedes, and then turned into the even narrower side road with a swaying lurch as his car's suspension tried to adjust to the sudden downgrade in conditions. Two car-lengths along, he found his way barred by a vine-covered gate.

A push of a button silently lowered the tinted window. He rested his arm on the frame as warm, thick air rolled in carrying the pungent scent of growing things. With one finger he pushed his sunglasses down, the better to pierce the green and yellow shadows and vines that prevented him from finding a pattern in the ornate gates' grillwork.

Remy shifted to park and pushed open the door, letting more humid air rush in and overpower his car's air conditioning. He slid out and stretched—it had been a long ride from New Orleans—then slipped off the jacket of his gray Armani suit and draped it carefully over the seat back. Only then did he approach the gate.

A thick layer of vines clung to the gate, and on either side, a fence marched into shadow in an unyielding line. Remy tugged at the vines at the center of the gate, until he could see the pale, yellow gleam that marked the road through a line of oak and cypress trees dripping with the gray ghosts of Spanish moss. A few more tugs and he found

7

and traced the letters scrolled into metal.

Oz.

The estate had been named to remind Magus Merlinn of the years he spent in Australia, and perhaps the Wizard designation had grown from that. It certainly wasn't because Magus had Klan associations. It wasn't even clear if he'd been given the title or taken it. What was certain, he'd been a wizard at creating success out of nothing. Ten years ago, he'd turned his attention to the governor's mansion, with a run for the White House to follow, but a bullet had stopped the legend. Yesterday, a homemade knife in a prison yard had stopped the Wizard's killer.

Was it a coincidence that rumors of a revival in Oz had started sometime before yesterday, though no one could quite say when or where they started? All Remy knew for sure was that in the good old boy taverns of power, rumors about Dorothy's return bearing the Wizard's standard had started to circulate as the first candidates hopeful of replacing the sitting governor started testing the waters. What no one seemed to know was who she intended bestowing that standard on—or if she planned to carry it herself.

Remy rarely did a straight news story anymore, but politics were king on his talk radio show and a scoop on Dorothy's plans wouldn't hurt his ratings any—or at least, that's what he'd told himself during the drive to Oz. The crazy plan he kept pushed to the back of his head as he looked at the firmly barred gate. It looked like it hadn't moved since the Wizard last passed through it in a fancy wooden box. Remy had to wonder about the reliability of his source.

He gave the gate a shake, then stepped back. Was it locked or rusted shut? He had some WD-40 in his trunk, if rust were the problem. He checked the closure, but found no chains or padlocks holding it in place and, despite the wads of plant crap on the gate itself, there was adequate clearance between gate and ground.

"Damn." He shook it again, but couldn't tell what the obstruction was. Unless a tornado miraculously appeared and lifted him over it, Oz was going to be tougher to crack than he expected—if Dorothy was even there—

Before he could finish the thought, a shrill shriek broke the silence as the gate pulled from his hold and began to ponderously swing open, exposing the road. Weed-choked and broken in spots, but still clearly yellow, and clearly brick, leading to the heart of Magus Merlinn's lost Oz.

"I'll be damned." With a last, wary look around, Remy slid behind the wheel of his car, engaged the gears and pulled through. Behind him, the gate closed with an ominous clang.

"Death, taxes—and Remy Mistral. I told you he'd come." Dorothy Morgana Merlinn watched the car pass from the camera's view, then looked down at Titus, working the security monitors. "Can I see him again?"

In a few moments, he had one monitor showing a replay of Remy at the gate, even as the monitor next to it showed his car moving carefully along the road toward the house.

Titus leaned back in the chair and looked up at her. He was a small, lethal man with light brown hair and cool eyes. Only once had he failed his primary task as bodyguard. Dorothy didn't blame him for what happened, but she knew he blamed himself. "How did you know that ill wind would come?"

She smiled. "A mistral is a cold wind, not an ill wind."

Though when she looked at the close-up, freeze-framed face in the monitor, it wasn't cold she felt. Titus fine-tuned the picture until the broad, high forehead, ending in strongly marked brows as dark as his hair, came into sharp focus. His eyes were dark, too, and deep set, perfect for brooding or piercing other people's secrets—or unlocking female hearts. His nose was straight and almost elegant above a full mouth and firm chin. No, it wasn't cold, but heat she hadn't meant to feel. She couldn't afford the luxury, not if she wanted to lay Magus's ghost to rest and reclaim her life.

Titus blew out a sigh filled with frustration. "I wish I knew what you were up to."

He looked up, his gaze sharpening as he tried to bore through her eyes into that place where her thoughts and desires simmered. She turned to more fully accommodate him. If she could deflect him—

His mouth twisted wryly. "That's the first time you ever looked like him."

He didn't sound pleased, but she smiled as she felt power push back the unwelcome heat, or maybe it mixed with it, turning it into something stronger than each was alone. If Mistral wasn't cold, she would be, until all Louisiana felt it and knew the truth of what happened ten years ago.

She stood up and reached for the door, two steps away. "Good. I don't want anyone to doubt I'm his heir this time."

His eyes flashed with remembered pain. "Just . . . be careful, chere."

She looked away from him. "I'm always careful. We won't fail this time."

"He doesn't have a snowball's chance in hell of even making it through the primaries. He's made too many enemies."

"Which is why he's driving his lovely car up our miser-

10

able yellow brick road right now—probably cursing us and himself every inch of it. Ambition's a bitch."

"But not as dangerous as revenge, chere."

"I don't want revenge. I want justice." She pulled the door open.

"Justice." He shook his head. "That's even more dangerous. And dang near impossible to get."

She smiled at him. "Why, sometimes I've believed as many as six impossible things," she quoted lightly, before she stepped out, letting the door swing gently shut behind her. She started across the weed-choked yard, her gaze sweeping for fire anthills. Even after ten years away, there was so much she remembered, but what she remembered the most right now was her first—and last—meeting with Remy Mistral.

Then, like now, change was in the air with an electorate primed for reform and longing for a candidate with a touch of magic to believe in. Enter Magus Merlinn aka the Wizard, whose magic touch had transformed several failing Louisiana businesses into jobs for voters. He'd been convinced the same magic could transform the state's unwieldy bureaucracy into something more responsible and responsive to the failing economy. Magus had the gift of engaging people, not just in his ideas, but in him—and his only daughter was no exception. She smiled, remembering the surly eighteen-year-old she'd been when she first met her father, angry about the years he'd been missing from her life, still grieving for her mom. Right away he'd made it clear he didn't take guilt trips. She could take what he was offering or not. Her choice. Or so it had seemed. When Magus smiled, the choices always narrowed to what he wanted. And thank goodness for it or she'd have missed her short time with him.

Unfortunately, her youth had made her ill-prepared for the bumps and jolts of politics, the hordes of media types howling around the hot campaign—or the bullets that stopped Magus's drive for the mansion.

As she always did when Magus filled her thoughts, she touched the place on her chest where a bullet had passed through Magus and hit her. Like the fictional Dorothy, there were risks in hanging with a wizard.

Which brought her full circle to Remy Mistral, who'd been part of that media frenzy back then. She remembered hearing one of Magus's aides commenting that he wouldn't be in the pack long. Even as green as she'd been, she could tell he had a breakout personality. To her young eyes, he'd seemed lit from within and vibrantly real in a mass of mostly plastic people.

She'd never expected him to notice her. Even if she hadn't been plain and colorless, who could see anyone but the magnificent Magus? But he had noticed her, his dark eyes finding her in Magus's shadow for a heady, disturbing moment. Then he'd dismissed her with casual and complete indifference.

It stung then, and it still did, she had to admit. It was hard to acknowledge to herself the crush she'd had on him, but she'd come here to face *all* her demons. Maybe it wouldn't have mattered so much if Magus hadn't been killed so soon after. Like circling buzzards over dead meat, Mistral had blown through her life and intruded on her grief. His final, punctuating comment had been to dismiss her again, as a person and to question whether she was Magus's daughter and could take over his legacy. His contempt had been the bookends of her father's death—and the frame, or maybe it was the lens, through which she viewed that terrible time.

What, she wondered, had changed his focus and kept him in Louisiana? Everyone had been so sure it was only a matter of time before a national news outlet picked him up. Instead, he'd moved into talk radio.

And now here he was, looking for her, finally curious about the Wizard's daughter. Once again, she felt that tug of uncertainty. She'd managed her father's affairs, despite of and over the objections of the naysayers, always with Mistral's words stinging in her ears. Time had wrought its changes on them both, and now fate had returned them full circle to where they'd started.

The sitting governor was almost at the end of his two terms, leaving the field once more wide open. Even better, the voters' passion for reform had not abated and there was a definite anti-incumbent feeling simmering beneath a lot of surfaces, if the New Orleans mayoral race was any indication. And with the desire for reform, came the desire for the return of a Wizard, according to the letters she'd received. The power, his power was still there, waiting to be harnessed anew. Some of Magus's old cronies looked to be making their move on his legacy. It was now or never.

She wasn't the Wizard—the long years in exile had taught her that again and again—but she was his daughter, with the inalienable right to bestow his power where she wished. They'd find it out soon enough.

As for Remy Mistral, that he'd once been contemptuous of her probably wasn't a good reason for setting him up. But it was a reason.

Remy stopped in front of the plantation house and shut off his engine. The sudden silence resolved itself into the barely perceptible shrill of a thousand-and-one-insect chorus beneath the green cathedral that pressed in around

13

the house, the rustle of larger life in the underbrush, and the fleeting trill and flutter of birds.

Remy opened the door, the creak of the metal a welcome imposition in the reverential hush. The Wizard's wake was long over. It was time his ghost realized that. He slammed the door, then turned to study Magus Merlinn's Oz.

At least he'd resisted the obvious green. To Remy's surprise, it was a smaller, far less pretentious version of the plantation houses one usually expected. It had been built in an era when homes were more serviceable and still likely to be flooded by the nearby Mississippi River. The line of columns marching sternly down the front veranda only hinted at grandeur to come and the peaked roof boasted a mere three gables. The raised veranda that circled the house, left visible the enclosure of the ground level, a modification possible only after the river had been tamed. A plain rectangle of a house with nature as its main adornment didn't seem right for the man Remy had known as the Wizard.

"Not exactly the Emerald Palace, is it?"

He looked, and quickly found the owner of the voice echoing his thoughts so perfectly. She was standing in the shadow of a towering oak tree, much like she'd stood in Magus's shadow back then. She lifted the baseball cap from her head, ruffled her titian hair into a fluffy halo around the thin oval of her face, then replaced it with the brim toward the back as she strolled toward him.

It took a few moments for Remy's brain to grapple with the differences between what he vaguely remembered about the Wizard's Dorothy—which wasn't that much—and what she'd become.

She seemed taller and was as thin as he remembered, though her figure had filled out more than memory recalled. Time and—he thought cynically—thirty million dollars had produced more assurance. A shorter haircut exposed more of her face, particularly the strength of her pointed chin. Her nose was narrow, well-aligned and dusted with freckles, and she had calm, violet eyes. Her mouth was full and lightly sensual.

She'd never be beautiful, but she had achieved striking. Magus would have been proud, Remy decided, and his enemies will be—surprised. She was graceful in movement, but her body turned vaguely awkward and coltish when not. The yellow sheath sundress she wore suited her disturbingly well when she stopped beside him. The clean scent of her perfume joined the flower-drenched air in assaulting his senses and he felt the jolt of desire in his midsection before he could rein it in.

"No," Remy said, pleased he sounded matter-of-fact. "It's not the Emerald Palace, but I like it."

"Magus liked to tell people he brought here that he was a simple man." Beneath the auburn veil of her lashes, she slanted him a look that might have been ironic.

He laughed, short and sharp. "Right."

Trouble was he could almost hear Magus saying it. He might even have believed he was a simple man. No one really knew what Magus believed. He was too much in motion, the pattern of his face shifting too quickly for analysis—though many had tried since his death, including him. They all agreed he lived and died an unsolvable puzzle.

Her mouth thinned, stretching into a smile that lit her face with a hint of her father's charm.

"I'm glad you weren't completely blinded by his light." She stepped past him, crossing to the wooden steps that led up the veranda. One foot on the first step, she paused, and arched her brows. "Coming?"

The angle of leg and body was sharply pure and a heady enticement in the sultry air—air that made her dress cling to her skin. She was a different kind of dangerous than Magus, but still . . . dangerous. Not that he'd let that stop him.

"Of course." Determined, but casual, Remy followed her up the steps and into the house through wide and tall double doors. He looked around him with interest, but felt his gaze drawn repeatedly toward Dorothy, who was turning out to be as enigmatic as her father. What was going on? Why hadn't she been surprised to see him? What was she thinking?

Dorothy knew he followed, felt his confusion, but didn't look back as she led him through the wide, central hall past elegant salons that opened off either side, past the period antiques that broke the long sweep, to the circular stair spiraling down to an old-fashioned kitchen with a brick floor and a fireplace.

He hesitated in the doorway, his dark eyes wary, until she nodded towards the straight-backed chairs that circled the scrubbed, wooden table. "Grab one of those."

With the warm, yeasty smell of cooking bread filling the air, she took an inventory of the refrigerator's contents, and then looked at him over the open door. "Cold drink or milk?"

"Diet Coke if you have it." The chair scraped briefly on the uneven floor, then creaked as he settled himself on the bare, wooden surface.

She set a cold can down in front of him, feeling the echoes of her pre-Wizard life call to her. She'd spent most of her life without money or a father, waiting tables with her mother and, eventually, when her mother became too ill, by herself. It wasn't until her mother died that Magus appeared in her world.

She turned from Mistral and the memories, opened the top of her bread machine and set about releasing the loaf inside. Behind her, she heard a pop and a hiss as he opened his cold drink. She hacked off a couple of thick slices as fragrant steam rose around her, piled them on a plate and set it in front of him.

"Help yourself." She pushed the pale yellow stick of butter and a knife toward him and she saw a brief, quickly hidden flicker of confusion in his eyes. Yes, she'd been right to bring him here, rather than to one of the elegant, formal rooms upstairs, as they made the first move in their wary dance. She was stronger here, more herself, less Magus. She needed to hang on to who she was if she was to survive this foray into Magus's world.

I'm not the Wizard, she told him with her eyes, *but I'm still dangerous,* and felt a surge of satisfaction at the wariness that lit his eyes again. Like the East's wicked witch, did he finally recognize Dorothy as a force to be reckoned with? If he didn't yet, he soon would, she vowed.

"That was better than the bread my mother never made me," Remy said, wiping his fingers on the towel she tossed him. He took his time, then leaned back in his chair, thrusting his feet out. If she thought standing gave her the power position, it was time to prove her wrong. It was also time to take back control of this strange meeting.

She smiled coolly, her lids drooping sleepily over her startling eyes as she wiped her hands. "I'm glad you liked it, Remy Mistral."

So she did remember him. He'd wondered, and yet how could she not? He'd been around a lot back in the old days, and these days his radio show was inching its way across the South. There was talk of it going into wider syndication—

17

talk that Remy kept a tight rein on while he tested the political waters. Talk was cheap, as some of his listeners were quick to point out. All it changed was minds, not policies. Louisiana was long overdue for a change in policy. Business as usual wasn't working. He wanted to change that.

"I didn't think you'd remember me, you've been gone a long time, Ms.—"

"This is Oz. Call me Dorothy."

"Dorothy." He frowned slightly, not because he minded the theatrical, but because he preferred to initiate it himself. The situation reminded him of one of those old dances, the kind where the couples moved together, then apart in a stylized tease.

She gave him that cool, cutting smile again. "You could call me Anna, if you don't mind messing with the mystique."

That surprised a laugh out of him. "I never mind messing with anyone's mystique."

Their gazes clashed as she pushed away from the counter, pulled out a chair across from him and dropped into it. Chin on her hands, elbows propped on the wooden surface like an inquiring child, she asked, "What brings you to Oz, Remy Mistral?"

He wanted to tell her to call him Remy, but it felt like it would weaken his position for some reason. Instead he straightened, equalizing their positions again. Did she know what she was doing? He couldn't tell by looking into her eyes, but his gut said yes, she knew, in spades. He studied her face for a long moment, letting the silence draw out between them until he could hear the steady tick, then tock of a clock somewhere in the room.

Her gaze didn't falter or her body shift even slightly. One to you, he thought silently. "I was hoping for an interview."

"I'm hardly breaking news."

"Verrol Vance was killed in prison yesterday. That makes you news."

For a second her lashes swept down across her pale cheeks in a fan of auburn silk. When they lifted, her expression was oddly blank. "So I heard."

"You have good contacts. Mine said they were trying to keep it quiet."

She shrugged, without breaking eye contact. "Magus always did."

And she'd kept those contacts up? Or reactivated them? "It's been a long time."

"Yes." She relaxed back in her chair. "Which should make me . . . old news. Or at best, a sound bite—which you could have gotten on the phone."

Remy smiled. "Your number is unlisted—and you haven't been answering it."

Her chin lifted slightly, her answering smile tightened his gut dangerously. "True." She stood up, studying him soberly for a long moment. "So, you're still a reporter and not just a personality."

He stood up, too. "Did you doubt it?"

A short silence. "I . . . wondered."

"You don't have to anymore."

"I guess not." She stared at him, but Remy had the odd impression it wasn't him she saw. He opened his mouth to ask—what? Before he could figure it out, she turned and started for the door.

"It's too late for you to drive back to New Orleans tonight. I'll have a room made up for you." She paused and turned back. "We don't dress for dinner."

It was what he wanted, but getting it didn't feel as good as he thought it would. It was too easy, too . . . something.

"Thank you." She was in motion again, and what a motion it was. Her body was almost liquid, the gentle sway of her hips . . . heady. Made it hard to focus on her words.

"If it's a story you want, not just a sound bite, then you'll want to see it, I suppose."

"It?" He shook his head to clear it. He wasn't here to play sidekick.

"Magus's study." She stopped, turned and gestured toward the stairs.

Remy hesitated, then nodded slowly, as if it didn't matter all that much.

It was only as they wound back up the iron stairway, paced back down the wide hall, that it occurred to him to wonder why she was so willing to accommodate him. His defenses up, his gaze firmly avoiding her hips, he watched her stop in front of tall, narrow doors with big, ornate knobs. She twisted both knobs at once and pulled the doors toward her. Half-turning, she gave him a look that was almost a warning.

"Welcome to the heart of Oz, Remy Mistral. I hope you find what you're looking for."

She looked so ordinary, yet . . . not. She was the gatekeeper to her father's power, but did she know it? She stepped back, with a gesture towards the dim interior, and he felt his awareness of her fade as the magic that had been Magus reached out to draw him into the room. He was only vaguely aware of her crossing the room to the floor-to-ceiling curtains and throwing them back to reveal long, narrow windows, letting in the last, golden rays of evening light.

Above the desk, hung between the long windows, was a portrait of Magus, part in shadow, partly touched with gold. From it, the power radiated, growing stronger with each step he took toward it. It wasn't gone. It hadn't died with him. It lingered here, waiting for the right person to take it and shape it into a weapon of power again.

All he had to do was convince the Wizard's daughter that he was the man to wield it. He looked at her and found her watching him, her face an enigmatic mirror of her father's looking down from the wall.

Chapter Two

"So which do you prefer?"

Dorothy looked at Remy through the lit candles Titus had set on the table between them. They made the shadows on the wall behind him twist and dance, but they also helped to clear the staleness from the air. Opening the house hadn't just been about opening the past. They'd be hiring staff, if her plan worked, but for now, they were keeping things simple.

"Excuse me?" She paused with her fork halfway to her mouth.

"Dorothy or Anna?"

"Oh." She laid the fork down as she considered the question. No one had ever asked it before. "My mother called me Anna."

"And Magus called you Dorothy."

"Yes." She used the fork to push her food from one side of her plate to the other. Who was she? Did she even know? Her mother had kept the secret of her paternity to the end, a fact Dorothy was still trying to forgive her for. She hadn't even known her legal name, had never seen her birth certificate, until Magus showed up to take her to Oz. It was an Anna world, one of making do and trying to make ends meet—and often failing. Her mother had kept her in school, but it hadn't been easy. There'd been days they'd gone to bed hungry. How could her mother let them live like that? How could Magus let them live like that?

Neither one had seen fit to share their story, its beginning or its end.

"I've been Dorothy for the last twelve years," she said, finally. "It works for me." She'd needed it in the beginning, to keep reminding all the people who thought she couldn't handle anything, that she was Magus's heir, in fact and deed. It had consumed her, leaving her little time to think about who she was or what she wanted. In that interesting way life had of bringing a person full circle, she'd solidified her position just in time for the upcoming election. She'd proved to them, and to Magus's ghost, she could do it. That left only one task and then she'd be free to live her own life. Find Magus's killer and put his ghost to rest. Maybe then she'd know who she was and what to call herself.

His ghost wasn't something she could see. Anything less than corporeal wasn't Magus's style. If he couldn't be larger than life, he wouldn't be. That said, she still felt him, especially here, in his Oz. He wasn't at rest and until he was, Dorothy couldn't be, either. She'd have damned both her parents to hell, if she weren't sure they were already there. And if she knew Magus at all, he'd probably already taken over.

"Okay." Remy rounded up his last bite of food and popped it in his mouth, then leaned back with a sigh. "That was good."

"I'm glad you liked it." Unfortunately, she was a little too glad he liked the food she'd prepared, though she'd bet he didn't know that. She'd wondered if she'd remember how to cook, but it had been as if she'd never stopped. Oddly enough, she'd felt satisfaction in the preparation. It had soothed and cleared her thoughts, bringing her to a tiny place of peace that she hadn't even known she needed.

An unfamiliar tension began to build in the silence between them. He wanted to speak, but didn't know how to start. She wanted him to speak, but didn't know how to help him begin without tipping her hand. This had to be his move or he wouldn't play. Remy Mistral would want to lead in this dance . . . or at least think he was.

She slowly pushed her plate back, then lifted her napkin and dabbed at her mouth. She knew he watched her, but kept her gaze down until the tension reached unbearable. Then, and only then, did she slowly raise her lashes and meet his gaze.

White-hot, it seared her briefly, before he reined it in. Despite the muggy heat of the room, she missed it. For that instant, she felt . . . super-charged. And it told her what she needed to know. Remy was hungry, very hungry. She'd felt the same desire in Magus all those years ago. Now how to set it loose?

Remy toyed with his glass, the hand holding the crystal, long-fingered and strong. The urge to break the silence twisted her insides but she refused to give in to it. She couldn't afford to give him even the thinnest edge of the wedge.

He took a drink, lowered the glass, his gaze finding her again, but minus the heat. "Are you going to run for governor?"

She thought about stalling, because now the moment was here, she wasn't sure how it would end. She could almost hear Magus telling her to sit up straight and have some balls. Apparently, he still hadn't noticed they weren't standard equipment on his daughter.

With only instinct to guide her, she pushed back her chair and stood up. "No, I'm not." She'd be as honest with him as she dared. There'd be less to remember. "Shall we repair to the salon? I'm sure Titus has something cold laid on for us there."

She noted his relief before she turned and followed him toward the door.

"Titus? Magus's bodyguard?" There was an edge to his voice, but whether it was disapproval or surprise, she couldn't tell. He stopped at the door to let her pass through first.

"That's right. He's my bodyguard now."

"Is that wise?" he asked, as he walked beside her down the long hall toward the soft glow coming from the salon off to the left.

"I trust him." She could swear she heard the whisper of silks and satins as the past moved out of her way so she could turn into the salon. She bypassed the seating, heading straight for the window. The air was so weighted, so ominous, it was like a weight on her shoulders. The window was slightly open, in hopes of any fugitive breeze that might find them. Insects beat against it, frantic for the light just out of their reach. They reminded her of what it had been like to be in politics.

"Why did you come back?"

His light-footed approach might have surprised her, but the wooden floor creaked and gave her warning. She turned to face him. To get what she wanted, she had to give him something.

"To find out who hired Verrol to kill Magus." She waited a beat. "But you already knew that, didn't you?"

"Knew?" One dark brow arched. "Suspected, but didn't know. I'm a reporter, not a psychic."

Dorothy smiled slowly. "Are you sure about that?"

He looked startled for a moment, and then smiled with real amusement. It suited him dangerously well. She'd

25

heard he had charm, but he'd never bothered to use it on her. There'd been no need. While his face was still lit with humor, she asked, "I hear you're considering a run?"

He froze, before nodding slowly. "I am."

She turned slightly, so she was no longer looking at him. "You'd be good at it. You have passion and that vision thing. Not unlike Magus." She hesitated. "Are you here for my endorsement?"

She looked at him then. He looked thoughtful and a bit wary.

"I didn't think . . ." he began, but stopped.

". . . that I was adult enough not to carry a grudge for your past . . . third-estate excesses? You disappoint me, Remy Mistral."

"Not for the first time, I'm sure," he shot back, his face still closed and suspicious. "Actually, there are more . . . credible candidates, former friends of Magus you could endorse."

"True." Point for him.

"Have they asked?" His tone was casual but his eyes weren't.

She chuckled wryly. "Every year since Magus died."

Remy chuckled with her, but his gaze stayed pointed and hard. "Anyone you particularly like?"

She shrugged. "Magus liked you. I think he even trusted you—as much as he trusted anyone."

"And you still do what he wants?"

His tone challenged her hackles to rise, but she kept them down with an effort. "Within reason." She turned away from him. "Of course, everyone is assuming that my endorsement would mean something after twelve years. Do you think anyone but the politicians remembers Magus? Or cares what his daughter thinks?"

She waited, insides braced. If he wasn't honest with her, she'd stop it now.

He didn't disappoint. "No." He stared at her for a long moment, then said, "But they could be reminded."

"Perhaps." She rubbed a finger down the screen, as she felt her way through the minefield of what they weren't saying. "As a curiosity, maybe even mildly interesting, but a voice of authority? I don't think so."

"No, but momentum could be built. You've managed Magus's holdings, kept some of them in Louisiana making jobs for people here. If you didn't matter, all those old friends wouldn't have tried, now would they?"

"No, I suppose not." She allowed herself to look uncertain. She slanted him a look. "I just assumed they were after the money."

He grinned. "That, too."

He was too dangerously appealing when he grinned. It softened his intensity, without making him any less dangerous. She turned away from him, and from her own vulnerability and sat down in a wing-backed chair that Magus had used to good effect in the past, as she had cause to remember. He'd looked like royalty when he sat here.

After a pause, Remy followed her, eliminating her slight, royal advantage, by dropping down onto a nearby couch. He leaned forward, his intensity hitting her in a wave. She struggled against it, keeping her back erect with an effort.

"Don't you understand how amazing Magus was? Don't you realize that what he built, that what he did and stood for, resonated with people? Getting killed for it made him bigger, not smaller. He was martyred for change, for the hope he gave to ordinary people that government could be honest and real and useful."

"What I remember . . ." Her voice came out stronger

than she'd meant it to and she pulled it back to cool. ". . . is that the father I barely knew was killed in front of me. And the person who planned it has gone on breathing and living and spending time with people he cares about. That's what I remember, Remy Mistral."

Their gazes clashed like cymbals, leaving unseen sparks to fall around them both. Now he knew what she wanted and how bad she wanted. What she didn't know is what he'd do with it.

His gaze narrowed sharply. "Do you . . . know who did it?"

"I have a few ideas, a short list of names," she admitted. "What I don't have is proof." She lowered her lashes, needing a respite from his gaze.

"What you need," Remy said slowly, his voice suddenly soft as silk, "is someone to get in their way—the way Magus did."

She didn't tense, but it wasn't easy, as he stepped in to take the bait she'd prepared for him. When she felt in control, she slowly lifted her lashes. "The thought had occurred to me."

"I thought it might." He held her gaze for a long beat before he said, "I'm willing to be your bait." He spoke slowly, as if he hadn't completely made up his mind, but Dorothy knew he had. She could feel his resolve beating like his heart beneath his impeccable suit, not frantic like the mosquitoes, but definitely insistent.

"For my endorsement and some well-placed contributions to your campaign?"

"The . . . bargain I'd like to propose is a bit more complicated than that."

She let the silence draw out for a moment as she studied him. What could he have in mind? She leaned forward, gesturing to the tall pitcher of lemonade and two crystal glasses on a low table, protected from marring the antique surface by a silver tray. Remy had never been a heavy drinker. His personal discipline was one of the things she'd admired about him.

He hesitated, watching her pour him a glass. As she handed it to him, he said, "Lemonade? You do remember me."

"I'm afraid it's far more sordid and uninteresting than that. Magus kept dossiers on everyone. When I found it, it made me wonder . . ."

"Wonder what?" Remy leaned toward her, quick interest in his face.

"If he felt death coming. He certainly had his affairs in order." More than in order, actually. He'd left detailed instructions for her, enabling her to look almost prescient during that rocky transition from his control of his business to her control. By the time his instructions ran out, she knew what to do.

"Knowing Magus, it wouldn't surprise me," Remy said thoughtfully.

Or he'd planned for her to manage his affairs while he was governor, which made him merely arrogant. Either way, she'd had much cause to feel grateful for his foresight, while feeling like a puppet on strings that led to a grave.

There was a short silence, one that allowed the tension to return and begin to build again. Dorothy sipped her lemonade slowly, enjoying the sour bite and the chill of it as it slid down her throat. More than anything she needed to keep her cool.

She felt him watching her, gathered her defenses and turned her body so that she faced him. She had to fight the urge to fill the silence with something, anything, but what she wanted him to want. Their gazes connected and this time, she realized, he wasn't going to play until she asked. He didn't know that she wanted him to win this one.

"What complicated bargain did you have in mind, Remy Mistral?"

She faced him with her hands clutching the cold glass, her back finishing school straight. She'd never been "finished," but she was a fast study.

He leaned back slightly, his legs thrust out and crossed at the ankles. The folds of his expensive pants fell in perfect lines, as if they obeyed Remy. He was almost too much like Magus.

"There are going to be several candidates claiming Magus's legacy. Your endorsement would help a lot, no question, but . . ."

Where was he going? Dorothy only kept a frown off her face with an effort. "But . . . ?"

"You're Magus's heir."

"But I don't want to run," Dorothy pointed out. "All I can do is endorse—"

"There is another way to confer Magus's power." He stopped, holding her gaze with his for a long moment before saying, "Marriage would."

The glass Dorothy held slipped from her hand, shattering into pieces against the hardwood floor.

Chapter Three

No question that Remy had given Dorothy's dangerous dance some surprising new steps. What startled her was the fact that it didn't seem that alien. Magus would have liked the boldness of it. What surprised her is that she did, too.

She crossed to the antique vanity table and sank onto the padded seat, slowly facing her own gaze in the aged, slightly mottled mirror. Behind her she could see her four-poster bed with its vintage mosquito netting pulled to each side. Everything about the room was to period, though the fabrics were copies, not originals, thank goodness. Vintage was good to a point, that point being when they stopped being comfortable or easy to care for. Probably because of her less-than-vintage upbringing, she thought wryly.

In a distant sort of way, she wondered who had decorated the room. It had been like this when she arrived in Oz and when she left it wearing mourning black. The colors were good, with her favorite green dominant. Had Magus known or was it just luck?

There was so much she didn't know and wouldn't ever know. It would have been easy to re-create him as the perfect father, to set him on a high pedestal and imbue him with any trait or motive she wanted. She could even make up her own reasons for why he didn't come near her for eighteen years. He wasn't around to dispute anything. Fantasy father would have been a much more comfortable ghost to deal with the past ten years. Unfortunately, or fortunately, her mother had taught her to keep her feet firmly on the ground, to keep her fairy tales in the pages of child-hood books and out of her life.

Those feet had come off the ground a bit when Remy revealed his plan. Even now, fantasy thoughts, straight out of the pages of a romance novel, whirled in her head. She stared at herself, then slowly and carefully began to debunk each one.

Remy didn't love her. He wanted Magus's power and access to the money to fuel his campaign. It wasn't personal. How could it be when he didn't know her?

She didn't know him, either. There was a huge difference between the infatuation of a seventeen-year-old and the real, grown-up love she was capable of now.

Attraction wasn't love, either.

If she wasn't very careful, she could screw up both their lives. She had to keep her mind on her goal, which was to expose the man who contracted Magus's murder and quit living in Magus's shadow. She wanted her life, not Magus's life. Remy wanted Magus's life, or at least what Magus had wanted. That meant they were on different paths, moving toward different things. And if she looked into the future, she couldn't see Remy giving up what he wanted for a life of obscurity. Nor could she see herself ever being happy in the limelight. Opposites might attract, but they were both grown-ups and didn't have to act on that attraction.

She almost felt the thump as her feet connected with the wooden floor under the vanity. Only then did she allow herself to consider Remy's proposal. Even without the rosy glow of fantasy, it had merit, or was that despite it? Being attracted to him was a definite complication, but was it insurmountable?

In some ways, it would be like dancing on the head of a pin. She'd have to pretend she liked him, while not letting on she actually did like him. A single misstep in one direction and the plan failed, possibly fatally. A misstep in the other and she got her heart broken.

Okay, those were the risks.

On the other hand, Remy's plan had more potential for a successful outcome, even weighted with all those emotional components. If she was able to be cool and logical, which she granted she wasn't really in a position to know for sure, it had the potential to apply the most pressure—if Magus had been killed for political reasons. And if he hadn't?

Dorothy considered that possibility again, though she'd done it thousands of times before—and come to the same conclusion. It had to be political. Or why choose that time? Why wait until Magus was rising in the polls? Why wait until pundits were beginning to call him unstoppable?

She'd gone through his businesses with the proverbial fine-tooth comb, looking for another motive and had come up empty. Magus, despite his ruthlessness, had pursued his businesses with an almost fanatical sense of ethics. Maybe he'd always known he'd go into politics and didn't want to give anyone any fuel for scandal. After the breakup of his marriage, he'd lived the life of an ascetic as far as she could tell. There'd been no bimbo eruptions on his entry into the political field or after his death.

Within his businesses, he'd treated his employees better than his only daughter. He'd believed that good treatment and good benefits paid off in spades. Only the unethical and dishonest had problems with him. Once she'd assured people she didn't intend to change things, the loyalty he'd built flowed to her. There'd been some jockeying for position after his death, but not as much as she'd expected. Magus had chosen to surround himself with people who were bright and intelligent, and top-notch at what they did, ambitious to excel, but not into power for power's sake.

Maybe it was because of his years in Australia, that down under Oz, that he was both colorful and down-to-earth. Somehow he'd managed to be both mysterious and accessible to those he worked with. Like her, they fell under his spell and were happy to be there.

When he began his campaign, he'd managed to connect in the same way with the voters he met as he traveled around the state. People loved him. It was as simple as that. And now Remy was willing to bet his freedom that they'd love her, too.

She looked down at her hands, spreading her bare-of-adornment fingers and studying them as if they belonged to someone else. Gone were the cracked and broken nails of working as a wait and the dry skin of too much immersion in harsh chemicals. The skin was smooth and soft, the nails perfectly manicured, meticulously cared for. She ran a finger along the fourth finger on her left hand, trying to imagine it with a gold band. She didn't have to try hard.

She slowly looked up again, speaking aloud to her reflection: "Who are you fooling, Dorothy? You knew you were going to agree the moment he said it. You should run as far and as fast as you can. This could really hurt, but you've been hurt before and it didn't kill you."

Of course, in the past she hadn't been baiting a killer.

Remy suggested they do the interview from Oz. The atmosphere was great and it would seem more a part of the mystique that Magus had so enjoyed creating.

Dorothy was happy to agree. For her it meant putting off the moment when she'd have to emerge from seclusion and once again face the howl of a press corps on the hunt. For a short time after Magus's death, as new heir to his empire, she'd been a target of the press, but by being rigorously un-interesting, they'd gradually faded away. For several years now, she'd only been covered by the business press. Now she was preparing to not only be interesting, but to give the press beehive a giant whack with a stick. Smart. Real smart.

At least she'd know real fast if Magus was still inter-esting and, by default, her.

"I don't understand why you're doing this," Titus said, during a rare moment alone with Dorothy. "You hate the press."

Poor Titus. He liked his world straightforward and aboveboard.

"How did you ever get mixed up with Magus and Oz?" she asked, before she could stop herself. Because she was so private herself, she was rigorously careful of the privacy of those around her.

He looked startled for a moment, and then said slowly, "Your mother offered me the job. We went to the same high school."

She couldn't have been more surprised if he'd an-nounced his parents were bugs. "I didn't know."

He shrugged. "I expect it's all in the file Magus kept on me."

"I expect it is," she said, tacitly letting him know she'd never read it. The real truth was, she'd never thought of reading it. Titus was just there, like Magus's ghost. But now that was changed. He'd been in high school. With her mother. He'd been a teenager. Amazing. "Your parents . . ." She let the question trail off, in case it wasn't wel-come.

"They died just after I graduated. So I went into the Navy."

"I'm sorry."

"It was a long time ago."

That wasn't what she meant, but she let it stand. She knew what it was like to have wounds poked at. "Do you know why . . ."

Again she hesitated, as his brows lifted in polite inquiry.

". . . my parents separated? Why he never tried to contact me?"

His cool, closed gaze softened slightly. "I was his bodyguard, not his confessor."

"Did he have one? A confessor?" She kept hoping that she could get some of her questions answered, but he slowly shook his head.

"Not that I ever saw."

"I guess my parents had that in common," she said, unable to stop the hint of bitterness that colored her voice. It seemed that her parents' secrets would always stand between her and her memories of them.

Titus looked like he was going to say something, but was diverted by a discreet beep from his cell phone. He looked at the message, then at her. "We have more company."

"Who?"

"Bubba Joe Henry."

"Really?"

Bubba wasn't his real name, of course. That was Robert Joe, but half the men in the South were Bubbas, Dorothy had found. The trick was keeping them all separate, hence the "Joe" add-on. What made this particular Bubba's arrival interesting was his position on her list of possible suspects.

"Do I have time to see him before the interview starts?" She looked at her watch, trying to do the math in concert with her racing thoughts.

Titus nodded. "You still have something over half an hour."

"Let him in, then. I'll see him in the sitting room." Pity the library was taken. She'd liked to have seen him with Magus's face in the background. She resisted going to the long windows that overlooked the drive where he'd arrive and instead seated herself on an elegant velvet couch. In the past, this had been the room where the ladies of the house received their guests, so it was an overtly feminine room, while still managing to be quite impersonal. Dorothy knew she'd never taken possession of it during her short time here, and it appeared her mother hadn't, either. Or her presence had been swept away when she left. It would have been nice to have something of her mother here, something that would help her build a bridge between the past and the present that included her mother. Sometimes it felt as if she'd not just died, but been erased from Dorothy's life without a trace. Other than some old snapshots, she had nothing. Anything of value had been sold to pay medical bills.

She heard footsteps in the hall and quickly straightened her shoulders and lifted her chin. As Bubba Joe entered, she rose to her feet, her head slightly tilted as she waited to see how he intended to play the scene.

He stopped in the doorway, his gaze drifting slowly around the room before finally settling on her. He was a tall man, with a ruddy face and light, wavy hair that some women seemed to find attractive. Dorothy had never seen the appeal, finding his ready smile a bit too practiced for her taste and too much calculation behind his light blue eyes. She'd heard he had charm, but she appeared to have been born armored against it. She'd also heard that he saw the governor's mansion as a path to the White House. He wouldn't have liked Magus forging ahead of him, using up his window of opportunity to power.

He'd come alone, thank goodness. His wife was the

coldest fish Dorothy had ever met. Thin and pale and ruth-
lessly determined as any man around, Suzanne Henry was
also rumored to be charming and intelligent. Not to mention AC/DC in the bedroom. There was the stink of scandal
about them both, but nothing ever seemed to stick to them,
not unlike another famous presidential couple.

Bubba Joe and Magus had maintained the appearance of
a friendship, but he'd disappeared pretty quickly from Dorothy's life after the funeral. She knew from the file Magus
didn't trust him and would have done what he could to
block him from ever running for office. She also knew
Bubba Joe didn't like being thwarted. Oddly enough, he
hadn't moved to fill Magus's position ten years ago. Ten
years was a long time to put ambition on hold. He hadn't
wasted the time, though. He'd held a couple of offices in
the state house and senate, avoiding any national service so
he could run as an outsider when the time came.

An outsider. A man who'd never held a job and been on
the public payroll his whole life. It was a crazy business, she
decided for the millionth time.

"Little Dorothy, all grown-up," he said, his tone as
warm as if they'd parted yesterday as dearest friends. "You
look amazing."

Dorothy figured he'd play the hypocrite. At least he was
going to spare them both a fake explanation of why he
hadn't called. He strode confidently forward, grasped both
her hands and raised them toward his mouth for an almost
kiss, and then planted a real kiss on either cheek, leaving
her feeling like she needed another shower. She stepped
back just enough to forestall any of the groping she'd heard
he was famous for, and then gestured toward the seating,
the movement general enough to let him pick his own chair.

"Please."

No surprise when he picked a wing-backed, throne-like one.

"You look wonderful." He made the compliment sound vaguely lewd. He rested his ham-like hands on the delicate sides of the chair and gave her a reproachful look. "Back in town three days and you didn't call."

Nothing like going on the attack to prevent having to explain. He was good, but she'd been tutored by Magus.

"No." She smiled pleasantly at him, before adding with facile friendliness, "I'm afraid I haven't much time. I'm doing an interview in twenty minutes."

A slight, quick frown drew his brows together and an ugly look flashed in his eyes before he reapplied his genial mask. The smile kept its edge, however. "So the rumors are true. You are considering a run for governor."

"I'm afraid I promised Remy Mistral an exclusive on that question."

This time his smile didn't crack, but Dorothy felt an aura of menace filter into the room. That he didn't like to be thwarted was, apparently, an understatement.

"I backed off before, Dorothy, but I'm not this time. Magus was . . . well, the Wizard. But you're no wizard. You'd do better to throw your support behind someone who can win. It's . . . safer."

"Magus didn't teach me to play it safe." Dorothy hesitated. "I'm surprised you waited so long to run. I rather expected you to already be moving on from the governor's mansion."

"Suzanne felt the time wasn't right," Bubba Joe said stiffly. "As you know, there is an ebb and flow in politics. Or perhaps, you don't." He tried to leer and sneer and failed at both.

The hair on her arms rose in warning. This was not a

man to underestimate. Dorothy forced a smile. "How is Suzanne?"

"She's fine." He hesitated, shifting slightly in the chair. "You went up to Angola, I hear."

"You have good sources."

"Naturally." He licked his thick lips. "And now Vance is dead. Doesn't that tell you something?"

"It tells me that the past isn't dead, either. That there are still secrets to find and expose."

"You should let the past . . . and Magus . . . rest in peace."

"Neither seems willing to oblige. Can't you feel him here? I know I do." She'd poked the tiger. Now maybe she could spook him.

"You're a wealthy young woman. You could walk away." He sounded firm and almost kind, but spoiled it by looking around uneasily. "There's the whole world to spend it in. He can't make you—"

"Oh, but he can. He is. Don't you think I've tried to stay away?" She hadn't expected to go this direction, but it felt oddly right. And it was a huge hoot. Until the room turned cool, as if Magus himself were trying to be heard. She saw Bubba Joe stiffen, his gaze darting around the room as if afraid that Magus were suddenly going to appear. Maybe he would. Magus had always had a sense of humor. She rose slowly to her feet, as if she were half-specter herself. She paced slowly to the fireplace, then turned to look at Bubba Joe. "Do you think he knows now who hired Vance to kill him?"

Bubba Joe jumped to his feet, the ruddy color draining from his face like from a sink.

"Did you have something you wanted to tell me?" she asked.

"I came here because Magus and I were friends. One hears . . . things. Nothing definite, but things. It's not safe for you to do this. Magus, if he is . . . well, he should know better. Care more about you!"

"I expect the dead can't be much different from what they were in life. He always managed to pay back the good and bad, didn't he?"

She could see the struggle on his face as he slowly regained control of himself.

"Suzanne was wondering if you'd have dinner with us sometime this week?"

Her presence would start rumors of support, even if she didn't offer it. It was a clever move on Suzanne's part. "My schedule is rather full right now, but I'll let you know if something opens up."

It wasn't what he wanted and it was clear he hated to leave without something. She rose, to emphasize that the conversation was over.

"Give Suzanne my regards."

He nodded shortly, but didn't move. "You won't reconsider?"

She shrugged. "I'm afraid I can't."

His look turned insolent. It flicked up, then down her body in an insolent and invasive appraisal. "Then watch your back, honey. This is a tough business."

"I'll have her back," Titus said from the doorway, his face tight and cold.

Bubba Joe looked like he dearly wanted to taunt Titus about his previous failure, but the sight of the gun holster was most likely a deterrent. He closed his mouth and stalked out.

Dorothy waited until the door snapped shut and his engine fired outside.

"Well, I managed to rattle him."

"You think he was involved?" Titus looked surprised.

She shrugged. "I don't know. He isn't a nice man. Maybe he's just trying to scare me into not running."

"Are you going to run then?"

"She promised me the answer to that first." Remy joined the conversation. "I see from the slime trail that Bubba Joe Henry has been and gone. He on your list? Because he should be."

"He's certainly in my top three," Dorothy admitted, catching an odd look on Titus's face before he could replace it with inscrutable.

"Well, you can tell me about it later. It's show time."

"Can I have one minute?"

"Sure." He left as abruptly as he arrived.

"So you've been discussing the murder with him," Titus said. "Is that wise?"

"According to Bubba Joe, nothing I'm doing is wise." He opened his mouth, but she cut him off quickly. "Can we do this later? I need to find my balance again for the interview."

Their interview was going to be filmed for release on the radio station's sister television station. That meant she had to prepare to be both seen and heard.

She turned away from him, considering her face and what expression to put on it. Unbidden, a memory of Magus emerged from the past. She couldn't remember the event, there'd been so many of them, but she'd been with him long enough to stop thinking about how the hordes of press affected her and study how they affected him. And how he dealt with them. At times, it almost seemed as if he drew energy from them, growing even larger in the onslaught of attention. His eyes would light with interest. He didn't see them as the enemy or even as a necessary evil. And he'd known the face they saw was the one that their audience would see. Princess Diana had possessed the same gift for warmth that still maintained a proper distance. It worked for them because it was real and honest. No false notes because they weren't pretending.

Dorothy had been pretending so much for so long, she wasn't sure she could be real and honest. She patted some powder on her forehead and chin, studying the sober expression in her eyes. It was going to have to do and might actually be all right. At least it was as honest as she could produce right now. She tucked the compact back in her purse, picked up her hat and adjusted it, and then headed down the hall, drawn toward the room Remy Mistral was waiting in.

In the doorway, she paused, her gaze sweeping the room before it was caught by Remy's. The interest she saw there surprised her for a moment, until she remembered their deal. She didn't have to work nearly hard enough to produce a matching interest. The air between them sizzled softly, just enough to catch the attention of those around them. The rumors would be flying before the show ended.

His gaze traveled down, then up, approval mingling with desire in his eyes. She was glad she'd chosen the simple, yet classic slip dress and the Princess Diana hat, with its fuller brim that drooped over one eye. They felt right with the languorous warmth uncurling in her midsection.

He came to meet her, tucking her hand under his elbow as he drew her into the room with him. His touch swept her with a "little woman" feeling, a sense that she was fragile and that she'd been created to lean on him like this. It was an odd feeling, after ten years being solitary and strong, but rather pleasant. It permeated her walk, turning it slinky, almost beauty queen. She chuckled silently. *Right.* With her cleavage? Rein it in, girl.

"What?" Remy asked, for her ears alone.

She couldn't possibly explain. "I'm just enjoying our performance. I didn't expect that."

Remy's smile turned wry. "Did you think it would be hard to pretend to like me?"

She stopped, turning slightly to face him. "I've spent the last ten years learning how to hide my feelings from the rapaciously curious."

He looked thoughtful and a touch relieved. "I hadn't thought of that. Being a media type, I'm not so nice." He finished with a cocky grin, then gestured her to one of the wing-back chairs that had been placed in front of the fireplace where Magus's portrait hung.

As she sat down, she noticed he sent a look toward the portrait that was almost defiant.

The intrusion of Remy's world into Magus's had changed the flavor of the room somewhat. The brash flash of the equipment warred with the stately feel of the room and its old-world furniture.

But beyond the fixtures was the personality clash of old and new. Remy with Magus. Magus still dominated, but Remy had a different kind of power, was potent in a different way. His was the power of voice and of ideas. And he had the advantage of actually being alive. He also had *it*. Sex appeal in spades in a nice package designed by Mother Nature or divine providence, or possibly both working together.

Dorothy dug her toes into the soles of her shoes, trying to keep her feet on the ground as both past and present swept over her in a wave. After a brief, inner struggle, she was able to push it all to the back of her mind. She'd deal with it later.

Lights, mikes and makeup were checked and then Remy turned his hundred-watt smile on the camera, while directing his thousand-watt voice into the mike.

"Good afternoon, Louisiana. This is Remy Mistral on KPRX and as usual, I'm that cold wind blowing across the state on this hot day in May. There's a lot happening in politics today, but the big news is that Dorothy is back in Oz and the foundations of power are a-buzz with wondering why. You lucky listeners will be the first to hear Dorothy herself tell us not only why, but when, where, how and who." He looked at Dorothy and smiled. "But not until after this station break."

He looked at her as he surrendered control of the airwaves to the obligatory commercials. Are you ready, his eyes asked? Was she? Could she ever be? Ready or not, it was starting. And she had no one to blame but herself.

The commercial break ended far too quickly.

"In case you've been in a coma for the last fifteen years, I'll recap who Dorothy is and who the Wizard was." He talked fast, shooting facts out as bare, unadorned arrows in every direction, reducing both their lives to a two-minute recap.

It was both humbling and sobering. She'd thought it would at least take three. Even at that clip, he managed to play all the right notes, hitting emotion and logic with just the right amount of force, building carefully to the moment when he brought her into play.

"So, Dorothy. Welcome to Cold Wind."

His smile uncurled her toes and she almost forgot that she could only be heard, that seeing was for later.

"Welcome to Oz, Remy Mistral," she said, giving him a smile that she hoped was both sexy and slightly intimate, but could have very well been simply goofy. "And all your listeners as well."

"How does it feel to be back?"

She wanted to shrug, but didn't. Instead, she drew out slowly, "It feels . . . right. I'm sure my father would be pleased."

She looked up at the portrait on the wall between them.

"You visited Verrol Vance in prison two days ago. Was that why you came back to Louisiana?"

"Well, it was certainly one of the reasons."

"I'm guessing you asked him who hired him to kill your father. Did he tell you?"

"No, but he was going to."

"You seem quite sure."

"I'm a million dollars sure." Dorothy paused. Remy's eyes widened. She probably should have mentioned it, but she hadn't wanted to kill the spontaneity of the interview. And he might have tried to stop her. He didn't ask the next question, so she answered it anyway. "That's how much I offered him to tell me."

Remy made his recovery. "Not much use to him in jail."

"I also promised him a pardon."

"Really?" He was trying not to look annoyed now and mostly succeeding. "To deliver a pardon, you'd need to run for governor . . . or support someone who would deliver on your promise."

Dorothy nodded in what she hoped was a thoughtful manner. "If he hadn't been murdered, one of those scenarios would certainly have been necessary."

Remy started to look amused. "Does Vance's death mean you're no longer interested in Louisiana politics?"

She had to admire the delicacy with which he drew out the moment.

She waited for a count of five before answering him. "Not at all."

"This brings us to the million-dollar question . . . and another commercial break."

As she and Remy stared at each other, in the background she could hear someone talking about a must-have bed, followed by the amazing properties of garlic, then there was a flurry of bad commercials for some local businesses. Behind the commercial chatter was the discreet buzz of the curious around them and deeper than that, the gentle hum of the desire that fueled the gossip.

"A million bucks?" Remy gave her a crooked grin, because the cameras were still running. "That's a lot of money."

"I had a lot of time to save it up." Dorothy smiled serenely back.

Through his smile, he muttered, "I wish you'd given me a little warning before dropping that bomb. That was almost an offer of money for information."

Dorothy arched her brows. "Really?"

That was all they had time for, before the program resumed again. Remy leaned toward her slightly, his face turning serious.

"So, Dorothy, could you answer the question that most of Louisiana is buzzing with? Are you going to run for governor?"

He'd told her to count to twenty before she answered. It wasn't easy. The silence screamed to be filled. Eighteen . . . nineteen . . . twenty . . .

"No, Remy Mistral. I'm not."

"Is that a huge sigh of relief I hear rippling across the state from the hopeful throng?"

"I hope not," Dorothy said. "Because I'm hoping that you'll accept my support for your run for governor of the State of Louisiana. And I'm quite sure I'm not the only one, am I, callers?"

Chapter Four

Darius Smith was a tall, rather sinister man. Both height and aspect suited him, as he preferred being feared to being liked. His skin was pale, stopping just short of albino, and his eyes were icy blue. He had very thin lips and long, thin fingers and toes. He was cold inside and out, and he made all his decisions from a neutral place and based completely on expediency.

He had no knack for endearing himself to the electorate and no desire to do so. It was, therefore, no surprise he worked mostly behind the scenes. It was power he craved, power he sought assiduously. When it flowed to him, he was content; when it flowed away, he became dangerous. He had a variety of methods for getting what he wanted. Murder was on the list, but only as a last resort. It was messy and dangerous. Occasionally someone came along, though, that made it worth the risk and the mess.

He snapped off the radio and the last bombast of Remy Mistral and his so-called cold wind of truth. He was annoying enough to be worth almost any risk, even before he'd decided to run for governor. If he was able to align himself with the Wizard's daughter, well, it was almost a moral imperative to stamp him out.

Dorothy. It was a pity she'd come back. There had been so much tragedy in her young life. He hadn't expected her to care this much about a father she'd known so briefly. He hadn't expected this kind of loyalty, considering her maternal roots.

Emma Merlinn. She'd been fascinating, but had certainly lacked the attribute of loyalty. It was still hard for him to believe she was dead. She'd been so alive, so super-charged in those days when they were all young. All of them had lost their heads over her, but he was the only one who'd learned how inimical passion was in the well-ordered life. And if she'd chosen him instead of Magus?

Darius pushed his chair back from his huge, sterile desk. The wheels rolled silently, smoothly, until he stopped them and stood up. The air in the room was cool and devoid of scent. It was a place of metal and wood, designed for efficient use of space and time, not for looks.

He paced to the bank of windows that looked down on the New Orleans city street. No sound from outside penetrated the inside. There was nothing and no one in his sterile world to distract him from the past. From remembering Emma and how he'd felt when he was with her, what it had felt like to be thoroughly intimate with her.

With her, he'd felt less distant from the human race. He'd almost felt . . . redeemed. His mind wrapped reluctantly around the word. It implied he'd done something wrong, rather than just what was expedient, but it was the truth. He always faced the truth, no matter how hard, about himself and others. Clarity must precede action. It kept him from an unseemly and foolish reaction. He disliked losing control.

He could still remember what she looked like, despite the nearly thirty years since he last saw her. What was it about her that had made her so enticing? She wasn't the most beautiful woman he'd ever seen, but she was the only one he couldn't forget, no matter how hard he tried.

Certainly her red hair was striking with violet eyes, but they were just body parts, meaningless without what was inside her animating it all. Intimacy with her had been . . . amazing. Unforgettable. In the years since, he'd failed to experience anything like it. He hadn't even minded the loss of control at the time. The satisfaction that followed was ample compensation. He'd had sex with women since, but not intimacy or satisfaction. Sex merely provided physical release, a hollow thing when one knew what one was missing.

Magus clearly had never appreciated what he had with Emma or she wouldn't have sought Darius out. His vision had always been too narrow, and too quick to shift, once a goal was reached. He could never be satisfied. The fault surely lay with him, because Emma had been without flaw in the bedroom. Death may have obscured reality for some people, but Darius wasn't one of them. Magus would have tired of being governor as quickly as he'd lost interest in his wife, had he lived to be elected.

When Darius learned Emma was dying, he'd thought of going to see her. He was glad he hadn't, that his memory of her was untainted by cancer's ravages or the march of time, though it was still hard to imagine the Emma he knew waiting tables and taking care of a baby. Motherhood must have changed her. Perhaps, he thought wryly, it blindsided her. It was obviously the reason she left Magus. According to the detective he hired to find her, she had Dorothy six months after leaving Magus. Maternity had muted her essence, if the pictures the detective took were any indication. A pity. If she'd come to him, as he asked, would she still be alive? Or was the cancer an inevitable part of her future? And if she had come, would he have taken her? Shrines weren't meant to be inhabited, just visited occasionally.

He shifted restlessly, turning from the view and pacing back to his desk. It wasn't usually this hard to rebury the past. Why was it resisting him today? He'd had her. That was enough, particularly when he knew he wasn't the only one who wanted her. Both Bozo and Bubba had wanted her, too, but she chose him.

And Emma? Who knew what she felt or who it was she wanted? In the end, she'd slipped away from them all, and apparently never looked back.

It was the only time in his life he felt real hate for someone. Magus appeared to be little affected by her leaving, almost seemed not to have noticed she was gone. Interesting that the only two strong emotions Darius had ever felt were centered on the same family. Love and hate, he'd heard, were two sides of the same coin. Had he come to hate Emma? He didn't think so, but he'd never achieved clarity where she was concerned.

That's why he'd never acted. He could never decide what was the expedient thing to do with Emma. And now her daughter was back. Stirring up the past, digging into old and buried secrets. Reminding him of what he'd never had, stealing his clarity, just like her parents. Though Emma had been the biggest thief. She'd stolen his heart. And here he hadn't thought he had one. Unless it was just his pride she'd taken?

He started pacing again, trying to get ahead of the unsettled feelings Emma's memory always brought in its train. With an inner shake of the head, he cleared back the memories of what had been, homing in on the now. And Dorothy. Emma's daughter.

Odd he couldn't remember much about her from ten years ago. He did recall wondering how she could be Emma's offspring, she was so unlike her mother. He'd lost interest at that point, all his attention on stopping Magus's drive for the governor's mansion.

He walked back to his computer, sat down and pulled up the company Web site where Dorothy's picture was posted. Now he could see that Dorothy had the look of her mother, though distilled and thinned by her Wizard blood. They both had titian hair and violet eyes, but Emma had had the purer profile, he thought. And the fuller figure. How had he missed the similarities ten years ago?

He grabbed the file of newspaper clippings about Magus and flipped through them until he found one with Dorothy standing just behind him. Even in the flatness of black and white, Magus overshadowed her, rendering her almost invisible.

He shut the file. Well, she'd been young then, very young. Decidedly a fish out of water in Magus's hectic and very public life. She appeared to have overcome that past. She'd managed Magus's companies well, earned her place on the various boards. Did that make her Magus's daughter or Emma's?

He needed to see her in the flesh to answer the question. Only then would he know how to deal with the threat she posed to the protégé he hoped to place in the mansion in Baton Rouge.

But was that his only interest? Was it possible that he'd find the mother in the daughter? It was an intriguing thought. Could the past live again? Emma had desired him. They'd only had the one night, but what a night it had been. Was it possible that satisfaction could be achieved again? If daughter were like mother, perhaps his long wait was over?

Unless . . .

Emma left Magus around three months after their affair. What if Dorothy were *his* daughter? Was it possible? He'd never wanted a child but, if he and Emma had made a child together, she might be interesting to him. If he saw her, could he tell?

In any case, his sources told him that Bubba Joe and Bozo were both going to see her in Oz. Did they fear her or the past, he wondered? Or both?

He frowned thoughtfully. Obviously he hadn't looked into the past thoroughly enough ten years ago when Dorothy made her first appearance on the scene. It wasn't like him to be so inattentive when secrets were his preferred currency. Who, he wondered, had the most to hide from that time?

Number two on Dorothy's list of suspects was waiting for her when her hour on Remy's three-hour show ended.

Bozo Luc. Bozo was not his given name. That was Gaspar. It was also not an insult. In the bayou country it meant "nice guy." It was the Yankees who turned the original meaning into a clown or buffoon. Bozo was charming, but not nice, nor was he a buffoon, though he wasn't above playing one when it suited him. He was a small, dark man, with intense eyes and a thick smile that both repelled and attracted. He'd wed, bedded and buried three wives. Rumor had it he was looking for number four. Unlike Bubba Joe, he'd inherited his power base from his daddy. The Lucs had been milling around the bayou practically since it was settled, or so the story went. Though they'd begun as fishermen, they'd inevitably diversified into oil and gas. According to Magus's file, Bozo wasn't so much into the accumulation of power as he was a believer in his divine right to rule. The end result might be the same as Bubba Joe's if he managed to get into the governor's mansion, but his motivation was different. Magus always focused on motivation when dealing with people.

When Bozo grabbed her hands, he first held them tightly, and then pulled her close, not touching, just studying her face with an intensity that was unsettling.

He could be looking at her as a possible new wife, she supposed, but surely she was a bit old for his taste, which seemed to trend younger with each marriage. She'd have thought she was too much of an outsider for the Lucs. Of course, he wouldn't be the first old family suitor to overlook the mongrel background of a potential spouse, but he didn't really need her money or Magus's name. He probably owned the votes in the lower parishes.

"Chere, you look . . ." Words apparently failed him, so he threw his arms wide, while still managing to hold on to her hands, before shrugging elegantly. He had enough French in him to get away with both the grand gestures and the affectations. There was, however, an odd discontinuity between his actions and the look in his eyes as he continued to study her. A slight, very slight frown between his eyes seemed to indicate he was either displeased or puzzled.

What he concluded, he kept to himself. Did he have some other motive for approaching her, and what could it be? Dorothy gently reclaimed her hands and used them to direct him toward seating. Like Bubba Joe, he chose the throne.

"What brings you to Oz?" Dorothy couldn't quite bring herself to call him Bozo. In her head, she knew it wasn't an insult, but it was hard to go against her upbringing. Her mother had been inflexible on the subject of good manners in the presence of friend or foe.

"You surely aren't going to back that blowhard, Mistral, are you, chere? Your papa must be rolling over in his crypt." His Cajun diction was perfect for sounding mournful and disappointed, and he looked like a father facing a child who had disillusioned him. Or maybe a priest trying to call a lost soul to repentance. The priest analogy would have worked better without the hint of decadence in his dark eyes. "Come out with me tonight and we'll talk about it. For your papa's sake."

"She's going to the Zoo-to-Do with me," Remy said dryly from the doorway. Over Bozo's head, his amused gaze met hers. By the time Bozo turned to face him, Remy's face was coolly respectful, however.

"Indeed." Bozo's dark brows arched in inoffensive astonishment. He was clearly wondering what on earth Dorothy saw in Remy. His dark, mournful gaze turned her direction again. "As Magus's oldest, and closest friend, chere, I stand by to offer you counsel during this difficult time."

His tone implied that she desperately needed it. And that he was the only one who could give it.

And where were you during that "difficult time" after Magus was shot, she wondered, but didn't ask. Bozo would only consider it bad manners. And so would her mother, for that matter. She could almost hear Bozo telling her that the past was the past. Are you unable to forgive, chere? She didn't need another huge helping of reproach from his dark gaze.

Remy pulled her hand through his arm, facing Bozo firmly and pointedly by her side. "And what would you advise her to do, sir?"

Bozo didn't seem happy at being addressed as a sir. Magus had noted in the file that Bozo thought he was young at heart and that made him young in appearance. Yeah, right.

Their gazes clashed, bringing something dangerous into the room. It was a reminder to her of the power Bozo wielded because of his birth and by choice. Dorothy had kept him on the list, because of the file, but now he'd earned his right to be there.

As if he sensed her sudden discomfort, he smiled amiably, charmingly. "So you think to take us all on, do you, Mistral?"

Remy shrugged. "I've been taking you on since I got my first job."

"But now the mosquito aspires to become the bug spray. Change isn't as easy as you think it will be. The old ways work for Louisiana."

"But not that well for her people. And they are . . . expensive."

"The best things always are."

"We'll have to agree to disagree on that, Luc."

"Interesting election in New Orleans," Dorothy said. "Makes one think change can happen."

"Funny things happen when real people vote," Remy added, his tone lightly mocking. "It's almost a revolution."

"A cold, fresh wind of change," Dorothy added, even knowing it wasn't wise.

Bozo's dark eyes flashed a warning . . . and amusement. It was an odd combo and only he could have pulled it off.

"You are still very young, chere," he said, with an almost gentle smile, before his gaze shifted back to Remy. Amusement faded, leaving only warning. "If you aspire to the Wizard's shoes, you'd best be careful, Mistral. Louisiana isn't known for its cold winds, just its hot passions."

Dorothy had read somewhere that politics was the business of Louisiana. She'd thought it absurd then, but she didn't anymore. Like Mardi Gras, it was considered great fun, but still a very, very serious business.

Not unlike the governor's race, where it seemed two of

the three top suspects were jockeying for first place on her suspect list. The level of aggression in the room bumped up another notch as the two men squared off, like two dogs with only one bone. It was time to diffuse it. She'd found out what she needed to know. Bozo deserved her suspicions.

"You've come a long way. Can I get you something, sir?" she asked.

Bozo shook his head, stepping lightly toward them to once again capture the hand not held by Remy. "I had no idea you were so like your father, chere. You're much too charming to suffer Magus's fate. Please, be careful."

He sounded like he actually cared.

"If you know something about that, I'd be most grateful if you'd tell me."

"Let the past alone, chere." His tone was deadly serious. He kissed her hand lightly, then lowered it to rest on Remy's bent arm and stepped back. He glanced around, as if remembering something about the room. It must have been a good memory, because it softened his gaze again.

A most unwelcome thought pushed its way into her mind. Had Bozo and her mother . . . ? She tried to bury the crazy thought, but it was hard to do while looking into Bozo's eyes. This room had never been her father's domain.

"Do you remember my mother?"

His brows arched. "But of course. You are somewhat like her, but not enough, chere. She knew when she was in over her head and strategically withdrew from the game."

With a last warning smile, he turned and padded silently out of the room, leaving Dorothy with the feeling that any frightening had been one-way. She gave an involuntary shiver.

Remy looked at her sharply. She gave him an over-bright

smile. "What's a Zoo-to-Do?"

Vonda Vance was an innocuous woman, in look and in deed. She'd never aspired to notorious. It had been thrust upon her, beginning that day Verrol walked into her library. She still wondered what he'd seen in her. Criminals and killers chose bimbos, not librarians, didn't they?

She was, she though wryly, the anti-bimbo. Flat-chested and no-hipped, with coloring so bland she was a virtual chameleon—able to blend into any wall with ease. There was some almost mystical quality about her lack of color. Occasionally she'd seek out shading in a makeover, but within minutes of application, her makeup would slowly fade away. Bright colored clothes didn't fade, but they did make her look more pale and insipid. She made up for her lack of exterior adornment by having a lush interior life. Until Verrol came along, it was the most interesting part of her life.

Verrol's eyes seemed to have been gifted with the ability to see the unseen. Perhaps that is what had made him so good at killing. Well, that and his own ability to disappear into the background. Of course, she'd had no idea of his sideline as a killer when she married him. She'd been easy to fool, so trusting and willing to be blind to any irregularities that would help her maintain the illusion theirs was a normal life. He went to work like any other husband. She'd thought he was a researcher for a lobbyist. He always seemed to know a lot about what was going on, the insider stuff that didn't make it into the newspapers. It was exciting, enticing, and in the end, an alternate way to escape the dull reality of her existence.

When he was arrested at the rally after shooting Magus Merlinn, with a gun in his hand, it had been much easier to look back and see the clues that what she'd believed about

Verrol had never tracked with reality. Until that point, she'd considered herself a competent observer of the passing scene and rather a hand with a mystery. It was still hard to realize that her imaginative life had been more real than her outer life.

It would have been so much easier to denounce and re-nounce him, but she'd married him for better or worse, though knowledge hadn't killed love. She hadn't expected that. So she'd dutifully made that once-a-month trip to visit him within the grim confines of Angola. It hadn't been en-tirely without interest. The museum was quite fascinating and there were no illusions about the reality of prison life. There she knew exactly what she was dealing with.

By keeping her mind on how different the criminal world was from her own, she was mostly able to keep the aching loneliness for Verrol at bay. She'd always had a disciplined mind. Life had pretty much required it of her. But nothing in her life had prepared her for desire, for the wonder of curving her bony body into Verrol's spare one, or the sweet security that came from being hugged by him.

On some level, she knew her world was hopelessly out of sync, as if she'd been caught between two dimensions and was unable to live completely in either one. Logically, she was sure there had to be a way back to her own life, but her heart, even after ten years without Verrol, remained un-cooperative. And now he was gone. *Dead.*

Because he'd been absent for the last ten years, it was hard to process the permanence of this new reality. How easy it would be to pretend it was just a nightmare from which she'd soon awaken. He was still in prison, shuffling through afternoon exercise or in the library writing his weekly letter to her, filled with promises that they'd soon be together again.

She'd never known where he found his optimism. He'd chosen a bad time to commit murder. The country was big on accountability. The jury had given him life without possibility of parole, hardly breaking a sweat in the process. She didn't blame them. She used to be them until Verrol. How could they know what they hadn't experienced? How could they know that he was more than a murderer? How could they know that knowledge didn't necessarily kill love? Or was it just need she felt because she knew that no one would ever see her like he did, that she'd never again have love in her life?

Verrol's lawyer, Clinton Barnes, had been kind when he brought her the news. The people at the library had tried to be kind, though no one had any idea what the proper number of days off were for the death of a husband who was a killer. And they couldn't understand that she wasn't relieved he was dead, that for her it wasn't over yet. Beyond the loneliness were the funeral and another painful period of media attention, followed by a future stretching out into an endlessly bleak landscape.

If only there was more she could do than just bury Verrol. As if her brain had been waiting for that thought, it directed her gaze to the letter Barnes had brought her.

"Verrol wanted you to have this if anything happened to him in prison," he'd said, his dark gaze both worried and curious as he handed it over.

Since he'd brought the letter, it had sat on her desk, unopened. She wasn't ready to deal with what might be in it. What if it answered the question everyone had wanted to know for ten years? Did she want to know who hired Verrol to kill Magus Merlinn? What good would it do now? If he'd told back when it first happened, it would have mitigated his sentence some. She'd begged him to talk, but he'd just shaken his head and told her not to worry. He was owed money and freedom and both would come in time. Yeah, that plan worked out well.

"I'd rather have had the last ten years, Verrol," she told the empty room. She picked up the letter, because it was almost all she had left of him. It was possible the letter was just a last good-bye or maybe an explanation of how and why he'd become a killer. He knew her well enough to know she'd want to understand. It was a way for her to find closure.

And if it was about who hired him? She looked into the deep, dark places of her heart and found a longing for the person who hired Verrol to be punished. She wasn't proud of it, but in the dark of many a night, she'd railed against the unfairness of how things had played out. Why should that person have been able to continue living and loving while she slept alone for ten, long years? And now, not content with taking her past, her future had also been taken away.

Sometimes she wished she'd never met Verrol, but how could she regret the things she'd learned? Even with the pain of it, at least she'd lived life, not just read about it in books. No, she didn't regret meeting Verrol. She only regretted losing him and who she'd thought he was.

Slowly, tentatively, she picked up a letter opener. Once she opened it, there would be no going back. She wasn't the kind of person who could know something and not act on it, even without her personal feelings in the mix. For good or ill, this would change her life in some way. For a moment, she teetered on the edge, but in the end, how could she not open it? It was Verrol's last communication with her.

She inserted the point under the envelope and pushed it

along the closed edge. The paper crackled slightly with age as she pulled it free and unfolded it.

At first, all she could see was that it was in his handwriting, just like all the other letters she'd received from Angola, only on nicer paper. So he'd written it before prison, possibly before he was even arrested? Tears swam across her view, blurring the words that followed: *"My dearest Vonda . . ."*

Dear, but not dear enough. Oh Verrol. If only . . .

Resolutely she wiped the tears and pushed back the regrets. She made herself focus on the words and not their dear shape and style. At the end, she began again. It was clever, the way he'd diverted attention away from the real clue.

And he'd given her one more chance to decide whether she'd go forward or back. How well he knew her and how much she missed feeling understood and known. She rubbed her forehead as longing tried to overwhelm her. Somehow, some way, she needed to stop living in the past. If that meant confronting it, then so be it.

And Verrol's mama? No one had known her connection to Verrol then or, apparently, now. Interesting that Verrol had chosen her to be his answer-keeper. She studied the words again. Had he left something at the library as a false clue? It would be just like him. He'd had a puckish sense of humor.

With a wry grin, she sat down. If she was brutally honest, and she always tried to be, she'd admit she was intrigued by both the answers and the money. How could she not be, she thought, looking around her dreary, lonesome apartment. She wouldn't, she couldn't take the money, but she was tempted. May God forgive her, she was tempted. Had Verrol known she would be? Or had he just hoped she'd reach out and take the freedom he was offering her?

"Oh, I can't think!" She rubbed her forehead again, trying to stop the headache before it got a foothold there. Almost impatiently, she looked for a distraction, spotted the remote, grabbed it and turned on the news. It was a shock to see there, on the screen, the Wizard's daughter.

"Did Vance tell you who hired him to kill your father?" someone was asking her.

"No, but he was going to." She looked calm, reflective and just the right amount of sad.

"You seem quite sure."

"I'm a million dollars sure." Dorothy paused. It felt as if she looked out of the television straight into Vonda's soul. "That's how much I offered him to tell me."

So that's why Verrol was dead. Vonda sagged back, as anger flared. How could she put him in danger like that? Anger quickly faded to shame. Of course she wanted to know who really killed her father, not just who pulled the trigger. And she'd been willing to let Verrol walk out of prison for that knowledge, with a bucket of money. Instead he was dead. Whoever did this thought he'd silenced Verrol, but he hadn't.

She looked at the letter again. His words were so like him, she could almost hear him saying them. How could he be dead? *Dead?* Gone. Erased to keep a filthy, little secret about who really wanted the Wizard dead.

What a pitiful reason for taking a life. And the money Verrol had taken to kill? I'm a hypocrite, too. I can forgive Verrol, but not who hired him.

She rubbed her face again, studying Dorothy through her fingers.

In a strange way, they were in the same boat. They both wanted justice. They both wanted the secrets to come out.

And the million dollars of "clean" money Dorothy was obviously dangling out there as bait? It shamed her, but she had to admit that was part of her justice. It wouldn't be a bad bargain for Dorothy. She'd been going to pay for the information anyway. She'd get her answers, and Vonda would get a ticket to a different life, one away from people who knew her as the "killer's wife."

She gave a half-laugh that broke in the middle. The killer's wife and the Wizard's daughter. Sounded like a bad book title.

It was also someone's worst nightmare.

Chapter Five

Luckily Dorothy had a little, formal something in her closet, since Remy hadn't given her much warning about tonight's big do at the Audubon Zoo. Fortunately, that something was also light and cool, and perfect for the hot May night. The same shade violet as her eyes, it slinked its way lovingly down her body, finishing in a slight, sassy flare at the ankle. Her shoes looked uncomfortable and weren't, thank goodness, since the party would be ranging all over the zoo, both on the pavement and off. Her hair had been styled to a point of wild abandon, while her makeup gave her a mysterious, almost exotic look. In fact, she looked and felt nothing like herself. The odd part, she didn't mind. Was it because of Remy or just events in general?

He did look smashing. It would be too easy to look adoringly at him, with his stocky frame nicely covered in a well-fitted tuxedo and a sexy, satisfied smile creasing his face. It was getting harder and harder to keep her feet on the ground, so she looked away from him instead, watching as Titus pulled the SUV into the space indicated by the uniformed cop. A bus would take them to the zoo's entrance, since Titus, in his role as bodyguard, didn't want to let her out of his sight. Around them thronged the beautiful, the not-so-beautiful people, the rich or those who knew someone who could buy them tickets. All of them streamed through the fading light of day toward party zero. As Dorothy joined that stream, it felt as if her world had been reversed, with the unreal relegating real to a minor role.

Around them were tall oak trees dripping with Spanish moss and age, their limbs bent and sweeping the ground as if herding them along. The silken, sultry air slipped across her skin like a lover's caress, but was almost too thick to breathe in and heavily weighted with the scents of a New Orleans night. There was the smell of flowers, of course, and also the richly pungent odor of green stuff, but also the spicy bite of the food awaiting them inside the zoo.

The music from the do was too loud for the buzz of insect life to be heard, but they were felt in gentle passes against her face or the occasional diving bite on bare skin. In between beats of music, there was the sound of many voices, punctuated by laughter in a variety of pitches.

There was a festive feel to it all, but it was still an odd sort of party, Dorothy decided. Despite the density of the crowd, they were all strangers, leaving her feeling very alone, even isolated. She could probably count on one hand the people she knew. And one of them was probably a killer. Remy had more acquaintances that he could nod or exchange greetings with, which made her feel disconnected from him, too. Titus was the specter at the feast as he stalked behind her.

It was, she decided, like moving through a very vivid dream. The flash of lights, the chatter of people, the multitude of colors, the distant sounds of the zoo animals, and the ebb and flow of the crowd brought some things into sharp relief and left others blurred or in shadow. There was clarity and confusion warring for dominance, with no clear winner possible.

She knew she was under scrutiny by those in the know, but it wasn't really her they were looking at. All they were seeing was the illusion she'd created in her hotel room this evening. Smoke and mirror effects, bought with Magus's money.

Before returning to Louisiana, she'd gone back to the diner where she and her mother had worked. It had felt as alien as this place did. No one had known her there, either. She was dangling between two lives, two worlds, trying to find a place to plant her feet and build a life, if she survived her dangerous dance with Remy Mistral and their suspects.

As if her thought made them emerge from out of the crowd, she first saw Bozo with a top-heavy blonde, then Bubba with his cold-fish wife. Beautiful people pretending to do their best to help the Audubon Institute continue their good works on behalf of things beast and growing green. In reality, they were there to have a good time. To dance and drink, to see and be seen.

And if she could be anywhere else right now, where would that be? As if in answer to the question, Remy's grip on her arm tightened, pulling her closer to the lean, hard length of him. The jolt of it was a plunge back into the present.

"Show time," he said, looking at her with pretended interest as the newspeople milling around the entrance caught sight of them. It felt like they were hit with a thousand watts of light, immediately blinding her. She gripped Remy's arm, tried to keep her face equally interested and focused on him as they pushed through the awful din of shouted questions. Just when she thought she couldn't take it anymore, they passed through the gates to freedom. She waited while Remy handed over their tickets and received programs in return, and then they were in the nighttime zoo.

She'd been here only once before, making a solo appearance for Magus. A daytime, Cajun thing. There'd been special food booths and pockets of music in a variety of styles. Despite the cushion of handlers steering her around, she'd enjoyed it very much. The zoo was beautifully laid out and invited exploration.

This zoo was nothing like that memory. It didn't even seem like the same place, with areas of deep dark surrounding places of brilliant light. Her first, awful thought was how easy it would be to kill someone here. There was too much of everything: people, noise, light and dark. And in the dark, out of sight, wild animals watched them, or at least it felt like they did. Yes, they were caged, but that didn't comfort somehow. All around her, the humid air throbbed with the emotions of the excited crowd.

At her side, Remy stopped briefly to consult the map in the program. "Looks like the closest food area is this way. You snooze, you lose, if you don't eat early and often. You hungry?"

He'd been looking around, his gaze alert and interested, but now he was looking right at her. For a moment, it felt like she zoomed in from some distant place, arriving intensely aware of everything, but mostly him. And the sharp bite of hunger, kicked up by the luscious smell of food.

She nodded. "Yeah, I'm hungry."

It was a short walk along a lighted path. Dorothy kept looking past the light, trying to pierce the intense dark and being defeated by it. At first she thought it was distant thunder, growing closer, but as they emerged into a circle of light and food, she realized it was voices. Hundreds of voices, some bright, some frantic, all intense and all rising in a vain attempt to be heard.

Around the circle were tables, each area defined by a particular chef from famous local restaurants, each serving up petite portions of their signature dishes. Across from them, Dorothy saw a chafing dish of Bananas Foster flare up against the dark sky before fading back into the silver chafing dish.

Without conscious decision, they moved into a line and were soon blending the tastes of jambalaya, tender steak, and a variety of seafood dishes. The tastes and smells were as intensely heady as the setting. As she spooned up frosty ice cream topped with the Bananas Foster, she watched Remy meet and greet a couple. Their words were lost in the din, but when their gazes flicked her way, it wasn't hard to figure out the subject. She smiled and moved to join them. She never heard their names or what they said to her, but she shook hands and smiled, nodding agreement to who knew what.

With Remy's hand warm against her back, she let herself be steered out of the bright circle to another lighted path. "What did I just agree to?" she asked with her mouth against his ear.

Remy chuckled. "Nothing important. We're doing good. After tonight, the rumors will be flying. Won't be surprised if we're secretly married by morning."

He consulted a map. "The tents are this way." He steered her past a sign that pointed to the snake house. "And the dancing, if you're up for it."

It was only now, when they were clear of the crowd, that she again became aware of Titus following silently behind them. Dorothy looked back. "I hope you tried some of the food."

He pretended he hadn't heard, as his gaze swept from side to side. "This place is a security nightmare."

"You'd be in a better mood if you'd eaten something." Dorothy felt her tension level ease as his kicked up a notch. Now they emerged into another area of lights, but this one was characterized by tent-like booths in long rows. Each one had tables inside the tented area, food and drinks set up, portable toilets in the rear, and with the name of the sponsor printed on a banner swathed around the base. As they made their way along the rows, searching for the one sponsored by Remy's radio station, Dorothy saw Bozo and Bubba again, in separate booths kitty-corner from each other. They seemed to be taking care not to look at each other as they went through the political meet-and-greet with anyone they could get a hold of.

Beside her, Remy tensed. "Barnes."

His tone caught her attention. He was nodding warily at a short, stocky man with very little hair. The man's expression hovered between cynicism and interest, the interest directed at her, or so it appeared. He gave Remy an expectant look. After a short hesitation, Remy obliged.

"Dorothy, this is Clinton Barnes."

Dorothy held out her hand. "I've seen you before, haven't I?"

"He was Vance's attorney," Remy said dryly.

"Oh." Dorothy felt her jaw slacken slightly and pulled herself together. She shook the hand he extended toward her and felt the scrape of paper against her palm. When he released her hand, the paper was still wedged between her index finger and her thumb. Dorothy clutched the scrap, trying not to show her surprise. "I'm sorry about your client."

"Do you really think he was going to talk?" he asked. "I never could convince him to, not even to reduce his sentence."

Dorothy shrugged. "It seemed to me he was going to. Obviously someone else agreed. I guess he never told you?"

Barnes shook his head, but his eyes told her he knew something. "It was nice to meet you. I liked your father and was very sorry about what happened."

"Thank you."

He moved off and Dorothy turned to look at Remy. "That was interesting."

"Yes," he said, but something happened when their gazes connected, that diverted her attention from Barnes. Heat began to build, a delicious heat, that should have been uncomfortable when the hot night was already a factor, but somehow wasn't. Her surroundings moved away, leaving her alone with Remy for a brief moment, and then she felt someone look at her. It was like being touched with ice. It traced down her back, turning her body leaden and afraid. With an effort, she managed to keep her face from changing, but she couldn't stop herself from stiffening. Remy noticed, his gaze tracking past her to scan the crowd, until he too stiffened.

"It's Darius Smith," he murmured, his lips close to her ear so she could hear him. His breath was warm and comforting, but not enough against the icy blast that emanated from Smith. "Number three on our list of suspects."

Dorothy drew breath sharply and deeply as Smith approached. His gaze was an icy blow, but with something else at its heart, something that made her uneasy and feeling oddly exposed.

He must have been around before, but she didn't remember him at all, which seemed odd now. What she knew about him came from Magus's file on him, which was very little, strangely enough. It was just a spare recital of facts and figures, that was as chilly and remote as Smith himself. It was the first time he'd left her unprepared and she wondered why, as Darius approached them, tall and cadaverously thin, but with a panther-like grace and menace. Because she felt like a staked-out doe, she lifted her chin and stood her mental ground.

He stopped directly in front of Dorothy, something in his stance tacitly shutting Remy out of the conversation. The air was dark and hot, but she still felt cold, a cold so deep it felt like she'd never warm again. His gaze plowed into hers, as if taking an answer to a question she didn't want to know, let alone acknowledge. Her throat dried to parchment and her whole body seemed to go numb with shock from the mental assault. She couldn't feel Remy gripping her arm anymore. She couldn't feel the ground under her feet. There were just those icy, blue eyes and the roaring in her ears that sounded like glaciers wrenching loose to crash into the depths of the sea. It took enormous effort to lift her brows in haughty inquiry.

The thin lips curved slightly in a humorless smile. "Darius Smith. I knew your parents."

Something unwholesome flickered hot, but brief in his eyes. He took her hand before she could react and lifted it to press a cold, but lingering kiss on the back. Ice spread from the spot, but there was an unwholesome heat at its core, like a stealth bomb finding its target. It refused to let her be wholly indifferent to him and she hated it and hated his obvious satisfaction. His vaguely animal scent spread out like an oil slick into the air around her. It wasn't cologne. It was the man. It was a direct contrast to the obscenely expensive suit he wore with casual grace.

His hands reminded her of spiders; the fingers were long and thin, but devoid of color and dead-looking. His touch transmitted no warmth from contact.

"You have the . . . look of your mother. She was an interesting woman." The pale, pink tip of his tongue traced around his mouth, as if remembering something tasty. His tone was coolly intimate.

It was like being licked by a reptile. The words were innocuous on the surface, but slimy nonetheless and his eyes stripped with insolent detachment. After her meeting with Bozo, she should be through with shock, but she wasn't. What on earth could this man, or Bozo for that matter, have found interesting about her oh-so-practical, down-to-earth mother? It was like finding out that the sun had really been rising in the west or that Jupiter, not the moon, orbited Earth.

He studied her thoughtfully for a brief eternity, before flicking a contemptuous look in Remy's direction. To her surprise, Remy seemed unfazed by Smith. Dorothy felt violated and angry—and even more estranged from her memories of her mother. Maybe ignorance really was bliss after all.

"So, Mistral, you think to blow your way into the mansion?" Somehow Smith managed to make it both question and insult, with his phrasing and the hint of incredulity.

Remy grinned. "I'm guessing I won't be collecting *your* endorsement. Who will you be backing this time?"

"Always the reporter. That's the first thing you'll need to change," Smith said, his cool voice sneering slightly.

"You're still better at giving advice than answering questions. Oh well, I think I can guess. You've been grooming that protégé of yours for years. A pity no one likes him but you."

Smith's thin lips twitched slightly. The only indication that Remy's shot may have hit home. His gaze shifted back to Dorothy.

"Politics are a nasty business. I hope you'll be wiser than Mistral?"

The statement was mildly delivered, but still managed to sound like a threat.

"I'm my father's daughter, too, sir."

That seemed to amuse him as well. "Are you? Well, we'll see."

After another period of probing appraisal, he left them, slithering off into the crowd. He didn't need to touch anyone or speak. People seemed happy to clear a path for him.

"That is one creepy guy." Dorothy shivered. "Do you like him for hiring Vance?" Dorothy did. In spades.

Remy shrugged. "He likes to sound spooky, but I've never heard of him doing worse than the occasional career kill. He's careful, maybe too careful for final solutions."

Had the undercurrents of what Smith said really gone right past him, she wondered? Maybe it was a female thing. She felt like she needed a long bath to be clean again. And maybe a mind purge to get the picture of him with her mother out of her head. There was no way to reconcile that image with the one of her mother, worn and gray, waiting tables with an expression of bored interest. The one thing Dorothy had always been sure about was that her mother didn't like men. Not anymore. Her whole focus and drive had been survival from as early as Dorothy could remember.

She could feel the bile of bitterness surge through her, temporarily overpowering the emotional sliming by Smith. Had anything in her past been real? Even if her mother had had affairs, surely she would never have gone willingly into that man's arms.

"Are you all right? Did he upset you?" Remy moved to give her partial cover from the crowd. He looked both worried and a bit surprised. "That's just his shtick, you know. He likes to imply he knows things."

"And does he know things?"

Remy shrugged. "Sometimes. Sometimes not." His worried look deepened. "What do you think he knows?"

"That's the problem. I don't know much of anything." She bit her lip. "Did you hear what he said about my mother?"

"Sure. From what I hear, everyone found your mother interesting. She was a beautiful, high-spirited woman. If she wasn't in the society pages, it was because she was out of town." Remy tipped his head to one side. "You didn't know?"

"How could I? The mother I knew was worn out from trying to put food on the table, then dying of cancer. There was nothing beautiful or high-spirited about her. She was incredibly ordinary. She was gray and worn. She waited tables and harped on my manners. And told me we were lucky to have little money." She shook her head wryly. "It's like we're talking about two different people."

"Well, parents are never really real to their kids, are they?"

He didn't say she was overreacting and for that she was grateful. Maybe she was, but it didn't feel like she was. She tried to smile.

"I guess not." Maybe this life had so damaged her mother that she'd fled it and vowed to completely reject it? Dorothy wouldn't know, because she'd never talked about the past. If Bozo and Smith played large roles in that past, maybe she had good reason to leave it all behind. Maybe she hadn't wanted Dorothy to know all this? She gave herself a mental shake. There was no way to know now what her mother had wanted or felt. And Remy was right. She was in no position to judge her parents with any clarity.

"Are you sure you're all right?" Remy took her hand and gave it a comforting squeeze.

She felt the crackle of the paper Barnes had slipped into her hand. Smith had driven it completely out of her mind. Someone approached Remy, giving her a chance to unfold the sheet and read the brief note.

"Monkey house. Midnight. Come alone."

Dorothy crumpled the paper again. Why did people who wrote notes, always say that? Come alone. She looked at her map and found the monkey house on it. It wasn't too far off the beaten path, but still . . .

She looked at her watch. She had five minutes to decide what to do. Her first impulse was to ask Remy to go with her, but he was a reporter. Barnes wasn't likely to talk in front of him. And Titus? Yeah, his manner encouraged confidences.

She wasn't without resources. Titus had taught her some defensive moves. And she had a small, personal pistol in her sassy, little handbag that he'd made sure she knew how to use.

"I'd like you to meet Dorothy," she heard Remy say.

She looked up and smiled at the people he was introducing her to, without hearing their names or what they said. She wasn't even sure what she said, though it must have been all right. They smiled and nodded. After a moment, they found the KPRX-sponsored booth along the row.

She looked at her watch again. She'd lost two minutes to indecisiveness. Maybe it was hubris to believe she could handle the situation and it could come back to bite her on the ass, but it was her ass, after all. In the end, she was the one with the most to gain or lose.

She leaned close to Remy. "I'm going to check out those charming facilities in the rear."

Remy chuckled and nodded, then turned back to his

conversation. She noticed that Titus started to follow her, but stopped when he realized she was heading for the "charming facilities" courtesy of Port-O-Let. To give guests of the booth another layer of privacy, the bright blue cubicle was draped in a small, canvas cubicle in the corner. She slipped between the flaps and out of sight of both men. It only took her a minute to untie the flaps at the corner and slip out of the enclosure. According to her program, the monkey house was back in the direction they'd just come.

As she walked swiftly along the path, she knew she could still turn back. Titus was freakishly concerned about her safety, but the truth was, she hadn't even been mildly threatened until today. Even if her suspects wanted to launch a plot against her, they hadn't really had time to plan it, unless Barnes was in on it. It was always possible, but it didn't make a lot of sense. His client was dead. Now he had information to sell. Barnes had good reason to know how dangerous a spot of blackmail could be, so she was the logical choice. If he knew something, she needed to hear it. Having suspects was all good and well, but she needed some real, solid leads.

She reached the turnoff for the monkey house and paused to look around. The crowd appeared unaware of Dorothy's existence, as far as it was possible for her to tell. There was a street-type barricade blocking the path, but it was easy to slip around it. It only took a few steps before she found herself in deep, dense darkness.

She had to stop and let her pupils catch up. Since she wasn't a cat it only helped a little. As her eyes strained to pierce the darkness, her other senses switched to heightened awareness to help out. The noise of the party still shut out the small sounds, but now she could smell animals mixed with the other smells from the do, drifting in the night air.

Not being able to hear was almost worse than not hearing anything. It increased her sense of isolation. Almost, she turned back. If she hadn't remembered a small flashlight attached to her keys, she would have. There was no way she could go anywhere without some light. She dug around in her small purse and pulled out the light. It wasn't much, but the tiny, yellow circle was better than nothing.

Remy was chatting with the station boss and a sponsor while they waited for the bartender to get to their drinks when Titus tapped on his shoulder. He excused himself and stepped to the side. This had better be good.

"What?"

"Where's Dorothy?" Titus looked tense.

"She went to powder her nose." He nodded toward the facilities in the rear.

"Two women have gone in there and come out. Did something happen to upset her?" He looked accusingly at Remy. His attitude was not exactly the typical body-guard–client approved one.

"Not that I know." Remy looked around, but couldn't see her anywhere in the enclosure or nearby. It was odd enough to make him uneasy. Had something happened he hadn't noticed? "Barnes."

He'd thought it odd for the man to approach Dorothy. What if they'd agreed to meet somewhere tonight? He cursed silently. As soon as she mentioned the money, he knew it was a bad idea. Informants would be coming out of the woodwork after it, and no guarantee they had any info of value.

"Okay, maybe. Would—"

But Titus was already gone, sprinting through the crowds, indifferent to the spectacle he was making or the attention he was attracting. Remy shook his head before turning in the opposite direction. If he wanted to meet someone here, where would he suggest? He went about five steps and then turned around. He wouldn't direct them deeper in the zoo, he realized, but pick some place near the entrance and easy to find, but away from the party. If she got in trouble, no one would be able to hear her above the din. He cussed silently. What was she thinking?

When walking wasn't fast enough, he started to run, too.

Luckily the path was mostly smooth and the farther Dorothy got from the lights of the party, the more the quarter moon and the stars were able to help out. At the entrance to the monkey house, she hesitated. The thick, acrid odor of animal feces reached out toward her. Inside the dark entrance, one of the animals chattered its disapproval.

Out here, the party was a distant din. The blare of the music and all the chatter, no one would hear her if she cried out. This would be a great place to commit murder, she'd thought earlier. She didn't like being right. Away from the crowds, the softer night sounds seemed magnified. The underbrush seemed filled with rustles of who knew what. Not too far away she heard something snarling. It was a jungle, but a caged jungle, she reminded herself. She pulled the small pistol from her purse and made the necessary adjustments for defense. She kept it down at her side, hidden by the folds of her slip dress.

"Mr. Barnes?" she called softly.

"I wasn't sure you'd come," he said, stepping clear of the shadowy entrance. In the fragmented light, he looked like a puffed-out penguin in his tuxedo. His bald head was shiny with sweat, making it shimmer faintly.

"I wasn't sure, either." She kept her voice cool and her

distance from him. She was younger and would have no hesitation shedding her shoes and using some of her moves if he made a wrong move. "I'm hoping it's worth the distress I'm causing my date and my bodyguard."

He started to step closer and she stepped back. "That's close enough. This place is a little too private for my taste."

He looked startled, then rueful. "I never thought of that. I just didn't want us to be seen."

"By whom?"

He was quiet for a moment. "You said you offered Vance a million bucks to talk."

"That's right."

"He never paid me, you know. He always promised he would, that the money would be coming when he got out."

"From whoever hired him to kill my father," Dorothy pointed out. Were all defense attorneys this sensitive?

He shifted nervously. "I did my job. I deserved to get paid."

His client might disagree, but he wasn't her concern. "If you have information, I'm willing to pay for it. Who hired him to kill my father?"

"I told you, he never told *me,* but I think he may have told someone."

There was a sound, like twigs cracking in the darkness behind them. He jumped sharply.

"What was that?"

Dorothy looked back, but the dark night was unrelenting. "Probably a peacock or something. Don't they wander around?" Dorothy sighed impatiently. "Who did he tell?"

"He left a letter for me to give . . ."

There was a sound not unlike a cough or maybe it was a soft pop. Then a red hole appeared between his eyes. Immediately there was a gush of blood across his face. He looked startled and then his eyes went blank. He fell forward. It was instinct to try to catch him, but he was quite literally a dead weight. She jumped back just in time. As he fell at her feet, she heard another pop and thought she felt the rush of air by her cheek. She dropped to a crouch and lifted the pistol, pointing in the general direction the shots had come from.

Chapter Six

"I'm armed!" Dorothy's senses were on full alert, straining to see, to hear, or to smell the assailant. The semi-silence was indifferent and impenetrable. She longed to hide in the bushes along the side of the path, while at the same time, wanted to do anything but that. She'd never been wild about bugs, which seemed silly to be thinking about at the moment, but strangely logical, too. She felt like a light beacon against the path. Now she wished she'd worn the little black dress. Hadn't her mother always told her, a little black dress can't be beat?

The lack of reaction from the assailant emboldened her enough to reach down and feel Barnes's neck for a pulse. There was none and his skin was already losing its human warmth. Gradually, the various sounds in the night sorted themselves into categories. Party sounds far away, animal ones not far enough, and the stealthy ones of something large moving away from her. She swung the gun that direction, but couldn't pull the trigger. What if it was an animal? Or an innocent bystander? She couldn't fire blindly into the dark.

Now she heard footsteps, approaching quickly. She eased back toward the bushes, not yet in them, but trying to be of them until she knew if this was foe, not friend. Out of the darkness, she saw the round beam of a flashlight cutting into the night.

She hesitated before calling out, "Who's there?"

"Dorothy?" Titus sounded as frantic as he could sound. "Are you all right?"

The footsteps sped up, the beam dancing around until it found Barnes lying on the path in a pool of his own blood. Titus uttered one short and sharp cussword, then the beam shone on her, almost blinding her.

She shielded her eyes. "I'm fine. Did you see anyone on the path?"

Titus helped her upright. "Should I have?"

"It would have been helpful." She avoided looking at Barnes as she stowed her pistol.

"You didn't use it." It was more statement than question.

"I never saw which direction the shots came from."

More footsteps, running this time. Dorothy's insides curled into a ball of tension, but relaxed a bit when she saw Remy come round the bend in the path.

"I'm guessing you didn't see anyone, either." Dorothy suddenly felt cold. Shock, most likely. She tried to control the shudders, but couldn't.

Titus shoved the flashlight at Remy and pulled off his jacket, wrapping it around her shoulders.

"This was a stupid thing to do, going off like that."

Dorothy wanted to answer, but her teeth were chattering too persistently.

"Go get help," Remy directed Titus. He stepped forward, pulling her into his wonderfully warm embrace. Dorothy leaned her head on his shoulder, inhaling the scent of him gratefully. *I'll be strong later.*

Titus started to object, but stopped when Dorothy lifted her head from Remy's shoulder. "Please?"

He nodded stiffly and stalked off.

"What happened?" Remy asked.

Dorothy told him, using as few sentences as possible.

"Why didn't you have me come with you? I thought we

were partners." He sounded angry and worried, but his arms tightened around her and that's all that mattered.

"He said to come alone," she murmured into his shoulder.

"And do you always do what you're told?" He eased her back just enough so he could look into her eyes. Rueful humor softened the frustration in his eyes.

Dorothy managed a shaky half-smile and shook her head. As she looked at him something replaced both frustration and humor. It was warm and hot and it arced to her, pushing out the remainder of the cold that shook her body. She felt her body soften against his and her lips parted softly in anticipation. He was going to kiss her. Her mind knew it. Her mouth knew it. All of her wanted it.

His head started to bend, but she heard the sound of the approach of reinforcements. Dorothy sighed. Titus had terrible timing. Though Remy didn't let her go, she felt the distance grow between them. He wanted to be a reporter, not a lover right now. She pulled away from him, noticed a bench and said, "I'd like to sit down."

Remy probably didn't realize how relieved he looked. She smiled wryly to herself as cold stole through her again, already missing the warmth of his body. Memory tried to push its way back to center front, but she shoved it away. She'd deal with what had happened later.

Remy watched Dorothy across the clearing as it filled with crime scene techs and cops. No one liked murder and they especially didn't like murder at wealthy charity events. Money must be coddled to keep it flowing. Titus stood behind her, his body language screaming to them all to keep their distance. Remy tapped the shoulder of the nearest cop and asked, "Can I take Miss Merlinn home? She's had quite a shock."

The cop looked across at her. He nodded. "Just tell her to be available for questions tomorrow."

"She will cooperate fully," Remy assured them grimly. And she would. He was supposed to be the target, not her. If she'd kept her mouth shut about the money, he'd still be the target. Is that why she'd done it? Or was she just stubborn? Probably a little of both, he decided gloomily. And she'd seemed like such a nice, quiet girl ten years ago.

"We can leave, but you'll have to be available for questioning tomorrow. I told them you'd cooperate," Remy told Dorothy.

Her smile was a bit wan, but brave. "Of course."

He took her hands and pulled her upright. She started to hand Titus his jacket back, but Remy shook his head.

"I'm not cold anymore."

"There's blood on your dress," Remy said grimly. He didn't mention there was also some on her face.

"Great." She managed a wan smile and she looked exhausted, but unbroken. He wondered where her strength came from. She was much tougher than he'd realized. Perhaps she would surprise her enemies, too.

Titus stepped around him, getting between him and Dorothy. "There's another way out," he said, starting to steer her forward.

Remy stepped in front of him, staring at him for a long, hard moment. Titus bristled and looked at Dorothy, but she seemed unaware of either of them, her gaze distant and rather sad.

Titus slowly retreated. Good thing looks didn't kill. Remy tucked Dorothy's arm through his as they followed Titus down a path that led away from the festivities.

As they made their way back to the SUV, he found himself remembering that moment before Titus interrupted them and the soft, pliant feel of her body against his. He'd been about to kiss her and she hadn't seemed opposed to the idea. His body wanted to finish what they'd started, but not only was Titus behind them. While kissing her might satisfy a lot of urges, it was not the smart play. They didn't want the same things. It wasn't fair to her and it could become a snare for him. Maybe if she'd wanted to be first lady—but she didn't. She'd made that clear. He'd just have to remember their game needed to be played in public only. Now if he could just convince the rest of his body that his mind was right.

Bozo Luc stood to one side, calmly smoking a cigarette as what remained of Clinton Barnes was wheeled past, zipped into a body bag. He dropped the butt on the ground and absently ground it out with the heel of his custom-made, leather shoes. As the last of the smoke filtered out his nose, he headed for the exit, where a cop stood guard, taking down the names of everyone leaving.

When he saw Bozo, he straightened slightly and looked like he might be about to salute, but caught himself. "Sir."

Bozo nodded genially at the man as he passed, noting that the cop dutifully wrote down his name. Well, the formalities must be observed. In Louisiana, it was about the look of things, not the substance or the reality. If they did come question him, it would be for advice, of course. If it amused him, he might give some. The Lucs were always well-supplied with advice.

The entrance to the zoo was packed with emergency vehicles and buses trying to transport Zoo-to-Doers back to their vehicles. It was almost a novelty for them. Usually he only saw this sort of thing on television. Bozo beeped his driver, because he didn't ride buses. Even the most diligent chauffeur would have a time getting to him. He looked for a quiet spot and found it already occupied by Bubba Joe Henry.

"So, Barnes is dead." Bubba Jo puffed quietly on his Cuban for a few minutes. "Do you think it will scare her off? I heard she had his blood on her clothes and face."

Bozo shrugged slightly. The smoke ignited a craving for a smoke, but he didn't think he'd have time and repressed it. "It's not as if this is her first. Sadly, I think it will make her more tiresomely persistent. She appears to be a determined young woman."

A quality he himself possessed. Why had he not previously considered the timing of her birth? Certainly Dorothy had been most uninteresting ten years ago, but still, he should have considered the matter. His affair with Emma Merlinn had been brief, but certainly within the proper—or would that be improper—parameters. As many a young person had discovered, it only took once for those inconvenient surprises to occur.

Surely Magus ascertained paternity before allowing her into his life, though? He'd known Emma had an affair with someone. He'd come to Bozo, his friend, spilled his guts, and then they'd gotten drunk together. Bozo had, naturally, taken care to be less drunk and managed to avoid an unwise confession. Magus had wanted to know with whom, but Bozo had managed to persuade him to let it go.

He remembered being surprised that Magus cared. He'd seemed so indifferent to anything Emma did to get his attention. The poor, passionate and decidedly neglected lady had been ripe for the plucking. He'd almost hesitated the night she came to him, but she was old enough to know what she was doing. He'd fantasized about her, naturally, but she'd managed to exceed his expectations enough to make him wonder who'd been tutoring her in passion's arts. If Magus had been such a good teacher, no wonder she'd been desperate for it.

He'd been between wives at the time, so it had been a nice, albeit brief, diversion. It was the first, and only time, he'd been a woman's one-night stand, an intriguing reversal of his usual role. What was it about Emma that he still remembered every detail of that night? Had he been a less pragmatic man, she might have haunted him. He'd never found a woman her equal in that respect and he'd certainly tried. Perhaps, had she stayed, she'd have eventually disappointed, too. Maybe it was the briefness of the encounter that gave it its power?

Fortunately Dorothy didn't seem to have inherited Emma's wildness, though it might be lurking there beneath that very controlled surface. Be interesting to find out—as long as she wasn't his daughter. Kinky was all good in its place, but there were lines even he didn't cross.

The situation was worth looking into. If Magus had ordered a paternity test, there'd be a record of it somewhere, probably in that dump of a town where he'd found her. Or close by. He wouldn't have wanted word to get out that he was unsure what DNA flowed through the blood of his only child. The Wizard must always appear to be in control.

A pity they'd wanted the same thing. Occasionally he missed Magus's friendship. No one had ever understood him quite so well. One couldn't, however, allow a mongrel to occupy the governor's mansion, particularly one who didn't understood how things were done.

And what if Dorothy wasn't the Wizard's daughter? It would be a most interesting development. He'd bet she wouldn't like the world knowing about her mother's indiscretions. The Wizard's charming little fiction about a fight would be exposed. And if the voters knew she wasn't really the Wizard's daughter? Would that be enough of a look behind the curtain?

It could go either way, he supposed, unless played right. Her paternity wasn't the problem, but the lack of honesty. Yes, that was it. Honesty was it, well, the appearance of it, anyway.

Maybe he needed to shape the outcome a bit? What was truth, anyway?

"What—" Bubba Joe began.

Bozo cut him off. "There's my transport."

Bubba Joe watched Bozo cross the pavement and slide gracefully into his ride, a stretch limo that seriously upped the congestion in front of the zoo. The guy walked and talked like a girl. Thought he was bloody royalty, that nothing could touch him, and that he deserved the governor's mansion simply because of who he'd been born.

Bubba had been born with a cheap spoon in his mouth. His mother had been, quite simply, trailer park trash of the trashiest kind. Fortunately, she'd fallen down her trailer steps and broken her neck just after he graduated high school with ill-gotten honors and an unearned scholarship in his pocket. He'd been able to pretty up her image a bit, just enough to appear self-made and humble without actually having to be either of those things. The truth was, Suzanne had made him and made sure he didn't forget it. She was the original ice queen, but it didn't matter how she was in bed because she'd been born with an instinct for politics that made up for any other shortcoming she might have. And she was happy to look the other way and clean up any messes his flings might cause his political future.

Bubba Joe shifted restlessly as more cops streamed out the door, mingled with, but not part of the guests. Suzanne had just put an end to his latest affair, leaving him without the means to satisfy his considerable libido—or mute uneasy thoughts that wanted to revolve around Dorothy Merlinn. He'd gone to see her, hoping that being face-to-face with her would put an end to his fear she might be his biological daughter. He tried to ensure he shot blanks when he played, but Emma had taken him by surprise. He didn't think she even liked him. Actually, he was pretty sure she didn't like him then or later. Bubba Joe knew enough about revenge plays to recognize one when he saw it and he was happy to oblige a lady. She'd tried to change her mind, but he put an end to that nonsense. You play with him, you pay. No cheating allowed. When he'd heard she was pregnant, the timing was close enough to make him uneasy. Affairs were not the accepted sideline of politicians, but illegitimate children were something else entirely.

Thankfully Emma chose to disappear rather than make a fuss. She'd been smarter than her daughter seemed to be. And if Dorothy was his daughter? Even his possible paternity wouldn't help her if she got in his way. He'd stood aside for the Wizard ten years ago, but he was standing aside for no one this time. He wasn't getting any younger. No way was he waiting eight more years to be a stinking governor, not when he could see and almost taste the presidency waiting out there for him. The party was hungry for someone like him, someone who could charm the voters, energize the electorate and eliminate the competition.

At first, he'd thought about trying to track down the paternity test he was sure Magus had had done, just to be sure, but now he didn't think so. Magus would never have left her his money unless he was sure. Which meant she was fair game—for anything. Maybe there was something of her tasty little mother there.

★ ★ ★ ★ ★

Darius sat quietly in the back of his limousine. The evening had certainly been unexpected, to say the least. While Barnes's murder had been remarkable and timely, he had to give Dorothy top honors for interesting. No question she was Emma's daughter. Whether or not she was his, was still up in the air. She could be, but it was hard to see Magus letting himself be fooled, unless he hadn't known Emma had strayed? Of course, Darius had wondered through the years why she came to him that night, why she left and why she never came back. And he wondered why she left Magus and the state. If Magus had found out or she'd told him, that would explain her precipitous departure and Magus's disinterest in his only child. Ten years ago, Magus claimed they had a fight and she never told him he had a daughter.

Whether Magus knew or not, Darius would bet real money there'd been a paternity test. Magus never took anything for granted. Darius made a note to have this researched. If it was out there, one of his people would find it. It might prove useful.

For now, he'd assume Magus had known Dorothy's paternity, for a perfectly selfish reason: she interested him. And it had been a long time since a woman had.

He had no doubt he could pry her from Mistral's grasp. If she didn't come willingly, well, there were many ways to deal with intransigence.

Dorothy was relieved when Remy didn't try to talk about what happened until she had a chance to change. Remy waited in her sitting room while she changed out of her bloodied dress. As she stripped it off and washed the blood from her face, shock made a comeback. Memories flooded her mind, memories of Magus's death. The bullet that passed through Magus's head had thumped into her shoulder, knocking her back a step, but not knocking her out. She'd had ample time to fully imprint all the awful details of her father's death. Blood and brain matter had splattered her face and clothes because she'd been standing on a riser, slightly higher than he was as he gave his stump speech. She didn't see the bullet enter, but she did see it exit his head. And the hole it left when most of the back of his head came off. She'd seen him crumple like a puppet whose strings had suddenly been released. Stared down into his sightless eyes, and the bullet hole between them, for what seemed like an eternity, before mercifully losing consciousness.

With images of both deaths flashing like strobe lights inside her head, she stumbled into pajamas, then a warm robe, her teeth chattering uncontrollably. Maybe she took too long. She'd lost track of time by the time Remy tapped on the door, and then pushed it open. When he saw her standing there, her arms wrapped around her middle, he strode in, gathered her up and carried her out in the sitting room. He deposited her on a settee, then found a blanket and tucked it around her. A food service tray was sitting there with a pot of hot chocolate.

"I figured you need it," he said, pouring her a cup and pressing it into her hands. He kept his hand wrapped around hers as he guided the cup to her mouth. The warm, sweet brew flowed down her throat, spreading heat along its downward path. "Bring back some old, bad memories, did it?"

She nodded. "For some reason, I didn't expect it. It's not like I knew Barnes."

"It's death you know, all too well," he said. "AC is set to *Ice Station Zebra* levels in this damn room." He found the controls and adjusted them, then turned to study her.

Dorothy produced a wan smile for his efforts, and was happy to change the subject. "I liked that book, but thought I was freezing the whole time I was reading it."

"Something else we have in common," he said, finally sitting in the chair near her.

"Else?" Dorothy arched her brows.

"Besides the desire to find out who hired Vance to kill your father."

"Oh, that. Not a lot to build a fake relationship on." With the slow retreat of shock, came the return of her sense of humor. "Reminds me of *Best in Show*. What was it? Soup and peas she and that old guy had in common?"

"And talking and not talking," Remy finished, with a grin. "Another one for our 'in common' column."

"Talking and not talking?" Her smile felt natural this time. It was too easy to like him. She thought about the moment he almost kissed her and felt her face flush. She lifted the cup to hide it.

"The movie," he chided her gently.

"Right." As a different kind of warmth built from her middle out, she found herself remembering Remy's mouth hovering above hers instead of blood and horror. She liked the memory much better, but in its own way, it was just as dangerous. So she kept the cup close to her mouth as she asked, "So, who do you like for Barnes's murder? All our suspects were there, unfortunately."

There was a pause, as if Remy were thinking of not letting her change the subject, then he said, "And all of them positioned to see Barnes talking to you."

She was relieved and disappointed. "So one of them knew what he was trying to tell me?"

"Or suspected he knew something."

"That's cold, killing him for mere suspicion." Dorothy

shivered as she remembered how close the bullets had come to her, though it had its comic side, too. She, Titus, the killer and Remy had all been milling around in the dark within a few feet of each other like the freaking Keystone Cops and not known it.

"You're sure he said Vance left a letter to give to someone?" Remy frowned thoughtfully.

Dorothy nodded. She lowered the cup to the table, taking extra care as a sudden thought sent excitement surging through her. "Wasn't Vance married?"

Remy arched a brow thoughtfully. "Yeah, he was."

"I wonder if she'd talk to me?"

"Why do you think she wouldn't?"

"Well, it is my fault Vance is dead."

The phone rang sharply. Dorothy picked it up. "Yes?"

"You have a message, ma'am, but the caller wouldn't leave it in the voice mail system," the desk clerk said.

"What is it?" Dorothy grabbed the pen and paper next to the phone.

"A Vonda Vance asked you to call her." He gave her the number.

"Thank you." Dorothy re-cradled the receiver. "Vonda Vance wants to talk to me. What do you remember about her?"

"She's a librarian, by all accounts a nice woman, had no clue what Vance really did."

"I don't remember her," Dorothy said, pulling up pictures from the trial from the file of her memory.

"You wouldn't. She was pretty nondescript. Kind that blended into the wall. Lucky for her. We lost interest in her pretty quickly."

"I thought I was pretty nondescript back then, too," Dorothy said.

"Yes, but you were the Wizard's heir. There was no place you could hide. I'm sorry."

She shrugged. "Do you think it's too late to call her?"

"It's two in the morning."

"Oh, right." She slanted him a look. "I'd still be waiting up if it was me."

Remy pushed the phone toward her. "Give it a shot."

She looked at the phone longingly. She was so close, if Barnes had given this woman a letter from Vance. What other reason could she have for calling? But her mother had taught her it was rude to call a friend after ten. To call a stranger? Infamy.

"I'll wait for morning. Rats." She looked at the clock. "Now I won't be able to sleep in."

Remy grinned at her. "Life's tough." His expression changed slightly.

"And then you die." She shot it back without thinking.

They both sobered. Dorothy looked away first, lifting the cup to her lips again to hide their sudden need to tremble. She gave herself a mental shake. If they were right about Vonda Vance, by tomorrow it could be all over. She'd know who did it. She was quite sure it wouldn't be the butler.

He turned off the tape recording of the clerk's call to Dorothy, silently cursing. Vance should have known better than to involve his wife in this, but he hadn't. It shouldn't surprise him. Vance had ample reason to want an insurance policy, but why had he chosen Vonda? He knew, better than anyone, the danger. Idiot.

And Vonda? Well, she was no fool. She obviously knew the value of the information and who'd be in the best position to pay for it. She wasn't the type to try her hand at

95

blackmailing a killer. She might be naive, but she wasn't stupid.

Barnes must have given it to her today. Interesting, that. Be more like him to keep it and use it himself. Unless he suspected Vance had told his wife about the letter? Made sense. Or maybe Barnes realized it was too hot for him to handle. If he'd just kept that perspective, he'd still be alive. He was beyond idiot, but then, Vance hadn't paid his bill. Those unpaid, billable hours must have been eating at him all these years.

"I should have considered Barnes's greed, but it had been so dangerous. Much easier to let events play out and then pay Vance as agreed when he got out of jail and let him pay Barnes." Even hiring the idiot for legal advice had seemed too risky.

And now Vonda had to be dealt with. It was a pity. She was a nice woman, but she should have stayed out of her husband's business. He checked his weapon, screwing the silencer back in place. Then he gathered up his jacket and left the room, closing the door silently behind him.

Vonda stayed up well past her bedtime, waiting for the Wizard's daughter to call her back. When she turned on the news, she understood why.

So Barnes was dead. *Murdered.* For the first time, it occurred to her that the letter might put her in danger, also. It shouldn't have taken so long for her to realize it, but she could castigate herself for stupidity later. It seemed obvious Barnes was after the money, too. Had he told Dorothy about Vonda and the letter? The fact that Dorothy hadn't called her, seemed to indicate he hadn't. But she couldn't assume anything.

She got up, overcome with a desire to flee, to hide. She

could be overreacting, but better that than dead. She pulled the letter out of the pocket of her dressing gown. She was not going to let Verrol be silenced again. She had to hide the letter, and then find a place to stay for the night. Leda would welcome her, but she didn't dare put her at risk. She'd call Dorothy in the morning and together they could retrieve the letter. Maybe she was letting her imagination run away with her, but there was no way she could stay here alone tonight, not after seeing that body bag leaving the zoo.

Which brought her to—literally—the million-dollar question. Where could she hide it that no one would find it? If it were daytime, she'd put it in her safety deposit box, but it wasn't. And if the worst happened? She wanted the right people to find it. She had a fire safe, but that would be the first place anyone would look. She'd probably read thousands of mysteries in her lifetime. Surely she could come up with something good?

As she packed an overnight bag with hands that persisted in shaking, life suddenly seemed more precious than it ever had, even when Verrol was still a physical presence in her life. She took so many things for granted. She wouldn't anymore. She'd be brave and bold, all the things she only managed in her imagination. And after the killer was exposed, she'd do all the things she daydreamed about doing. And maybe she'd do some things she'd always been afraid of doing. Like that bungee cord thing.

In the meantime, there was the letter. It was the key to everything. Okay, start simple, Vonda. First she switched its envelope with another letter from Verrol. She needed to hide it someplace hard enough to be believed, but not impossible to find. She discarded several places, before deciding on the Sherlock Homes, hide-in-plain-sight method. She slipped it under the blotter on her desk, leaving it just slightly askew, like she'd shoved it there in a hurry.

To the real letter in its new envelope, she added a short note that said simply, "Leda, you'll know what to do with this when you read it." This she placed in a Ziploc bag. She was thinking maybe the freezer or the toilet tank as a hiding place when she heard stealthy movement outside in the hallway. As she stared at it, someone very gently and slowly tried the doorknob. Her first reaction was to scream, but luckily terror tightened her throat, making that impossible. She grabbed the phone and had punched 911 before she realized it was dead.

Her next impulse was to hide, but there was nowhere to hide in her tiny apartment. Nowhere to run—that wasn't entirely true. Adrenaline sharpened her thought processes to a razor point of clarity. She grabbed her purse and the suitcase with the vague idea of fooling the invader into thinking she was already gone, then backed into the bedroom, without taking her eyes off the door. It took all her willpower to close the door and shut off the sight and sound of attempted entry.

Now fear made her fast. She went to the window, pushed it open and eased out the screen. The fire ladder was curled under her nightstand. She secured it over the edge, tossed out bag and purse, and threw her leg over the edge. When she had both feet on the metal rung, she pulled the curtains over the window.

It was surprisingly hard to navigate the rope. It hung straight down the side of the building and moved with her. She bounced and swayed with each step. At the bottom, she eased her feet down into the shrubbery that ran along the side of the building, testing the noise factor before putting her weight down. Above her she clearly heard the muffled sounds of someone searching her apartment. Bad time to wish she had a cell phone. It was tempting to find a door to bang on, but this time of night, who would let her in? And would it alert whoever was in her apartment?

First she needed to hide the letter. At the least, it would be a bargaining chip, if the searcher wasn't fooled by her red herring. She hid her suitcase and purse in the shrubbery a few feet down from her window, then started around the house, keeping close to the building. At the corner, she stopped. What if whoever was up in her apartment hadn't come alone? Her car might be staked out. Okay, so avoid the parking lot.

It was terrifying to be out in the thick, hot dark. She'd never been a brave woman, except in her imagination. Now the night seemed full of eyes, and who knew what wildlife? She wasn't far from the bayou. What if there was an alligator taking a stroll in the dark? She'd read just last year of someone who had an alligator turn up in their pool. The apartment complex had a pool. Or there could be thieves or even a rapist prowling around. It would be just her luck to flee from a killer and into the arms of a rapist.

She gave herself a shake. Maybe it would be better if she didn't think and just did. The next building over was where her friend, Leda Tasker, lived. She didn't dare seek refuge with Leda and bring danger to her, too, if she could draw danger away from her. What she had in mind wouldn't precisely endanger her, but when Leda found the letter, she'd know what to do with it if . . .

Vonda pushed that thought away. Focus on the task. That was the way to deal with it. There was one open space to cross. Fortunately the moon was on the wane. Just enough light to see, but hopefully not be seen. She did what she'd come to do, then worked her way around Leda's building, too.

The night wouldn't be so terrifying if she was in her car. Maybe by now it was safe. Or she could hide nearby and just see if anyone seemed to watching her car. She circled all the way around, now moving along the back of the complex, where the smell of garbage was almost overpowering. It was also a lot more scary back here, where no windows overlooked the dismal view. She crouched between two, broken-down cars, wrapped her arms around her middle and tried to slow her breathing. She was hyperventilating. Not a good time to pass out.

Inside her apartment, it seemed like the city was never quiet. Seemed like cars were always driving by. Tires squealed. People talked loud as they walked to the building or played their music too loud. Why did everything have to go quiet tonight? Any normal sound would have been so gratefully received by her straining ears right now. And then her straining ears did hear something. Stealthy footsteps. If her throat weren't totally closed with fear, she would have whimpered. For a moment all thought stilled, but when the footsteps seemed to be coming her way, adrenaline gave her some flight impetus. She flattened out and slipped quietly under the car. It was both better and worse.

Now she could see movement and occasionally a dark silhouette against the darker bulk of the building. The figure stopped now and then, bending to poke into the shrubbery that marched forlornly around the building. At the corner, when the wan moon cast a pitiful light into the shadows, he stopped, turning slightly as if straining to hear. In that moment, she saw light hit something metallic in his hands. Something that appeared to be shaped like a gun.

She stuffed her fist in her mouth to stop the scream trying to push its way up from the bottom of her stomach where her heart had dropped.

"Vonda?" The voice was soft, but well-known to her. She sagged in relief. Safe. She was safe.

Chapter Seven

Remy closed his suitcase and snapped the locks. No matter how expensive the hotel, it was still just a hotel. Their suite had been sumptuous and comfortable, but he'd be glad to get back in his apartment and away from Titus's brooding presence. They'd each had one of the suite's three bedrooms. Remy found it ironic that Titus had taken the middle room. He'd probably stayed up all night listening to make sure Remy didn't creep into Dorothy's room. The whole situation reminded him of a Neil Simon farce.

No question the guy was a weird duck. His presence was flat, but persistent. Remy didn't know a lot about him, except that he was just *there*. Dorothy had mentioned something about him going to high school with her mother. It was the only personal detail he knew about the guy. And, actually, he didn't want to know that. He just wanted him out of his face.

He did a quick check, and then left the room. In the sitting room, Dorothy was using the phone. She acknowledged his presence with a small wave toward breakfast. Remy examined the offerings, chose some fruit and a bagel and sat down to eat.

Dorothy hung up the phone with a slight frown. "Something's wrong. Vonda isn't answering."

"Maybe she already went to work."

"Would you, without leaving that number, too?"

She had a point. Her voice was calm and controlled, but was she? Remy studied her face, trying to assess how all this

102

was affecting her. She'd been back, what, three days and already two people were dead. He hoped Vonda wasn't number three. "Maybe she changed her mind?"

From what he'd known about Vonda he didn't believe it, but people changed. Life happened and some people took it well, some didn't. Life had definitely thrown her a curve ball when she found out her husband was a hired killer.

"You think she may be trying to blackmail the killer? That would be so dangerous." She shivered.

Was she remembering Barnes or her father? He shrugged. "It's a possibility. Or she just went out for breakfast. You left a message on her machine?"

Dorothy nodded. "I'd like to go see her. Wait for her or something."

"Let's give it a bit longer. I'll see if I can track down an address and in the meantime—"

The phone cut across his words. Dorothy all but jumped on it.

"Yes?"

She listened for a moment, looked both disappointed and surprised. "Certainly, send them up." She hung up the phone. "It seems I have a delegation from the state genealogical society. They have a presentation for me."

"They probably want money." That made her smile, not wholeheartedly, but it was something. He was glad for the distraction. She needed to decompress, get her balance back before they saw Vonda. She looked calm, but he could feel the seething tension beneath the surface of that calm.

Besides all the other mess, he'd heard her fielding a number of business calls, all before nine in the morning. She was, she'd told him, working toward turning her father's companies into co-ops run by the employees. She'd hoped to have everything completed before her return to

Louisiana, but there'd been some delays. She hadn't gone into detail, but he was a reporter. He knew she was selling control of the companies to the employees well below market value. Some of the members of the board were fighting her on it. He'd heard she wanted to make sure that the new management had enough money to keep the businesses healthy during the transition period. She had to have lost millions on the deal. Of course she had millions, but still, not many people could have walked away from all that money.

A knock at the suite door interrupted his thoughts. She answered the door herself, which was odd. Why wasn't Titus running interference, as usual?

Two women and a man entered the suite, introducing themselves with flustered eagerness. Dorothy invited them to sit down and offered them refreshment, which was refused with even more flustered effusiveness.

"We're so sorry to disturb you, Miss Merlinn," the thinnest one, who also seemed to be the leader of the group, said in a gush of remorse. "So kind of you to let us come up."

"It's truly not a problem," Dorothy said, with a reassuring smile. "And call me Dorothy. I don't know anyone who calls me Miss Merlinn."

She'd make a great governor's wife. Remy studied the tableau from a short distance as she put them at ease, and then graciously accepted the genealogy scroll of her family that they had prepared for her. She listened with apparent interest as they told her about their organization, then, without being asked, managed to give them a contribution and get them out the door in record time. There was no sign that she was seething with impatience and curiosity about Vonda Vance and what she might have to tell her. She might not like this life, but she was good at it.

104

He looked at his watch. He could only spare another hour before he had to get in prep for his show. Lots to talk about again today.

When the door closed, she turned with a rueful smile, still holding the scroll.

"Do you really not have a family line traced already?" Remy asked. "I'd have thought Magus would have himself traced back to some kings for sure."

"If he did, I never found it," Dorothy said. She tossed it on the table by the phone and tried Vonda's number again. He heard the phone start to ring and out of curiosity picked up the discarded scroll. He arched his brows in mute question, she nodded, so he untied the ribbon, and unrolled the heavy parchment.

They'd done a nice job of it, tracing not just Magus's line, but her mother's, spreading them artistically around on a tree with leaves for family members. He studied the names, following different lines.

"Any kings?" Dorothy asked.

"Just a couple of French dukes." Remy grinned at her before turning the sheet sideways to study her mother's line. "I didn't realize your mother had a sister. Where does she live?"

Dorothy's eyes widened. "I didn't know she had a sister."

Before Remy could respond, he heard the ringing stop.

"Yes, hello," Dorothy said. "Is Vonda there?" Her brows pulled together, putting a charming wrinkle between her brows.

You've got it bad, Mistral, when you start admiring wrinkles. Luckily she hung up the phone, the expression on her face odd enough to drive out everything but curiosity. "What?"

"That was a police officer. Apparently Vonda's apartment was broken into last night."

"And Vonda?" Remy asked sharply.

"No one seems to know," Dorothy said, her face suddenly white and drawn. She turned from him, wrapping her arms around her middle. "I should have left it alone. I should have just left it alone."

Remy approached her cautiously. Her back was unnaturally straight and brittle-looking. He touched her lightly, then turned her to face him.

"This isn't your fault. Crap happens. Trust me, crap would have happened with or without you. Whoever did this, well, secrets have a way of surfacing. One way or another. The only person to blame here, is the person who started it all. The killer."

She nodded, but he could tell she didn't really believe him. He didn't blame her. When secrets surfaced, it was because someone dropped a rock in the pool where they were hiding. Together, they'd dropped a big one. Truth was, he felt responsible, too. He opened his mouth to tell her that, when her head drooped forward onto his shoulder.

"I'm sorry. I just didn't know it would be like this. I guess I thought it would be like TV, where we just followed the clues and justice was done. Stupid, huh?"

Without thinking, he pulled her close. "Not stupid at all. We'll get through this. We'll find out who did it and stop him."

"Him?" She looked up at him, giving him an unobstructed view of her amazing, violet eyes and the sweet, heady curve of her mouth.

"Or her," he said, huskily.

He saw her eyes darken as they registered his change in focus. Thinking slowed to a crawl as his blood supply moved south for other duty. It wasn't smart, but it had been a while since he'd felt the clean, swift bite of desire. Had he really been proposing a marriage of convenience to her or had he, on some level, known she might be the right fit for him?

That was the last clear thought he had as she moistened her slightly parted lips with her tongue. The glistening oval beckoned, promising both respite from worry and a plunge into sensation. He bent his head. Their lips touched lightly. He pulled back, brushing his mouth against hers. He prepared to go in for the long haul, when they both heard the fumble of someone at the door.

By the time the door opened, they were several feet apart. Dorothy had her back to Titus, who stopped in the doorway. *That's twice. Third time, he smashed his face in.*

Titus's eyes narrowed sharply on Remy, then they flashed to Dorothy. "Everything all right?"

Dorothy pretended to be busy with papers on her desk. "Of course." She looked up, one brow arched. "Why wouldn't they be?"

Titus nodded, gave them both another look, then went into the other room, closing the door with just a hint of a snap. Remy grinned at her, and then looked at his watch. "I've got to go to work."

He gave her a look of apology.

She accepted with a smile. He had his hand on the knob when she said, "Remy?"

He looked back at her.

"How do we stop him?"

"By getting in his way."

Her smile was slow, but breathtaking. He wanted to cross the room and bury himself in that smile. He hung on to the knob like it was a lifeline. Probably because it was.

"Let's up the stakes then," she said, a grim note in her voice, despite the smile.

"What do you mean?"

"Let's have a party."

She made it sound like a rumble. "Okay," he said cautiously. "Where?"

"Oz. I think we should open Oz."

She was terribly calm, but Remy had the feeling it was the proverbial calm before the storm.

Kate Needham opened the Web page for the New Orleans newspaper, *The Times-Picayune,* and started browsing for stories about the governor's race. She didn't have to look far. The murder of Clinton Barnes wasn't the lead, but it was below the fold, front page. By this time she was familiar with all the players, but even if she weren't, the lead paragraphs had enough info to place Barnes in his proper context as Verrol Vance's attorney.

So, Vance was dead and now so was his attorney. And Dorothy had been with Barnes when he was shot. It was a throwaway line. Clearly the police were trying to downplay Dorothy's role in the incident. What had she been doing with Barnes, except trying to get information? She'd made it clear during the interview Kate had listened to via the Internet yesterday, that she was determined to find who had hired Vance to kill her father.

She just had to mention the money. Kate shook her head. Foolish girl, waving all that money in people's faces. So far all it had accomplished was to get two people killed. Granted, they weren't the two most honorable people on the planet, but Kate was sure Dorothy felt the weight of their deaths, nonetheless. Her face showed her to be a person of character and resolve, despite her resemblance to her mother.

Did she ever wonder about the past or about her DNA donors? Clearly she'd tried to make some kind of connection with Magus ten years ago. That had ended in disaster and almost killed her. Now she was getting herself involved with Remy Mistral. Why had she exchanged one driven, ambitious man for another? Like her mother, it seemed she was a slow learner.

Should she contact Dorothy, she wondered, just like she had every day since she found the article about her? She knew Henry was worried about her and it grieved her that it was so, but how could she ever explain to him what happened when she wasn't sure she knew herself. What was real? What wasn't? For the last ten years, she'd been Kate, just Kate, Henry's wife.

Sometimes this dark feeling had swept over her and she knew that something was lurking out there somewhere, something awful just waiting to pounce, but the shrink told her it was just the blues. People often had feelings of impending doom without it meaning doom were truly impending. He'd given her some antidepressants and sent her home. And while she took them, doom did move further away. But it hadn't left and it chose this week to pounce on her with stunning force.

Being hit by a train would have been easier than this. It was as if her life was this connect-the-dots puzzle and she hadn't even noticed that not all the dots were there. Now they were back, painfully back. She couldn't tell Henry. He'd hate her. So she'd gone to her shrink again. The one who told her it was normal. He'd given her a new version of "normal" this visit.

"Extreme stress, severe trauma can cause the repression of painful memories and sometimes memory loss."

"For so long?"

"There was, apparently, nothing in your life to remind you until now. Or maybe your mind wasn't ready to deal with it."

"I don't feel ready now!" she'd cried out. And she still didn't, but he'd assured she was. Easy for him to say. He just had to sit and listen and collect his money. He didn't have to live it or feel it. More than anything, she wanted to turn back the clock, not have clicked on the link that took her to the Web site with the story.

She felt the lie of it, even as she told it to herself. She might wish she hadn't done the things she'd done in the past, but the truth was, she couldn't regret being whole again. It was only now, in that fifty-fifty hindsight that she could see she had been less for not having all herself in her head the last ten years.

She heard the gentle whir of Henry's wheelchair behind her. Dear, dear Henry. Would he love the whole her as much as he'd loved the half her? It shamed her that she wasn't sure. Ten years of marriage should count for something, shouldn't it? Even count against some forgotten truths? Would Henry have loved her with her missing parts? She didn't love him the less for his lost mobility. But that wasn't about his character.

Her head drooped, even as she quickly closed the window on the computer screen. The wheelchair came closer until he was in her peripheral vision. His hand, less vigorous than when he'd proposed to her, but strong enough, gripped hers.

"Won't you tell me what's wrong, Kate?" His voice was so gentle, her body shook with the pain of it. His anger would have been easier to take.

"If these ten years are real, if you've been shaped by them, Kate," her shrink had said, "then you'll be able to tell Henry the truth."

But what was truth? She hadn't just forgotten her past. She'd made up a new one and apparently believed it to be real. How was that possible? The shrink had a word for it. So did Kate. *Crazy.* If she was having trouble believing it and she'd lived it, how would Henry feel?

"There's nothing you can't tell me, Kate." His grip tightened on hers. "Now that I'm . . . less mobile, if you've needed . . . more than I can give you . . ."

She whirled to face him. "No! Never that, Henry! Never that!"

"Then what?"

"It's so much worse than an affair." She pulled her hand free of his, curled both into fists.

"I love you."

"You won't for long."

"Can you trust me so little?" He looked hurt. He would be hurt either way. He held out his hand to her. "Kate?"

She took a shaky breath, and then took his hand. Where to begin?

"I . . . have . . . had a sister." Through his hand she felt surprise jolt through him. And this was only the beginning.

Titus would have yet another conniption, but Dorothy didn't care. For this visit, she didn't need any shadow but her own. It had been easy enough to get Vonda Vance's address. Those useful contacts of Magus's. The concierge got her a cab and he knew the address. The drive over was bumpy, but that was because of the city's infamous potholes. Any other time, she'd have enjoyed the drive through the city streets. She'd forgotten how interesting New Orleans was, with its mix of old and new, fast and slow.

Vonda's apartment complex was not particularly attractive, but it wasn't a complete dive, either. For some reason, this reassured her. At least her life hadn't been awful after her husband went to prison.

There was still a police car out front, but none of the other trappings of a crime scene. Dorothy paid the cab and went inside. Vonda's apartment was on the second floor. Gravity pulled against her as she climbed the stairs, releasing her reluctantly. At the end of the hallway, she saw an open door. Inside, a cop and a woman stood talking among the chaos of the tossed apartment. They both turned to watch her approach with a curiosity that increased as it became clear where she was heading.

"I called earlier," Dorothy said. "Did I speak with you?" She looked at the cop.

He nodded, looking a bit flustered. He was young, painfully young to Dorothy's eyes.

"You're Dorothy Merlinn?"

The woman with him jerked at the sound of Dorothy's name. "You're the Wizard's daughter?"

"I'm afraid so." Dorothy gave her an apologetic look as she studied her.

She was medium everything, build, coloring, height, weight and dress. The only exception was a pair of glasses hanging from her neck on a lurid, beaded chain. It was the kind of interesting incongruity that Dorothy loved.

"I'm Leda Tasker. Vonda was a friend and co-worker." She tried to look suspiciously at Dorothy, but her curiosity kept getting in the way. "He said Vonda called you last night?"

"She left a message at my hotel, asking me to call her," Dorothy confirmed. "Have you heard anything . . . ?"

Leda shook her head, worry pushing out everything else on her face. "They found a suitcase with her things and her purse in the bushes below her window with everything tossed around it."

"It seems she may have climbed down a fire ladder," the cop added.

Dorothy looked at the mess. "I take it this isn't normal for her?"

"Hardly! Vonda was very neat!"

Books were strewn about. Her CD cases had been opened, the discs dumped, the covers pulled out, and then thrown into a pile. Drawers were opened, the contents tossed. Cushions had been ripped open. The desk looked like a category five hurricane had hit it. Even the refrigerator hung open, the contents clearly searched, then dumped on the floor.

"Do the other rooms look like this?" Dorothy asked, dully. If any letter had been here, it had been found. Someone had, so far, managed to stay one step ahead of her all the way.

"But nothing seems to be missing," the cop said. "Money was still in her wallet, TV and stereo still here."

Leda looked tense and her eyes were wide with worry. "Do you know what they were looking for?"

Dorothy hesitated, wondering how much to say. She hated those mysteries where no one told anyone anything. "I think she had something she wanted to give me. I had the impression it had something to do with my father's murder."

"You think Verrol finally told her who hired him?" Leda asked. "You mean that idiot put her in danger like that? He's lucky he's already dead!"

"He may have thought she'd want to know. Or that it would be financially beneficial to her," Dorothy said carefully. "I'd have certainly paid her for it."

Leda looked fierce. "She wouldn't have wanted money,

just justice. She was a good person!"

"I would have wanted to help her, just the same," Dorothy said. "I would have liked to know."

Leda calmed. "If she got down the ladder, she might be hiding somewhere, afraid to come out."

Dorothy looked around, trying to imagine what she'd do in this place with a killer outside the door. She could feel the residue of fear now. She recognized it from last night. Also the enmity and the fear of the killer, fear of exposure and capture, perhaps?

The search had a methodical look to it. He'd felt he had time. But then it had gotten more frenetic. He hadn't found anything. He was getting frustrated. She went over and looked in the bedroom. The curtain had been ripped back, as if by an angry hand. He'd looked out, realized she'd fled, taking what he was looking for with her. She couldn't have been gone long. Perhaps he'd seen her shadow moving in the apartment before he came up? Because just getting the letter wouldn't be enough. The information was inside her head now.

Beneath the fear, Dorothy also felt resolve and courage. Vonda had shown presence of mind by going out the fire ladder. She'd have known why she was in danger and probably tried to secure the secret some way. But where would she put it that the killer wouldn't find, but a friendly would?

"You didn't find anything in her stuff, I take it?" Dorothy asked.

Leda shook her head. "Whoever was after her found it, as well. It had been searched."

Great. "What about your mailbox? Did you check it this morning?"

Leda looked startled. "No!"

She ran out of the room. The cop looked at Dorothy, then as one they turned and followed.

He watched from the shadows as Dorothy, the cop and a woman ran out of the building, then to the front of the next. The woman stopped at the row of mailboxes. Did they think he hadn't thought of that? He'd looked in them all and found nothing.

He saw their shoulders droop. They talked for a bit, and then started to walk, not back to Vonda's place, but around the building. They were looking at the ground. Did they think they were Indian scouts who could find footprints on cement? They turned the corner, out of sight. Curiosity had him starting the car. He had to keep his distance, but if he drove to the end of the complex, turned down the side, then around the corner to the rear of the complex . . .

Now they were standing between two cars, looking at something. He couldn't see what. Dorothy, sharp-eyed and reckless, was now walking around the area, looking at the ground very carefully. She'd find it soon, damn it. Yes, she'd stopped. An exclamation, the other two hurried to join her, but she was already following the trail. Around the garbage containers. To the fence. She placed a foot on the ramp of the container and climbed up.

Don't look, he thought. Let the cop look. . . .

She dropped down. Even from here he could see her white face. The cop climbed up to look at the body he'd dumped there, and Dorothy put her arms around the sobbing woman.

Three bodies in three days. Must be some kind of record. For both of them.

Remy came as soon as his show was over. The crime

115

scene had mostly been wrapped up, and the body removed. Titus had beaten him there, and was smoldering just off Dorothy's right shoulder. He wouldn't chew her out in front of Leda, but he made sure she knew how he felt.

Dorothy saw him and started toward him, then stopped. Where did playacting stop and reality begin? She didn't know. Fortunately, he closed the distance, wrapping her in a warm, comforting embrace. Over his shoulder, she could see a photographer snap a picture. She was glad he was there. Because he was, she could lay her head on Remy's shoulder without him misunderstanding it.

Remy didn't say anything about her solo foray into detecting, for which she was most grateful. She was a grown-up, even if Titus refused to treat her like one.

"You're having an interesting week, aren't you?" Remy murmured against the top of her head. This massive understatement had her pulling back to look at him. Because of Leda next to her, she didn't smile, but she knew he saw it in her eyes for a moment.

She turned to Leda, whose eyes were red and swollen from crying.

"This is Leda Tasker, a friend of Vonda's."

"I'm sorry about your friend," he said, shaking her hand. "She was always nice to us back then, even when we weren't always nice to her."

Leda's eyes filled up with tears. "She was a good person. She didn't deserve this."

"How . . ." Remy stopped, as if he realized there was no tactful way to ask the question.

"She was shot," Dorothy said.

"Then discarded like old rags," Leda finished bitterly.

"You said her apartment was trashed?"

116

Dorothy nodded. "It's hard to tell if the killer found anything. I know we didn't."

Dorothy wanted to burrow back into his arms. It was painfully hot, but she was so cold, it felt like she'd never be warm again. She couldn't get the image of Vonda's dead, staring eyes out of her head. She wasn't aware she was fidgeting until Remy caught her restless hands in his.

"What's this?" He held up the plastic tape dispenser she'd been fussing with.

For a moment, Dorothy couldn't remember, then, "I found it. On the ground over there. I forgot I had it. Someone must have dropped it."

As soon as she said the words, her thoughts jumped on them. *Someone?* It looked fresh, like new. There was no dust or anything to indicate it had been there long. What if Vonda had dropped it last night? She could feel excitement spike inside. She looked at Remy, could tell he had reached the same conclusion, but he shook his head.

He was right. If they found anything, they'd just have to turn it over to the police. Much better to get a look at it first. Luckily, Leda seemed oblivious to any nuances or enlightenment. Dorothy patted her back and handed her another round of tissues, while the police slowly, ever so slowly, withdrew from the scene.

"Leda," Dorothy asked casually, as if it didn't matter, "when you checked your mailbox, did you feel down inside or just look?"

Leda blew her nose before answering. "I don't know." She frowned. "I think I just looked. Why?"

"Would you mind if we checked again? I have an idea."

"What—?" Leda began. Dorothy held up the tape. "What? Oh. Oh!"

"Do you think she was able to hide it from who killed

her?" Titus asked, interest temporarily bumping out his annoyance with her.

"I think," Dorothy looked at Leda, "that she was a very brave person. It took guts for her to call me. I'd like for her death to mean something. That's what I think."

Leda smiled, a shaky smile, but the first real smile Dorothy had seen from her. "Me, too."

It didn't take them long to be back at the bank of mailboxes. Leda opened hers and felt around inside. Then, disappointedly shook her head. "Nothing there."

Titus started to step forward. "What about one of the others?"

Dorothy couldn't stand by anymore. "I'll check."

She and Remy started at opposite ends of the row, feeling inside each box. The one right next to Leda's, she felt something taped against the inside of the outside. Clever girl. No one would see it unless they stood on tiptoe to look in. And she almost hadn't felt it taped so securely to the side. She scraped at the tape until it gave way and pulled it free.

It was a Ziploc bag. With an envelope inside. All three drew close as she turned it over. It was addressed to Vonda Vance and the return address was Verrol's, with Leda's name and a note to her added to the outside.

"That's Vonda's handwriting," Leda said.

"Maybe we should go someplace more private," Titus said, his hungry gaze on the envelope.

Dorothy understood. He'd waited a long time for justice to catch up with the man who killed Magus, too. It was partly what kept them together. They both needed to move on, but couldn't until they knew.

"No one can see us from the street," Remy said. He took the package and pulled the letter free of its envelope, then carefully unfolded it. She and Leda each grabbed a side, so they could read with him. Titus watched tensely, as they all read the words Vance wrote to his wife:

My dearest Vonda,

If you're reading these words, then I'm dead. I want you to know that you are the best thing that ever happened to me. I love you so much and I'm so sorry for what I put you through. I know you want to understand how it all happened. I know that's important to you and I want you to understand. Just be aware that it may not be as cleansing as you expect. Some knowledge binds rather than sets you free. Please consider carefully before you dive into the mud hole that is my life, the life I tried so hard to keep you from ever finding out about.

I hope you will also forgive me for not doing as you asked, and revealing who hired me during the trial. As odd as it may seem, considering what I am, my word is my bond. It may not seem like much, but other than you, my word was all I had. However, my death frees me of that obligation.

I realize you didn't ask for this burden, but if you can, please finish this on my behalf. I'm not sure if it's revenge or justice, but trust me when I say either is well-deserved.

That said, if you can't do it, I understand. Burn this letter or put it somewhere safe. It's your decision. I know the money I was paid won't interest you, but there is a lot of it, and with it, all the answers to all the questions anyone might have.

To protect you, I've hidden the information and only you, or someone who knows you, will be able to figure out how to find it. Please take all precautions. This information is dangerous to you. It is selfish of me, I know, but it is only the thought of you out there, living and remembering me, remembering us, that keeps me going in here.

Okay, if you're still with me, the path to the information and money lies in our past and in our future. If you think back, you'll know exactly what I mean. Do you remember the day we met? I can't forget it. You took my breath away and just thinking of you now, it happens all over again. I think my cellmate is getting worried about me.

If you wouldn't mind, would you also please look after my mom. I know I've mostly been a disappointment to her, but with me gone, she won't have anyone.

I love you so much and I hope that someday you'll be able to forgive me for what I was, for what I did and for what I didn't do for us.

> *Your loving husband,*
> *Verrol*

She looked up, unable to speak, as the tragedy of it caught in her throat. She felt like an intruder into something personal and intimate.

Titus met her gaze. "Well, what does it say?" His voice was flat and deadly.

Dorothy shook her head. Leda gave a soft sob.

"What an idiot he was," she said. "If only . . ." She stopped, looking at Dorothy.

Dorothy smiled wryly. "Yeah. If only." She looked at the letter again. "What do you suppose he meant by the answers lying in their past?"

"Obviously, he thought it was something she'd understand, but not just anyone else," Remy said, his tone reflective. He looked at Leda. "She seemed to think you'd understand?"

Leda rubbed her head, obviously finding it difficult to concentrate. "Their past. I'm not sure. It could mean anything, couldn't it?"

"Let's start with something simple," Remy said. "How long were they married? Did you know them their whole marriage?"

Leda nodded. "Yeah, I've known Vonda since we both started work at the library. That's where she met Verrol. At the library."

"Do you think that's what he meant?" Dorothy asked. "He asks her if she remembers the day they met, right after he says the answer lies in their past."

Leda frowned. "How would he dare hide anything there? It's a public place."

"Are there any private parts of the library? Anything that might have been special to them?"

Leda sighed. "I suppose there could be, but you know, she didn't tell me everything."

"Maybe she thought you'd have noticed?" Dorothy said. "This isn't a good time to think about this. You've had a shock. We'll worry about it later." She gave Remy a pointed look. Something in his demeanor made her wonder if he had some ideas. He'd probably researched the couple as part of the coverage of Magus's murder ten years ago. He gave a slight shake of his head, as if telling her not to say anything.

"We have to turn it in," he said, "but I'm going to make a copy of it first. Leda, I think you need to be protected." He arched a brow in Dorothy's direction.

"We'll go to Oz," she said. "You'll be my guest. Can you call in sick to work?"

Leda nodded, looking a bit overwhelmed, but also relieved. "Are you sure?"

121

"She left the letter for you. That puts you in danger, I'm afraid. Even if you can't figure it out, someone might think you can."

The color drained from Leda's face. "They could come after me at . . . Oz."

"Not with Titus in charge." Dorothy smiled at her body-guard. "He'll take care of us both, I promise. You'll want to pack some things. I'll go up with you."

"We'll stop by and copy it, then drop it off and get some grub. Titus should head for Oz and get things ready." Again there was that feeling that he had something for them to do.

Dorothy expected Titus to object at Remy giving him orders, but all he said was, "If Miss Tasker is nervous, I can take her to Oz with me."

Leda looked surprised, hesitated, but nodded. "Actually I'd like that. I doubt I could eat anything, anyway. Thank you, Miss Merlinn."

Dorothy smiled. "Call me Dorothy. No one calls me Miss Merlinn. It sounds so . . . weird."

Leda managed a chuckle. "Dorothy then." She hesitated. "Do I click my heels three times or are we catching a tornado to Oz?"

Remy slanted her an amused and rueful look. "Definitely a tornado."

Chapter Eight

It was a relief when Leda and Titus finally drove away. Dorothy felt the weight of their expectations ease a bit. It made it slightly easier to deal with the guilt she felt about the violence resulting from her return to Louisiana. All rationalizing aside, she'd deliberately tried to provoke the killer into acting. That was the hard truth she had to live with. Okay, she'd tried to provoke it in her and Remy's direction, but that was just another excuse. Violence couldn't be contained or controlled. It could only be stopped at the source. If she could go back in time, she'd do it differently, but now she could only go forward. She looked at Remy. "The library?"

He nodded. "That's where their past began. We can grab some drive-through on the way. Don't know about you, but I'm starved." He opened the door for her, then went around and got in behind the wheel. "I can't believe Titus let you get away so easily."

"I can't, either. Maybe he's taken with Leda." Dorothy exchanged a mischievous look with him.

"That would make him too human," Remy said dryly. "He'd never stand for it."

Dorothy chuckled. Titus did like to cultivate a spooky, emotionless mien. Maybe it was a bodyguard rule or something.

They made a copy of the letter, dropped it off with the detectives assigned to the case, endured a brief lecture on tampering with evidence, then grabbed some lunch and arrived at the library in record time. She was surprised to meet Titus outside.

"I thought we got rid of him too easily," Remy muttered, as they approached him.

"What happened to Leda?" Dorothy asked in alarm.

"She changed her mind, decided she needed to stay and help make arrangements for Vonda's funeral."

"Oh." Dorothy was surprised, but she had sensed a lot of strength in Leda. "I'll call her later then."

"She said she'd call you in a few days. Or if she thought of anything," Titus said. "I guess we all had the same idea. I can cover this, if you have things to do."

"And miss the hunt?" Dorothy shook her head. "You know me better than that!"

His smile was rueful, but worried.

"What can happen inside a public library?" she asked him. "Besides, this time I think we're one step ahead of the killer instead of behind."

"Maybe," he said. "If we knew how he was staying ahead, I'd feel better."

The news of Vonda's murder had preceded them to the library so it was sadly easy to convince her co-workers they needed to look around the area where Vonda worked. They were far too shocked to think clearly.

At first they stayed together, working systematically through the reference area and even going through her work locker. They got nowhere very slowly and very dustily.

"This is crazy," Titus said, finally. "We need to split up. This is going to take forever."

Remy frowned. "As long as we stay within voice contact, I guess it would speed things up. Titus, why don't you go right, I'll go left, and Dorothy, you start in the middle and work your way—" he stopped. Their gazes connected and the cool air around Dorothy warmed a bit. She may have lost track of time looking at him. He was easy on the eyes. If only he'd be as easy on her heart . . .

Titus cleared his throat, shattering the moment, or whatever it was.

"I'll figure something out," she said. Her lips twitched slightly, but whether it was for Remy, who looked slightly embarrassed, or Titus, who looked annoyed, it was hard to say. Both men moved slowly away from her, both stopping often to look back. She gave each a sweet smile before moving into the stacks. When she realized that she was in the history section, her blood quickened and her awareness of either man quickly faded. Could their past also mean *the* past?

The place felt like it had been forgotten in the past. The air was musty and dry, and slightly humid despite the chill pumped in by the air-conditioning system. The books smelled old, too, and many of the spines lined up in rows were cracked and worn from use or years.

It was an interesting problem. How could Vance be sure that no one would look for a particular book, assuming he'd used one as a repository for whatever it was he'd hidden? These books couldn't be checked out. They had to be used in the library. But even the most oblivious researcher would probably examine any piece of paper inserted into a book. It was simple human nature.

What if he'd thought of that and put it in a book shelved out of order? It was still a risk. He'd have to assume that someone wouldn't notice the book and correct the omission. If this was the only place she had to hide something, where would she put it, she wondered?

She'd either go high or low, she decided. She got on her knees and checked the bottom two rows for anything that looked out of the ordinary, but didn't find anything. Okay, that left high.

"Dorothy?" Remy's voice was a bit sharp, as if she'd been quiet too long. "Titus?"

"I'm still here." She found a rolling ladder and pushed it into the opening of the aisle assigned to her. Once up the steps, she studied the top two rows in the first sections, but again found nothing that looked out of the ordinary.

"Titus?" Remy said, very sharply. "You all right?"

"Yes."

Titus sounded annoyed, though that wasn't unusual these days. This wasn't good for him. Despite the lingering imperatives of her past, she'd been able to move forward. His life had stopped the day Magus died. She'd been selfish. She'd allowed him to be her anchor without considering the effect it was having on him. His jealousy of Remy was her fault, too. She'd set him up as protector, confessor, and on occasion, a friend, her one constant in a life spinning out of control. Then she shut him out when she brought Remy into the situation. How would she have felt if their situations were reversed? She probably wouldn't have handled it as well, she realized ruefully. She was a punk.

He didn't know he didn't need to be jealous of Remy, that they were playacting. Well, Remy was. She wasn't sure anymore where reality began and ended on her side. There was too much happening for any kind of clarity. But even if Remy and she parted ways, at some point in her life she did want love. She wanted romance and a husband, a family, an ordinary life. She wouldn't need Titus then and actually she didn't need him right now. He was more in the way, because he was so focused on protecting her. She needed wings right now, not cement boots.

She hadn't learned a lot from Magus. He hadn't been in

her life long enough, but one lesson had been thoroughly learned. Life was about risk. Living *was* risk. The only real tragedy would be dying without having lived or loved. Feelings weren't always reciprocated. When she'd realized who she was and what she was worth, she'd known that finding real love wouldn't be easy. Maybe she wouldn't be loved, but she intended to love someone and to live her life fully and completely.

"Are you all right?" Titus asked her.

She looked down and found him watching her from the darker end of the row. As usual, his thoughts were his own, but his body language radiated his intent. He was hungry for any clue to who hired Vance. He throbbed with it.

"You look tired. Why don't you take a break?" She expected him to angrily reject the suggestion, but to her surprise, he hesitated before nodding.

"Do you want anything to drink?" he asked.

"I don't think anything is allowed down here," she said. "I want to check a couple more rows, then I'll probably take a break, too."

He nodded and left, the echo of his footsteps fading in the direction of the stairs. With a sigh, she turned her attention back to the unyielding line of books. This was crazy. No place here was really safe.

Unless. . . .

She lifted her gaze to the top of the cases, just barely within reach of her fingers. If she stood on tiptoe . . . She reached up, but felt only dust.

"Yuck." She got down, moved the ladder a few feet and tried again. More dust. Another few feet and she found more dust. At the end of the row, her tiptoes were getting tired. Her dust-coated hand felt dry as sandpaper. And she needed to pee.

On her tiptoes the last time, she felt along the top, straining to reach at least the middle of the case. Just as she was about to give up, her finger bumped something. Her first impulse was to call out, but what if this were a false alarm? She'd feel silly for having distracted Remy, particularly because she really wanted to distract him in her direction. She sighed, reaching up to try again, but still could only bump the edge. Maybe if she tried from the other side? She scooted the ladder around and this time was able to move the book in her direction and finally grab it. It was so coated with dust, the cover almost wasn't readable. Almost. Through the layer of dust, she could faintly see the title. *The Wizard of Oz.*

"Did you find something?" Titus asked.

She jumped. "I thought you were gone."

"I'm back," he said. "Did you find something?"

He sounded so odd, though she couldn't place how or why. She hadn't consciously planned to start cutting him out of the loop. It was instinct that had her shelve the book, as if she'd just pulled it out. "I thought so for a moment, but no. Nothing yet."

With a stab of worry, she realized she hadn't heard anything from Remy for a few minutes. "Remy?" No answer. "Titus?"

"Wait here." With the silence of a stalking cat, he disappeared around the corner, leaving only a disturbance in the dusty air to mark his passing. Instead of comforting, she found it disturbing he could move so quickly and quietly. What if the killer were as adept?

The air felt colder around her and she felt exposed and isolated, now that she didn't dare call out to either man. She quietly pulled *Oz* back off the shelf, wiped it as best she could. Trying to shield her actions with her body, she

128

briefly thumbed through the pages, but found nothing that jumped out at her. No papers or writing on the flyleaf, front or back. After a quick look around, she tucked it in the waistband of her jeans, against her back.

The silence grew more dense and menacing. She had to break it.

"Titus? Remy Mistral?"

Perched up on the ladder, she felt like a sitting target, rather than above the fray. After a brief inner debate about staying or going, she quietly climbed down and padded down the aisle in the direction of the stairs. She wanted to look for the guys, but she'd seen enough movies to know that was a bad idea. She needed help first and then they could search.

She reached the end of the aisle and stopped. What if someone were waiting for her to emerge from the stacks? She tried to quiet her own breathing, reaching out with all her senses for any hint of danger or an indication of a malignant presence. As she strained, she heard movement. Slight at first, but then more definite and in the direction Remy was working.

"Dorothy?" Remy sounded both groggy and worried.

Dorothy started toward him. It wasn't wise, but she couldn't help herself. She had to get to him. There was an impression of movement behind her, but before she could react, a hand came over her mouth. She struggled wildly against the strong smell that filled her nostrils, but it was a battle she'd already lost.

Strength left. Darkness engulfed.

Suzanne Henry found Bubba Joe staring out the window of his office. He'd been happy when Vance died, then the lawyer, but the news Vonda Vance was dead had turned him moody and dangerous. What she didn't understand was why.

"What's wrong?" she asked finally, even though she hated drawing his attention to her when he was like this.

He shrugged angrily, but half-turned to look at her, his gaze the half-shamed, half-embarrassed one he'd been throwing at her since the first time he strayed from their marital bed. Amazing that she'd cared back then. Briefly. Until she realized he was incapable of feeling shame or remorse. He just hated getting caught. For a short time, his view of himself as a great guy was disturbed.

He still had the remains of the charm he'd had back then, though he and it were starting to smudge around the edges, as if not just his character were losing cohesion, but his body was, too. He'd managed to slather a patina of sophistication over his trailer park trash past, but it was still there and popped out on occasion.

To her amazement, no one but her seemed to see the dark side of Bubba Joe. His utter and complete ruthlessness. His lust for power that was even greater than his lust for women. His inability to be anything but completely selfish and completely self-centered. The world revolved around Bubba Joe. And what he wanted he got.

She felt a chill as the pieces began to fall into place.

"You're the one who hired Vance, aren't you?" Every time she'd thought he'd gone as low as he could go, he'd find a way to go lower. These days it was all she could do to pretend to look adoringly at him when they were in public. Most of the time she had to pretend he was someone else. She'd gotten real good at pretending. Thank goodness she didn't have to fake it in their bed anymore. She wasn't that good.

He seemed to hesitate and she knew he was trying to

find the right lie to tell her. Like she couldn't see through anything he threw at her. If he needed to lie, that meant he was involved.

She sank into a nearby chair. "How bad is it?"

Usually it was women. Bubba Joe thought his confessions were good for her soul. If she were wholly engaged in cleaning up his messes, then she wouldn't have time to have political ambition for herself. Suzanne let him do it, because at least then he wouldn't have her killed. It wasn't a good thing to know too much of Bubba's business or get in the way of what he wanted.

Like Magus had.

Bubba Joe shrugged, looking predictably sulky. Truth was anathema to him.

"Vonda Vance? Clinton Barnes? They your work, too?"

"No!" He was so quick, so emphatic, she had to believe him, though it went against the grain. "I don't know who did that."

Bubba Joe looked puzzled and annoyed. It wasn't a good look for him. And he wanted to run the most powerful nation in the free world. Maybe we'll be to Mars before it happens, she thought wearily, and I can go live there.

"Tell me everything and give it to me straight." He wouldn't, of course. He couldn't. Suzanne had learned that as soon as something happened, he'd begin to shape it into a version more favorable to him. "You hired Vance, using what money?"

"I'd picked up some cash along the way."

Translation: he'd been pocketing cash given him by political donors who didn't want to be tracked on any reports. Funny how they always knew who could be bribed. It was like calves who knew their own mothers.

"Well, you remember how Magus was back then. Every-

131

thing was Wizard this and Wizard that. Oh, we just *love* the Wizard."

And how could a Bubba Joe compete with a Wizard?

"And then he passed you in the polls."

"He passed everybody. He was going to be elected! He wanted to be president!"

"And so you went to Vance." They'd hired him a couple of times for small things, mostly to deal with women. Usually he just had to scare them, but a few of them had disappeared. Suzanne preferred to think they'd left the area. Made it easier to maintain her moral superiority to Bubba Joe. But she hadn't been surprised when Vance killed Magus. No, she hadn't been surprised.

"You couldn't possibly have had enough cash to make it worth his while to spend ten years in prison. What else did you promise him . . . oh, my gosh! You promised him a pardon."

He was such an idiot, but she didn't say it out loud. She didn't need a fist to the jaw. Or worse. Bubba Joe used sex to control his women and when he was pissed, it wasn't good.

"Only if he got caught."

"And you didn't think that people, like the police, might find it interesting that you'd pardon a killer?"

"He wouldn't be the only one. You know how I feel about the death penalty."

Actually, she hadn't realized they were against it this year.

"Is there any evidence out there that would connect you to this?"

"Well, I had to sign an agreement with Vance or he wouldn't have done it. About the pardon. He didn't trust me!" He actually sounded aggrieved by that. And why am I surprised, she wondered.

"And you have no idea where it is."

"If I did, I'd have it by now, wouldn't I?"

"Well, we know where it isn't, or you'd already be in jail. Let's focus on what you do know about it."

Bubba Joe looked sulky again. "There's a timer."

"A timer?"

"Yeah, he said if anything happened to his wife, some kind of timer would kick in that would release the agreement to the public."

"Why would he feel his wife was threatened?" Like she didn't know. Good plan, Bubba Joe. Hire a killer, and then threaten his wife with bodily harm.

He shrugged. "He was a paranoid son of a bitch."

She rubbed her face. "Did he mention what this timer was set for?" Dear heaven, this was worse than she'd thought.

"He said I'd know when it ran out."

Suzanne frowned. "So it could be days?"

"It could be today."

"If it was today, we'd already know. Every day the cops aren't at the door is a day we can try to do something about it." He looked away from her. "Why did you wait to tell me?"

His face flushed red. "What can you do about it? His wife, his lawyer, they're both dead! There's nothing anyone can do about it!"

"What if someone else is involved? Someone who knew about the timer and what would happen to you if Vance's wife died?"

He stared at her for a long moment, his jaw slightly slack, before a look of comprehension slowly spread across his face. It wasn't a good look on him, either. "But who else would know?"

"Oh, I don't know. Maybe the person who told you about Vance in the first place? The only other person who knew you knew him?" She kept her tone neutral, but it wasn't easy when she wanted to shout, Duh!

She could see him thinking back. He didn't live a lot in the past, so there was some effort involved.

"Darius Smith? You think he's the one who did this?"

He's the one her money was on.

"I'll kill him!" Bubba Joe's color darkened dangerously.

Hadn't he learned anything from the Wizard's death coming back to bite him on the ass? Oh, why did she even ask herself the question? Of course he hadn't.

"That's certainly one course of action, but it might not be a good idea to kill someone while there's evidence of your involvement with Vance floating around out there," she said, even as her thoughts spun with the implications of Darius's involvement. If he was behind it, he'd take some delicate handling, assuming Bubba Joe didn't go behind her back again and just have him whacked.

No matter how she tried to spin it, this was bad, if Darius was involved. He loved knowing things and this was a thing worth knowing. If he did have the power, he could halt or slow the timer or hold it over their heads for as long as he wanted. With it, he could force Bubba Joe to stand aside for his protégé or even support him. Or worse.

She closed her eyes, pulling up an image of Darius in her mind's eye. He didn't have any apparent weaknesses. Didn't seem to be that interested in women, though he was a sexy devil in an odd, ugly sort of way. She wouldn't have minded giving him a ride, particularly if she could get him to lose control. She loved icy men with hot centers and hot women with cold hearts. A girl did have to have her hobbies if she was going to live with someone like Bubba Joe Henry.

"What are you smiling about?" Bubba said suspiciously.

"I was thinking we could turn this on Darius," she lied. His jealousy was both inconvenient and hypocritical. If he'd had any idea of her recreational coping techniques, if he thought she was getting it somewhere else, he'd be reasserting his marital rights in ways he knew she wouldn't like. "There has to be a way. There's always a way."

"I don't believe you." His voice was cold. She could hear the violence in his voice and feel his need to hurt.

It took all her discipline not to stiffen or show any sign of alarm. And then she had to push beyond that and distract him. There was only one way to distract him now and that was to act like she wanted to jump his bones. He loved depriving her of himself. It made him feel powerful.

She slowly lifted her lashes. She rose and forced herself to walk over to him and run the back of her hand along the side of his face.

"You're so sexy like this, Bubba Joe." She leaned into him, brushing her breasts against his chest. They recoiled in horror, but he didn't know that. "So strong. So powerful. It makes me crazy when you get like this."

That at least was the truth. Crazy sick to her stomach.

He smiled as he grabbed her hand, squeezing it until tears filled her eyes. "I'd like to help you out, baby, really I would, but you know I have to go."

"Later?" she asked, pleadingly. She knew the script.

He looked her up, then down, his cruel gaze dismissive of her female assets. "Sure. Later."

He stepped away from her. "I'll give you a few days to figure this out, then I'm acting, Suzanne. I'm not waiting for Darius Smith to take me out."

He wanted to kill Smith, she realized. He was hungry for it. She kept her lashes down, her body submissive. This was when he was most dangerous. Her body curled in against the thought of what he could do when he felt this frustrated and scared and hungry for violence.

"Sure, baby. You know I'll do my best." She lifted her lashes then, willing her eyes to look at him longingly. His gaze probed hers. It was almost as bad as having his fingers probing her private places with cruel insolence.

Without warning, he slammed her into the wall, pressing against her with the full length of his body. He ground himself against her, as he grabbed her chin and stabbed his tongue down her throat.

She endured it as best she could. She knew this drill, too. She couldn't respond in any way, not in passion or revulsion. Either would set him off. She had to be completely passive so he could dominate. His hand stroked the side of her neck, and then tightened on her throat until the blood pounded unpleasantly in her head. He didn't say anything, just stared at her with a cold, almost dead gaze. She could feel him teeter on the edge of violence, and thought, he's going to kill me this time, but then he slowly pulled back. His eyes told her it wasn't over yet.

She had one last bit of business to play right. She made herself reach for him with a murmur of distress. He hit her with his open palm, knocking her to the ground.

"Have some pride, Suzanne. You disgust me."

This was new, and she had to act on instinct. "I can't help it, Bubba Joe. I'm sorry."

He reached out and grabbed her hair, twisting it until she looked up at him.

"Do you want me, baby?"

She licked her lips. "You know I do."

"Well, I don't want you. You're old and dried-up. You're only good for solving problems. So do what you're good at and I'll let you stay." With his hand still twisted in her hair, he slammed her head against the wall twice.

She stayed limp, curling in on herself, as his lust for violence sucked up all the available air around them both. It clogged her lungs and slowed her heart to a crawl. He didn't want to stop. He wanted to keep hitting and hitting until some deep, dark place inside himself was satisfied.

"Are you going to do what I want?"

"Yes, Bubba Joe." She fought to stay conscious, to sound meek and calm.

"Good." He sounded disappointed.

He wanted her to fight him. So he'd have an excuse to kill her and believe it was her fault. She didn't dare look at him. She didn't know this part.

It seemed to take forever before his hold on her hair eased. Then she was free. She heard him walk across the room. He walked like he was powerful, content to know he'd completely dominated her.

He's going to kill me, she realized. Maybe not today, but sometime. She'd known he hated her, but hadn't realized how much. Would it have made a difference if she'd let her strength show? Or perhaps he sensed her inner rebellion and was reacting to it? Certainly his fear had ripped back the facade of his life, revealing the ugly, heartless core.

He had, she realized painfully, the soul of a serial killer. So far he'd used a third party to do his killing for him, but he was hungry to do it himself. She'd felt his longing too clearly to doubt it. Right now, he still wanted political power more, but just barely. She was alive because he hoped she could clean this up for him, like she always had. If she wanted to survive, it was time to cut Bubba Joe loose and save herself.

If Darius were behind this, then he was her best bet. He had the power to take Bubba Joe down and protect her from his retribution. And if he wouldn't play, well, there was always Dorothy. She'd wanted to know who was behind the killing since it happened.

"Dorothy?"

Remy's voice seemed miles away. She had the vague recollection he was in danger and struggled against the hands holding her down.

"I'm coming." She tried to call, but the words came out a dry rasp of sound.

"Lie still." He sounded closer now and undeniably grim. "Your head will clear in a moment. And then you'll feel as crappy as I do."

Her lids felt like lead, but she managed to lift them. Remy knelt by her, his face angry and hard.

"Titus?"

"He's down, too, but all right."

She sagged back in relief, but then stiffened again. "The book!"

"What book?"

"I think I found something . . ." It wasn't pressing into her back anymore. She felt the ground around where she fell. "It's gone!"

"I thought you said you hadn't found anything?" Titus sounded shaky, but also hurt.

"I wasn't sure," she said, avoiding his accusing gaze. "I didn't want to get our hopes up. No chance of that now." She struggled to a sitting position, despite her unpleasantly spinning head. "How is this happening? Am I bugged or something?"

Remy looked thoughtful. "I suppose it's possible we're

being tracked." He looked at Titus, whose body language turned defensive.

"I didn't think we'd need it. I have some debugging equipment. We'll know soon."

"Until then, I suggest we suspend any further discussion," Remy said.

Dorothy nodded. Right now she could hardly think, let alone discuss anything. Remy and Titus helped her upright and after a painful period of spinning head, she was able to walk under her own steam. "I wish I hadn't eaten," she muttered as Remy helped her into his car.

Titus looked like he wanted to object, but Remy just ignored him. "We'll meet you back at Oz."

"Someone should warn Leda," Dorothy said, before he shut the door. She was looking at Titus. He nodded and left. She looked at Remy. "Are you sure your head's clear enough to drive?"

He ignored her as he eased out into traffic. "Did you hear anything?"

Dorothy shook her head. "Not until it was too late."

"Me, either." He stared ahead, a deep frown cutting moody lines into his face. "This guy is really starting to piss me off." He braked suddenly. "Let's not wait for Titus and his magic equipment. I know someone here in New Orleans who can help us out. Okay?"

Dorothy nodded. She hadn't looked forward to the drive to Oz, having to watch their words the whole way. And wondering if they were being tracked. But she was still puzzled about one thing. Why had the killer or his confederate only knocked them out? Every other contact had been lethal to the people involved. And maybe that was her answer. The higher the body count, the higher the risk of being caught.

The good news, their efforts were obviously putting pressure on their opposition. The bad news? So far the opposition was winning. That was going to change now, she vowed.

Chapter Nine

Darius watched Suzanne Henry approach his table. He rose to pull her chair out and then pushed it back in for her. As she sat down, she looked over her shoulder at him, giving him an intimate smile that was both thanks and an invitation.

He sat opposite her, studying her curiously. She wasn't bad-looking, in a chilly bitch way. He'd fielded some signals from her in the past, but had managed to turn them aside without her realizing she'd been turned down. She probably thought he'd missed his cue. Now here she was, practically clanging like a railway signal. Today, he suspected, she wasn't going to allow him to miss anything.

Normally, he'd have no compunction in squashing her and her expectations like a bug, but Dorothy's return and the memories she'd stirred up had left him unsettled. Unsatisfied. Suzanne was as different from Emma as two women could be, something he considered a positive at the moment. He needed an outlet for his libido, not a pale imitation of Emma. He'd heard that Suzanne liked to play on both sides of the aisle. It made her mildly more interesting than the women who typically hit on him. He also had a feeling that the quickest way to find out why she'd sought him out now, was to give *him* what *she* wanted. He let lust off the leash a bit, and she got someone to talk to.

She rested her hand on the table, leaning slightly forward to give him some cleavage action. "It's so kind of you to meet me, Darius."

He reached out and covered her hand with his, caressing the back softly, while he pretended to appreciate the offered view. It surprised him that he even remembered how to seduce, all the little steps that built a response. It surprised him even more when it worked. Suzanne was, apparently, a fast stepper. At least he wouldn't have to play the game too long. He was interested in relief, not a relationship.

As they chatted their way through the preliminaries, he felt her bare foot push under the edge of his pants. She rubbed his leg in what she probably thought was a sexy circle. When she tired of this, she slid her foot up his leg into his crotch. He was so startled he didn't have time to control his reaction. He was only human.

Her gaze was locked on his like a smart bomb on a target as she continued kneading him to attention. He reached under the table and captured her foot, rubbing it gently, but indifferently. "If you're not careful, we won't be able to find a more private place to talk."

Her lashes swept low, then back. "It would be easier to discuss my . . . problem . . . in a more private setting, but we'll need to be careful. You know how Bubba Joe is."

He stroked his finger along the bottom of her foot and her body jerked in response. If he wasn't careful, she'd be doing a *When Harry Met Sally* moment. He gave her foot one last stroke before releasing it.

She licked her lips, pouted them for him, and then reached into her purse and extracted a key card. She was careful about how she slid it toward him, making the moment both personal and private. He met her halfway. She gathered herself together and presumably put her shoe back on. She slithered out of her chair and stepped close to whisper in his ear.

"Don't be long."

"It'll take me a few minutes to be able to walk," he told her, genuinely amused.

She laughed, looking surprised and actually pleased. Laughter suited her, softening the hard lines that her life with Bubba Joe had cut into her face.

He watched her walk away, weaving through the tables, confident and sexy. She was a dangerous woman, but she was about to become less so. He took out his cell phone and placed a call.

"Yeah, I need you. At . . ." He turned the key over and read off the hotel and room. "Bring the camera." He hung up, sipped some water while his body returned to normal, then stood up, tossing some money on the table to cover the meal he hadn't had. As he strolled out, he found he was enjoying the unusual lick of anticipation in his blood at what was coming. And for the opportunity she presented. He had a keen sense of when information was heading his way and it was telling him that Suzanne was big with news.

Bozo Luc opened the letter his informant had handed him and quickly scanned the contents. So, it was as he had suspected. Magus had indeed made sure that Dorothy was his blood, his DNA, before bringing her to Oz. He'd have done the same in his place, of course. What surprised him was the disappointment he felt. He had, he realized, liked the idea that his night of passion with Emma might have borne fruit. To his surprise, he found he still missed Emma. He hadn't realized it until now. Infuriating, of course, but also an amazing woman and totally wasted on Magus. Dorothy had her mother's fire, but she also had enough of Magus in her to make her . . . annoying.

It had clearly been a mistake to drop her ten years ago. She'd found her feet and her father's self-possession. He'd been so sure she'd never come back to Louisiana or have any desire to reclaim his political legacy, let alone hand it over to someone like Remy Mistral.

It would be easy enough to eliminate Mistral as an annoyance, but if Dorothy really cared about him, she'd be as dogged about pursuing his death as she was being about her father. She needed to be reeducated. It didn't have to be a final solution, unless she wasn't open to reason.

He looked at the results again, before he stuck them in his wall safe. They'd make a nice souvenir. And keep him grounded, if he were tempted to let his little game get too real. His informant had already altered the results at the source, to make it look as if he, Bozo, were her father. It would be almost impossible for her to represent Magus if the word got out and that would, by default, leave Mistral blowing hot air instead of cold. He doubted much time would pass before Mistral sheared off. He still had his sad little career on radio to go back to. It was clear he was using Dorothy to access Magus's political legacy and would have no need for her when it was gone. She'd need friends then and this time he wouldn't make a mistake. He'd be there for her. After all, he was her father now.

All that remained was for her to find out her new paternity. It was a pity he'd have to play loving father with her. She was, as his son would say, hot. And she was lonely. He'd sensed it in her when they met. He specialized in comforting the lonely and the hot.

Maybe he should have made her father Darius or Bubba Joe. They'd both assumed they were the only ones she went to in her efforts to pay back Magus for his inattention. It had all been so entertaining at the time. Emma sleeping with everyone in sight. Magus oblivious until the end. Emma had confided in him, because, well, people did.

They couldn't seem to help themselves. They always thought he had their best interests at heart, too. Strange. None of them ever stopped to ask themselves why on earth he would. Even Darius, who thrived on secrets, couldn't keep all of his own. He'd needed someone to talk to in the end. Had he gotten over his obsession with Emma or had he transferred it to Dorothy? It would have been funny to make him a father, but he couldn't have her turning to anyone else for help or answers to past puzzles. One thing his source had been clear about, she was deeply curious about the past and her parents, with precious few answers available to her. He could change that for her. He was good at fiction.

And would she still seek Magus's killer? He mulled it for a time, without coming to a conclusion. Even he hadn't been able to ferret out that mystery, though he had his suspicions. It had been such a stupid thing to do. Death was so messy and even the cleanest murder wasn't spotless. Secrets had a way of being found, usually by the wrong people. He wondered, idly, who had eliminated Vance, his wife and his attorney. As if the thought gave birth to the act, the phone rang. He waited for the caller ID. His brows arched in surprise. How interesting. He punched the speakerphone button.

"Hello, Bubba Joe," he said blandly.

"Did you do it? You knew Vance, too. I know you did. I know you used him to do jobs for you. If you did, I'll kill you myself." He slurred his words and ended with a string of curses.

"It would help if I knew what we were talking about," Bozo said calmly, wondering what had set Bubba Joe off. He wasn't usually so forthright about who and what he was. Civilization was a thinner veneer on him than even Bozo had realized.

"Vonda Vance's murder. Did he give it to you? Because if you think you can blackmail me out of this race, well, you don't know who you're dealing with."

Why am I sure he's not working off a script from his wife, Bozo wondered. He wasn't, of course, surprised. He'd always assigned Bubba Joe first suspect honors. But then Bubba Joe hadn't taken advantage of the opportunity and he'd wondered if maybe it was Darius. He was the type to take the long view. Clearly Bubba Joe had panicked back then and Suzanne had headed him off to deflect suspicion. But why would he care about Vonda's death, unless . . .

Well, Vance had never been a fool. He'd have known Vonda was his pressure point and acted to neutralize any threat to her. Interestingly enough, he had truly loved his almost-invisible wife. A pity she hadn't actually been invisible. She might be alive.

"I'm afraid I don't know what you're talking about," he said soothingly. "Have . . . it? What would that be?"

He could almost hear Bubba Joe thinking. If he was wrong and Bozo didn't know, then he wouldn't want to tell him. But what if Bozo was lying? The horns of a dilemma. Couldn't happen to a nicer guy.

"Don't mess with me, Bozo. You won't like what happens."

Bozo didn't like drunken threats. Maybe it was time to turn the tables on Bubba Joe. Evidently there was another player in the game. Vance had worked alone, or so they always thought. He found himself remembering Dorothy's interview and the calm way she'd talked about a pardon for Vance. Dorothy had gained a lot from her father's demise. Could she really care about a man who had so neglected her that she went hungry at times?

What if she were Vance's silent partner? It would be

pretty sweet for her if she could expose Bubba Joe, thus ending all speculation about who had hired Vance. She rakes in sympathy, still gets the money, and propels her candidate into the governor's mansion on a tide of sympathy. She seemed like such a nice girl, but was she really?

"What makes you think I'm the one messing with you?"

"Who else is there?"

It was too tempting. He shouldn't, but he would.

"What about Dorothy?"

"That's ridiculous!"

"Is it?" Bozo asked, keeping his voice soft and reasonable. "Who stood the most to gain from Magus's death? Who still stands the most to gain if someone else is exposed for hiring Vance?"

There was a long silence, broken only by Bubba Joe's raspy breathing as he thought about this. He'd never been particularly fast on the uptake.

Finally he muttered, "I already thought of her. Be sure I'll be talking to her, too. But if I find out you're screwing with me, Bozo—"

"I know, you'll deal with me. Go try to sober up, Bubba Joe."

The phone slammed down in his ear and Bozo laughed. So, there was evidence that would implicate Bubba Joe out there somewhere? Who, after Vonda, would Vance give such evidence to? Bozo had known him, but not well. One didn't, with the type of person he was. Was it possible that Dorothy was really his silent partner? If she was, then she was the best little actress he'd ever seen. Except for Magus, of course.

He looked at the paternity test again, the faked one. If Bubba Joe didn't take care of her, he'd have a little chat with the girl from Oz. He smiled slowly. Life was suddenly so interesting. And here, he'd been feeling so bored.

As Suzanne Henry waited for Darius to appear, her thoughts rioted out of control. Bubba Joe had picked the wrong day to pull her chain. After he'd left, it hadn't taken long to realize that he'd given her the power to take him down. Why had she waited so long to do this? She'd spent so many years believing her future was tied up in his, that she was nothing without him. But he'd made it all so not worth it.

And the beauty of it was, Darius would do it for her, so Bubba Joe would have no reason to suspect her at all. Maybe she could get Darius to drop his boring protégé and sponsor her instead. There'd be more side benefits for him.

She stretched on the sheets, loving the feel of them against her bare skin, loving the anticipation of finally getting what she wanted. That was something Bubba couldn't understand, the anticipation of waiting. He was the ultimate instant gratification cretin.

And if Darius wouldn't play? She shrugged. Well, there was always Dorothy. If she could get to her before the timer ran out. That was the big unknown. How much time did she have to explore her options?

She heard the key in the lock, then the door opened and Darius came in, letting it close slowly behind him. He didn't speak. Just tossed the key on the desk and started to undress. His eyes were cold, but interested. It was so sexy, it was all she could do not to writhe on the bed when he loosened his tie. Each button of his shirt was meticulously undone and then the shirt was shrugged off and tossed aside. His chest was narrow, almost boyish and bare of any hair. That was a pity. She liked hair, but she liked his chilly interest more. His belt came out. He sat on the edge of the bed, his gaze studying her waiting body like a surgeon about to operate.

She was about to die of wanting him. Maybe she would. Didn't they call it the little death?

"What are you waiting for?" She trailed a finger down his chest and felt the skin contract with pleasure. She smiled then. For a moment, she'd wondered if he was too cold, but he wasn't indifferent. And he was ready, if he'd just get his pants off.

"We'll talk later, but first, I hope you don't mind. I invited someone to join us."

"Join us?" She started to sit up, but he gently pushed her back down on the bed, sweeping his hand down her body with the indifferent precision of a master violinist. Somehow he managed to hit just the right places to shut off almost all thought.

"What are you doing, Darius?" she managed to gasp.

"I got you a present, Suzanne." His voice was wonderfully cool, the perfect complement to his hot touch.

The door between the rooms opened. Suzanne pushed up with her elbows. Through a haze of desire, Suzanne saw a young woman, probably the most beautiful young woman she'd ever seen. Everything about her was hot, from her fire-red hair hanging over her naked body to her dangerously high heels—the only item of clothing she'd left on—but her eyes were icy cold. She was, in every way, the perfect woman. She had her dress in her hand and she swung it once, before dropping it lightly on the desk. Then she bent down, giving tantalizing glimpses of her assets, and removed first one shoe, then the other. She set these side by side on the desk, before crawling into bed beside Suzanne.

Suzanne smiled slowly as she sank back into the bed. "Why, Darius, how sweet of you."

Who'd have thought the icy-on-the-outside, hot-on-the-inside Darius would be into threesomes? Live and learn.

There was a hint of evil to the smile he gave her, but there was too much exploding sensation to worry about anything else.

Remy's friend went over them and their car. He found both a tracking device on the car and bugs planted in their clothes. Unfortunately, he couldn't tell them how they got there. It could have been a chambermaid, he supposed, but it left Remy feeling uneasy about the people around Dorothy. Maybe Titus wasn't paranoid after all.

His head was completely clear and Dorothy was looking much better, though she was still mad at herself for losing the book.

"If only I'd left it on the shelf."

He turned the car in the direction of Oz and asked, "You say you flipped through the pages and didn't see anything?"

"No, no paper or writing, but it was very quick and there wasn't a lot of light down there."

"Try not to feel bad about it. We all got caught off guard." Remy rubbed the back of his head. At least their assailant hadn't whacked Dorothy. He and Titus hadn't been so lucky.

With a feeling of revulsion at himself and Suzanne, Darius pulled on his clothes. Suzanne's rapacious hunger had brought about the desired result. He'd achieved release, but satisfaction still eluded him. The fault lay in his mind, not in his body. He felt, he acknowledged painfully, as if he'd been unfaithful to Emma. And even more so to himself.

He paid off Cassandra and nodded for her to leave,

though he hated to see her go. She'd diverted Suzanne from giving him her full attention. She'd deliver the photographs to him later. For now, he needed to find out what Suzanne's agenda was. She lay on the bed, purring like a kitten, her hot hand still stroking his back.

"You're not getting dressed already, are you?"

He was quiet for a moment, as he struggled to control his body's response to her touch. Now he remembered why he hated losing control so much. It was so hard to get it back. Despite the desires of his mind, his body wanted release again. It cared only for sensation. He moved away from her, grabbing a chair and bringing it close to the bed.

"Now we talk, Suzanne." His tone was level, cool. Thankfully, she liked cool and controlled.

She pouted, but pulled and pushed the pillows until she could sit up. She made no attempt to cover her nakedness. The light from the open window fell unkindly across her, finding the places where age was taking its toll. If only he could leave.

She appeared to consider how to begin her pitch. What surprised him was that she shivered, as if remembering something bad, and appeared to actually shrink inside herself. He reached down and pulled the blankets up over her, glad for the excuse. She looked down, fingering a piece of fuzz on the blanket before finally looking at him.

"Bubba Joe almost killed me today."

She said it calmly enough, but remembered fear darkened her eyes. If she was telling the truth, Darius felt a stab of compassion for her and, ironically enough, sympathy for Bubba Joe's desire to have her out of his life.

"Why would he do that?"

She looked at him now, eagerness helping to push back

fear. "He's afraid. And when he's afraid, he gets mean."

"Afraid? Of what?"

Her gaze shifted. She still wasn't sure she trusted him. How could he help her along? He took her hand and squeezed it. So simple, but so effective. She gave him a grateful smile.

"Bubba Joe told me you're the one who introduced Verrol Vance to him." She couldn't look squarely at him, instead studying him sideways and from under lashes thick with mascara.

Was she going to try to blackmail him? After what she'd just let him do? If she was, then she had some balls he hadn't found during their recent encounter.

"I introduced Bubba Joe to a lot of useful people." He lifted her hand to his mouth and teased her fingers with his lips and tongue. The calculation in her eyes clouded with desire. She should have learned you can't successfully mix business with pleasure, at least not from the underneath position. For that you had to stay on top.

"But Vance killed Magus Merlinn. And now his attorney and his wife are dead. Murdered."

"I've seen the news." What was she after? She actually had him puzzled. He licked the palm of her hand and observed her body's uncontrolled shudder. Was there any place he could touch her that she wouldn't respond to? She was ridiculously easy. It was hard not to compare her with Emma, who'd required him to court her passion assiduously through their one, long night together.

She pulled his hand to her cheek and eased close, so she could lean on his knees and look up into his face. For the first time, she seemed unaware of him sexually.

"Darius." She paused for effect. "He did it."

"It?" It what?

"*It*. The million-dollar question. The one thing everyone wants to know. Who hired Vance?" She sat back with a look of triumph. "It was Bubba Joe. He told me he did it."

"Really?" Even his poker face needed to respond. He allowed his eyebrows to rise as he exhaled silently. "Shouldn't you be telling the police?"

"He'd kill me. I'd never get to be free of him. And there's no proof. Yet."

Yet? That was an intriguing way to put it. "I don't understand."

"He's so stupid. He threatened Vance's wife. Can you believe it? So Vance set a trap for him. Her death has triggered it. Any day now, evidence will be released, connecting him to Vance. I told him I'd help him try to find it, but then, I thought, why should I help him?"

She touched her throat, calling his attention to the bruises there that he hadn't been interested enough to notice in the throes of passion.

"If this doesn't take him down, it'll be something else. And he's going to kill me. I could see it in his eyes. It's not just about being governor for him. It's about power. And no matter how much he gets, it will never be enough. He needs to be stopped."

"I see." His mind was actually reeling from shock. He'd never thought he could get too much information. How intriguing that she'd come to him for help in dealing with her murderous husband. While murder was his last resort, it was always on his list of options when dealing with difficult people.

Was he about power, too? He didn't think so. He took no pleasure in killing, at least none that he could recall particularly from his early days, before he could afford to hire his killing done for him.

No, he wasn't about power. He liked the puzzle, the challenge of manipulating events. Life was so dreary otherwise. It amused him to play at politics. To see if he could foist his protégé on the state, then control him. Everyone thought he didn't know how lame his choice was, but he did. That's what made the game so interesting.

Still, it was funny that he and Bubba Joe both thought they were the only one who had hired Vance to kill Magus.

Chapter Ten

Dorothy walked slowly along the path to the cemetery, grateful to be alone for a few minutes. She hadn't been down to pay her respects at her parents' graves since the day she walked behind Magus's coffin. She'd been in Louisiana off and on over the years, taking care of business, but so briefly she hadn't had time to go to Oz. Or so she'd told herself. She wasn't entirely sure she was ready now. So many questions, even more since her return, still stood between her and her memories of her parents.

The path showed her neglect. In places the tall grasses pressed close or completely over the path, with the possibility of fire anthills hiding in their depths. She was intensely aware of the silence. Even nature seemed to be slumbering in the hot, midday sun. The hot, rich smell brought back so many memories of that awful day she'd laid her father to rest. At the time shock had cushioned her, but when shock faded, she was left with vivid memories to live and relive over and over since then, in all their nuances, and through all the stages of grief.

To some extent, she was passing through them again, though faster. Currently, she was deep in angry. Where did this person get off, just whacking people when he felt like it? At first, she'd wondered if she should back off, but not now. This person had to be stopped. This wasn't just about her father anymore. This person might be seeking public office. This person might be looking beyond the state to the White House. This wasn't merely a personal issue anymore. He'd taken it public. It was now firmly in the "no man is an island" zone.

At least no one had died today. Well, no one she knew, or who was connected to the case. The New Orleans murder rate was a separate issue and not within her purview, thank goodness.

She should call Leda and make sure she was all right, though if someone had been listening in on their conversations, they must know Leda knew less than nothing.

After a night in Oz, danger seemed distant from them and connected, instead, to New Orleans. Thanks to Titus's security measures, Oz was darn near an ivory tower.

She and Remy had discussed the party idea and had decided to limit the guest list to suspects only. Even that small group, however, necessitated a massive preparation effort. Oz had been closed a long time and she wanted to make sure they felt the full power of Magus's legacy and her return to wield it. She'd worried their prey wouldn't come on such short notice, but Remy had said grimly, "They'll come. Either out of curiosity, or because they can't help themselves."

She knew that he also wanted her to have this quiet time in Oz for her spirit to heal. In his own, third-estate way, he was a nice man. And they'd both agreed that a period of quiet would be more likely to up the tension level of their suspects, not lower it. Or maybe he'd just wanted her to believe that. In any case, he had to work today, but would be taking some of his vacation time starting tomorrow. They both felt that events were coming to a nice—or nasty—boil.

There was certainly a lot to do to get the house ready for public viewing. She'd had an excellent caretaker, but the house had stood empty a long time. She'd brought in her housekeeper from Dallas, because Helene Tierry, who'd been the housekeeper, retired after Magus died. She lived in town, but seemed content with her retirement.

Titus had offered to oversee the contractors working on the outside and she'd gratefully accepted. She felt awkward with him since she'd lied to him in the library. And she still felt strongly she needed to cut him loose, but didn't know how to do it. Since they'd come back, their relationship had changed. Their comfortable camaraderie was gone and she missed it, but at the same time was glad for it.

It made her feel crazy, but then the situation was insane. She and Remy were basically courting a killer by inviting him to freaking dinner.

Her personal assistant had flown in to help her with the details and a new groundskeeper was supervising the reclamation of the garden and yard areas. She supposed he'd eventually get down this way, too. She also had people going over the wiring and plumbing. Roots had a way of growing through pipes down in this country. She didn't want a backed-up toilet for her guests. Talk about messing with the mystique.

Out of the chaos, the yellow brick road had emerged. The landscape still had a wild, somewhat brooding aspect, but that was just rural Louisiana. Her favorite decision so far was to order the house painted a soft, emerald green. She intended the Wizard to be an unseen guest at the party, even if she had to occasionally cross the line into melodrama.

Gone for now was the brooding quiet of Magus's Oz. Dorothy was bringing it to life again, but when night fell, he was back, he was *there,* assessing her work and alternately approving and disapproving. If she were being haunted, it was nothing like she'd expected. And it didn't seem to include her mother. Of course, she hadn't been murdered, so maybe resting in peace was not an issue for her.

Knowing Magus, he wouldn't approve her intent to commune with the past today. He'd never been one to attach much importance to graves and had only been sentimental when the situation required. He'd consider it an unproductive use of her time, which was one reason she was so determined to do it.

In an odd twist, her parents had both died on the same day. They weren't buried side by side, since they'd been divorced, but at Dorothy's request, Magus had arranged for Emma to be buried the next row over, in the family graveyard. They'd ended up headstone to headstone, since Dorothy had had control over Magus's final rest. She could remember hoping it would force them to come to terms with each other.

The path curved around a stand of oak trees mixed with a few cypress trees. The gray ghostly Spanish moss hung down in her face and even the sluggish air seemed determined to slow her down. It still fascinated her how the cypress knees pushed up through the grass in tiny communities or maybe they were little clumps of gnomes planning nightly mischief.

Gently, almost imperceptibly, peace pushed out every other emotion. It was far too hot to be angry, or agitated. There'd always been something almost magical about the woods around Oz, as if she'd stepped out of time and possibly even place.

Moisture clung to her skin, making her linen dress cling, too. Her feet slipped slightly in her sandals, but none of it mattered. In the distance, the quaint steeple of a church broke the line of trees, then the path straightened and she could see the little cemetery with its mix of headstones and crypts. Little cities of the dead. Only not just the dead waited there.

A blue car was pulled into the dirt lot in front of the little church and a woman in black stooped to lay flowers on a grave.

Annoyance tried to rise, but it was too hot. She could only manage mild irritation and an even milder curiosity. Most of the family buried there had been part of the family Oz used to belong to. They'd died out, just after selling to Magus. The only new graves in twelve years were her parents.

Of course, people doing genealogy could still be related to the family, but then why would they come dressed to mourn? And from here, it looked like her mother's grave receiving attention.

The woman stood up and, as if she felt Dorothy looking, she turned to face her. Glasses hid her face, but the shape of the jaw was as familiar as her own. For the first time, she remembered the genealogy scroll and the previously unknown aunt. Events had pushed that little surprise completely out of her head. Now it surged back to the forefront.

Time slowed to a dream's pace as they studied each other. The hair barely visible beneath the hat was gray. A bit of filmy black lace covered her eyes. Gloves in this heat? Insanely high heels for the terrain. Designer dress, no question about that. The cut was wonderful, flattering and demure. Perfect for mourning. Never mind that it was twelve years too late.

Dorothy stopped when the width of her mother's grave separated them. The silence was reflective, not uncomfortable. Perhaps she should be angry or something, but it was too hot. Her heart counted out time in slow and steady beats that seemed to pause when the woman reached up and lifted the veil back to reveal eyes as violet as Dorothy's. She could be looking into a mirror thirty years from now.

159

"Hello, Dorothy," she said.

"You must be my aunt . . . ?" Dorothy heard herself ask with matching calm.

"Kate. I'm your Aunt Kate," she said.

"Bubba Joe thinks you're the one who had Vonda Vance killed," Suzanne said, as she tried to insinuate herself back into his arms.

"Why would he think that?" Darius asked as he caught her arms, softening his rejection by bringing both her hands to his mouth again. They were the least offensive part of her body at the moment.

"You're the only one who knew he was connected to Vance."

He probably should have thought of their connection himself, but since he'd thought he was the only one to hire Vance, it hadn't seemed like an issue. Interesting sensation, this being wrong. Not that he planned on getting used to it.

He had to hand Vance the honors for making the best use of the situation. He had collected two payments for doing one job. If he'd gotten his pardon from Bubba Joe, he'd have walked out of jail with a tidy retirement fund and a clean record. Darius had even shown him how to hide the paper trail to his money from the police.

"I'm still not seeing where I come into this, Suzanne," he said.

"He thinks you have the proof. That you're the one who will release it. We convince him you aren't the one, but that you know how to find it and then we wait for the timer to run out. He goes to jail."

"And you?"

"I'll need protection. Money to hide from him. I told you, he wants me dead." She pulled her hands free and

crawled close to him again, running her hand down his bare
chest to the place where his pants were hooked closed. She
started to undo it, but he covered her hand to stop her.
What she had to say was so much more interesting than
what she could do.

"But I don't have it," he said.

She sat back on her heels, studying him. He met her gaze
calmly. It helped that he was telling the truth. What she
couldn't know was that this information was as dangerous
to him as it was to Bubba Joe.

"You really don't, do you?"

"I can't think of any reason Vance would have trusted
something like that with me."

"I suppose not." She frowned and then smiled. "But I'll
bet you know who might have it." Before he could stop her,
she climbed in his lap, twining herself around him like an
unwelcome vine. "If we had it, we could control when it
was released. We could make Bubba Joe crawl and beg for
mercy."

The hunger in her voice told its own story about her life
with Bubba Joe as she started kissing his neck, his chest,
any place her mouth could find. Even as his body betrayed
him by responding, his mind remained aloof, considering
the question of who Vance might have trusted besides
Vonda. He probably knew more about Vance than anyone.
No one worked for him that he didn't know inside out.

He hadn't had Vance killed or been involved in the two
subsequent murders. Apparently Bubba Joe hadn't, either.
That meant there had to be a third player in Vance's game.
Who could it be? Did he know what he was doing? It was
possible it was the person he'd trusted with the proof, of
course. Maybe whoever he was had decided to make some
money on the deal. Or was that *she?*

Now there was something to consider. The only *she* in the situation was Dorothy. She certainly had had the most to gain from Magus's death. And had ample reason to hate him. He'd practically let her starve until her mother died, then used her for his political ambitions. Had she been as broken up about daddy dearest as she looked? Or just a very good actress? It was an intriguing line of thought to explore later.

With a start, he realized Suzanne was practically crawling all over him. He grabbed her chin, tipping her face up and halting her roving tongue. He'd never liked being licked. Her face was slack with lust, her jaw unattractively agape. She had an ugly soul. More than anything, he wanted to close his hand around her neck and squeeze it until her eyes went blank. Bubba Joe was right about one thing. She was a liability. And not particularly trustworthy. If she'd betray her husband, she'd have no problem betraying him.

As much as his mind hated her, his body betrayed him again. He pushed her on the bed with a savagery that surprised him. She wanted him. She was going to get him. When he finished, she lay quietly where he left her until he'd dressed again. Her thin, white body was already showing the bruises of their encounter when he finally looked at her.

"Are you going to be able to cover those up?" he asked, without expression.

"Bubba Joe will probably think he did it," she said, her voice flat and slightly bitter.

He was more like Bubba Joe than he thought. For a moment he felt shame. He sat down and awkwardly patted her. Comfort wasn't his style, but he was willing to try. Almost immediately she was sex kitten again, cuddling against him

162

with mutters of relief and forgiveness.

As he cradled her body against his, he realized that she'd done more than give him information and sexual release. She'd opened a dark door to his soul. All those years, he thought he sought control for control's sake. But that wasn't it at all.

He turned her until she straddled him again. If she would be insatiable, let it be for a purpose. A last purpose in her sad life. He might have felt some remorse at what he was about to do, but it was really a mercy killing. He knew he'd be kinder than Bubba Joe.

"My sister and I weren't . . . close . . . after our parents died," Kate said, smiling her thanks for the cold drink Dorothy offered her from the refrigerator. They'd come in the back way, avoiding the chaos of upstairs. Dorothy had told her the kitchen would be quiet and it was.

She paused to take a sip, trying to order her thoughts and edit them as she went. She should have prepared better for this moment. Henry had wanted her to wait, but she'd felt driven to come. She remembered all of the past ten years, but what happened ten years ago she was still remembering in painful chunks. And it all felt as if it had happened yesterday to her. She was raw and wounded and shocked and horrified by what she did remember.

"We'd always been different, pursued different kinds of lives. We just drifted apart. When the marriage broke up, Emma needed help, so we lived together until you were born, but I wasn't much into kids and we went our separate ways again. Didn't keep in touch." Kate had avoided looking at Dorothy, but now she looked up. "I didn't know. I know it's hard to believe, but I didn't know about the cancer and her death—" She stopped and swallowed painfully.

"What do you remember?" Dorothy asked. Her face and tone were neutral.

Judgment reserved for now. And when she knew it all? She shouldn't have come, but she was here. She took a steadying breath.

"I remember a newspaper story about Magus. It had a little bit about you, about your reunion." All of it crap, of course. Magus couldn't let the truth be known. She traced a pattern in the old wood of the table. "My life wasn't going real great right then. And I guess I thought Magus might help me out, for old times' sake. So I came. I was there . . . the day he was shot. The day you were shot."

She shuddered. It had been ten years, but for her the memory was fresh and sharp in her mind as if it had happened yesterday. "My shrink says I had a mental breakdown because of the shock of it and everything that had been going on. My brain just shorted out."

"I don't understand," Dorothy said. "Why would that be so traumatic for you?"

It wasn't easy to look into Dorothy's eyes and lie. "I'm not sure. There are still some pieces missing from that time. It's . . . odd what I remember and what I don't. I remember the rally too well and I must have talked to Magus, but I can't remember. I guess . . . we didn't talk back then?"

"I didn't even know you existed until a few days ago." Dorothy seemed uncertain how to react.

Kate didn't blame her. "I feel so ashamed. Henry, that's my husband, he says I couldn't help it, but it feels like I could have, that I should have." She twisted her hands in her lap. Her insides felt like they twisted, too. "I . . . wasn't a very nice person back then," she admitted painfully. "Apparently, when I blacked out, I just rewrote my reality. Made myself into a Kate I could live with again. Not long after that I met Henry. We fell in love and got married. I was happy, but—"

Dorothy's face wasn't unkind or kind, but Kate didn't mind. At least she was reserving judgment. It gave her time to build something. A beginning maybe?

"But?"

"On some level I must have known something was wrong. I always felt like there was something out there, just waiting to steal my peace. I used to go to the shrink. He'd give me antidepressants. Thank heavens for Henry. He kept me . . . sane."

She looked up to find Dorothy studying her, probably assessing her truthfulness. Well, she couldn't blame her. It had happened to her and she didn't quite believe it.

"I don't blame you for finding it . . . fantastic. And strange. I'm pretty freaked by it myself. I just feel terrible that I left you alone. I wasn't a great person then, but we are . . . family. Of sorts. You haven't been too well served by your family so far, have you?"

Shame ate at her insides. She felt a brief, bitter longing for the peace she'd felt just days ago. Why did she have to remember now?

Dorothy seemed to come to a decision, but what it was Kate couldn't tell. She smiled, though it was slightly cool. "Your Henry sounds wonderful," Dorothy said, almost wistfully. "Is he here with you?"

Just hearing his name, Kate felt the darkness recede a bit.

"He wanted to, but . . . he's ill. And in a wheelchair. He didn't want to complicate the situation even more. And we didn't know how long I'd be here."

Dorothy nodded, seemed to hesitate. "Wow, an aunt, an uncle. It feels . . . odd."

"I can imagine. I'm so very sorry. I wish . . ." She stopped. How could she wish the years with Henry away? She couldn't have had memory and Henry. That she did know.

Dorothy nodded again. "Well, look, you're both welcome to stay here. We could fix him up a wheelchair-friendly room. I think I like the idea of having an uncle."

Just an uncle? Well, what did she expect? The fatted calf? And what would she do when she knew the whole truth? Henry had urged her to come clean, but Kate couldn't. Not yet. She hadn't even told Henry everything yet. He'd have never let her come.

"I'll ask him. Thank you." She pushed back from the table. "I should get my car and check out of my hotel, if you're sure. I mean, I'm fine in the hotel."

"I'll have Titus get your stuff for you, if you'll give me the keys to your car and room."

"Titus?" Kate felt her throat go dry.

"You and my mother knew him in high school, he said."

"That's right." She hadn't expected that. Thank heavens for the warning. "So he told you about . . . us?"

"I never even knew about the high school thing until a few days ago. Neither of my parents seems to have been big on sharing and Titus makes them look gabby." Dorothy's smile was wry and a bit sad.

"I . . . could probably answer some of your questions. Not everything, of course, but some." It wasn't much, but it was something.

For the first time, Dorothy gave her a real smile. "I'd like that. There's so much I don't know." Then her expression changed, closed slightly, as she looked past Kate.

"Titus. My Aunt Kate has come to visit."

Kate froze; she wasn't ready for this, but there wasn't time to get ready. She turned to face her old school chum, her chin up. "Hi, Titus. How have you been?"

Chapter Eleven

Bubba Joe knew Bozo was right. He needed to get sober. He needed to think. Where was Suzanne? He needed her to think. He needed to punch her face in. He needed, he flexed his hands, to choke someone. Suzanne was the easy choice, so maybe it was just as well she wasn't around. The other person he really wanted to get his hands on was Dorothy.

Had she been playing him for the fool all along? All that crap about Magus haunting the place. She was good. But she was going to find out, he was better. He needed to figure out what to do, but he couldn't think. Coffee, he needed coffee.

He grabbed the bell and yanked it furiously. When the maid appeared, he snapped, "Coffee. Hot. Black. Lots of it."

She looked scared as she nodded and backed out of the room. Good. Be scared. Everyone be scared. Bubba Joe was making his move.

When she came with the coffee, he waited until she set it on his desk and poured him a cup, then lunged for her, but she must have been expecting it. She eluded him and fled the room.

He cursed the empty room. He'd deal with her later. He downed the cup and refilled it. His hands weren't steady and it spilled, but by the fourth cup, he wasn't spilling it anymore. And he was thinking more clearly.

He knew he could get Dorothy to talk, if he could get her

alone. Titus would be with her, but a couple of roofies and he'd be no problem. He always kept a supply on hand. It was so much better when his dates didn't remember details. *"I have no recollection,"* was one, sweet phrase.

Now, how to get her to come to him? She wouldn't come willingly. Wait. Hadn't he collected a souvenir from his encounter with Emma? Yeah, he had. Such an interesting one, too. And he'd tell her he thought he was her daddy. Okay, now his plan was coming together. . . .

He heard the front bell ring, then the slow steps of that stupid maid. After a short, muffled exchange, she knocked on his study door.

"What?" He didn't want to be disturbed. Not now.

"Policia," she said, her eyes wide and scared.

The police? Was this it? Had he run out of time? Something awful uncurled in his gut. Something that clawed, ripped and tore at him. It was . . . fear? It had been so long since he'd felt it, he almost didn't recognize it.

Two men appeared behind her, pushing past her into the room.

"Mr. Henry?" the taller one asked.

Distantly, over the pounding surf of fear, he noticed that they looked uneasy. He nodded, unable to speak.

"I'm afraid we have some bad news, sir," the shorter one said. The two cops exchanged glances, before he continued. "I'm afraid your wife is dead."

"Dead?" He couldn't process their words. They weren't here about him? Suzanne was dead? *Dead?* "How . . . ?"

"I'm afraid she was murdered."

"Strangled," added his companion.

As his fear for himself began to recede, he was able to notice that they were watching him closely. Funny that his fear for himself was the perfect shocked reaction for Suzanne. Dead. And he didn't get to do it. Well, it was safer that way, but it still sucked.

"I don't understand," he said, with perfect truth. It felt strange.

"Apparently she met someone in a French Quarter hotel." The cop was still watching him closely. "They had sex, then he killed her."

"Can you account for your whereabouts this afternoon, sir?" his partner asked.

They suspected him. It was almost funny. Good thing he hadn't needed to roofie his alibi. She actually liked it rough. This could have been so dang ironic.

"I can give you the young lady's name," he said, "and I trust you'll be discreet with it?"

"Certainly, sir." The two cops exchanged looks again, their faces going expressionless.

"We'll need you to come down and identify the body, sir."

Bubba Joe adopted a suitably serious expression. "Of course. I just need to make a phone call and I'll come right down."

The grieving widower. This might work for him, though it was going to be a bitch replacing Suzanne as his manager.

Remy found himself retracing his journey to Oz in the fading light of a setting sun, only this time he knew what was waiting for him there. He and Dorothy had talked by phone last night, so he knew her aunt had showed up. He was withholding judgment until he met the woman, but he found her story unlikely and her timing suspicious.

Yesterday, work had been pressure-cooked to a white-hot heat as speculation swirled about his run for the mansion and his relationship with Dorothy. He hadn't minded it, since he was mostly used to it, but he was glad to have a break before they launched their next salvo at the dinner party. It would be nice to be acting, instead of reacting, to events. And one hoped the guilty party was sweating it out somewhere.

What had started as an intellectual enterprise, a chance to satisfy his curiosity about a past event, had, at some point in the last few days, turned very personal. The quest to find out who was behind Magus's killing was no longer about a sleeping murder. Murder had waked with a vengeance. Someone was very afraid and striking out without mercy. What was even more troubling, for someone who cared about the future of the state as much as Remy did, was the realization that the killer might also be politically powerful. What if he, or she, were to become governor of the state? It wouldn't be the first time Louisiana had had someone unworthy in a position of power. The state had even survived some pretty scaly leaders, but it still pissed him off. Just surviving wasn't enough anymore.

The people in the state deserved better and they were trying to get it. There was an ebb and tide in human events, where all the pieces came together to make something happen. If that tide passed, how long would it take the people of this state to recover this time? He wanted to be governor, but this wasn't just about him. Not anymore. Whoever had killed, whoever was now killing, had raised the stakes.

He and Dorothy had dropped stones in a stinking, deep and dark pond and the resulting ripples were spreading well beyond any personal agenda he or she might have. The night of the Zoo-to-Do, he'd wondered if they should back off, or if he should at least try to persuade Dorothy to back off. He now knew he'd never be able to convince her to do that and he knew it wasn't the right thing to do. He wasn't perfect, but he was a man of goodwill. He couldn't allow evil to endure without doing something about it.

All of this meant he'd bitten off a lot. Beyond the obvious danger of their situation was the worry about how close he and Dorothy were becoming. He'd known it would be challenging to pretend to love Dorothy, but he'd thought it would be because she wasn't that lovable. Now he was finding it hard to keep his head. She was far more beautiful, far more fascinating, than he'd expected. And beyond that, she was a good person. It sounded like such a cliché, but she had character. She had integrity. She had a sense of humor, charm and natural warmth. She was definitely, infinitely desirable.

In short, she would be dangerously easy to fall for. He had to keep reminding himself they wanted different things, but it was getting more difficult, because it was quite clear they both wanted each other. He hadn't fallen yet, of course, but the line was blurring between where pretense began and reality ended.

He spotted the opening to Oz and this time he didn't shoot past. As he turned off the highway, his car didn't lurch and sway, though the remote Dorothy had given him for the gate went flying across the car. He muttered to himself, put the car in park and bent over to retrieve it. At first he didn't know what the cracking sound meant. He almost sat up to look, but then he got it. He twisted around, without exposing his body to fire, and saw another hole appear in the side window of his car. Even then it was hard to compute that someone was shooting at him. Someone was actually, freaking shooting at him.

He grabbed the remote and pointed it blindly at the gate, careful to keep a low profile. He counted to ten, the longest ten seconds of his life, then fumbled the car into gear and drove blindly forward. Two more shots thudded into the body of his car before he felt sure he'd pulled out of range. He stopped and took a cautious look over the edge of the door. Nothing happened, so he sat up.

He'd set himself up as a clay pigeon, but the truth was, he hadn't really expected to be shot at. Now he felt . . . pissed. Royally pissed. The killer had just made it very personal again. If it was the last thing he did, he was going to find him and stop him. Preferably with his fist first.

He took several deep breaths. He'd like to talk to Titus, too—

A jeep came careening down the road. Titus sat next to one of his security guys, his expression not a happy one. The jeep jerked to a stop by Remy's car and Titus jumped out.

"Go see what you can find out," he ordered the driver.

Remy waited until Titus could see the four bullet holes in his window before he lowered it.

"You all right?" Titus asked tightly.

Remy nodded sharply. "I expect my insurance rates are going to go up."

"I know someone who can fix it. Leave your keys with one of the guards. It'll be ready by morning."

"Okay." Remy stared at him for a long moment, before finally asking, "You riding up to the house with me?"

"I'll wait for Finlay."

"Fine." He rolled the window up again, trying not to notice that the cluster of holes were where his head should have been. His heartbeat had slowed somewhat during his brief exchange with Titus, but now it sped up again. It was one thing to *think* he was kicking the ant's nest, a whole other thing to *know* it.

He was conscious of Titus watching him. Man-like, Remy refused to let him see him sweat. He put the car in gear and pulled away, for the first time noticing the progress that had been made in the few days since he and Dorothy began their dangerous dance with a killer.

The yellow brick road had been repaired, the encroaching green trimmed back for an easier-to-the-paint-job passage. When he swept into the yard and found the house gleaming green in the golden light, he laughed out loud. This was a declaration of war, with a vengeance.

He parked his car with the bullet holes away from the house. He had a feeling Titus wouldn't tell Dorothy. He wouldn't want her to be worried about Remy. He was quite sure Titus would do nothing to further any bonds they might be building between them. What Remy didn't know was exactly how Titus felt about Dorothy. Remy was sure that Titus didn't consider himself merely an employee. Yeah, he'd been there for her for a long time, but that didn't give him the right to act like a dog with a favorite bone. For one thing, he was old enough to be her freaking father. And his last important bodyguarding job had ended with Magus dead and Dorothy injured. If the opportunity presented itself, he was going to suggest Dorothy distance herself from Titus.

He saw Dorothy waiting for him under the same oak tree as last time. Today she wore jeans, a white T-shirt and the inevitable gimme cap with the brim turned back. Her smile was wide and welcoming. It dug into a deep place inside him, warming him from the inside out. He forgot about the shooting and Titus. Driven by instinct and what he wanted, not what he should do, he started toward her. In his mind, she was already in his arms, his mouth on hers, his body home where it belonged. She didn't move, but there was nothing in her eyes to stop him. Three feet, then two feet separated them. One more foot . . . but before he reached her, the jeep with Titus and Finlay drove into the clearing, stopping him in his tracks.

He couldn't tell if she was disappointed. If she was, the expression passed so fleetingly across her face, he couldn't be sure. She'd gotten good at hiding what she felt. He supposed she'd had to, but it made him sad, particularly knowing he'd helped it to happen.

It was a pointed reminder of all the reasons they were wrong for each other. His body wasn't buying it, but for now his brain was back in control.

He started to say something to her, but stopped. He was tired of Titus being silent witness to everything they said and did. Surely he didn't need to be so omnipresent here in Oz? He looked at him pointedly, until he and his sidekick excused themselves and left. When he was out of sight, Remy looked at Dorothy.

"Any news?" Remy asked.

Dorothy nodded. "A very interesting call from Bubba Joe Henry."

Remy's brows arched. "Really? What did that slime bucket want?"

"He had something he wants to give me. Of my mother's." A troubled frown creased her brow. He wished he had the right to smooth it away. "He's hoping I'll meet him at his place in Baton Rouge tonight."

"No." Remy shook his head. "Absolutely not."

"That's what I told him, only a bit more ambiguously. I said maybe tomorrow, but he said he'll be busy making funeral arrangements tomorrow."

"What?"

"It seems someone murdered his wife today," Dorothy

said evenly. "He didn't seem too broken up about it, though I'm sure he will be tomorrow for the cameras. Anyway, he told me if I'd feel more comfortable, to bring Titus. He's sure I have no secrets from him."

"I still don't like it," Remy said. "What's his angle?"

"The only way to find out is to go. I should be fine with Titus." She stepped closer. "I told him I wanted you to be there, but he said no. I think you make him crazy."

She smiled at him. It was a great smile. It seemed to come from deep inside her and couldn't be contained by her mouth. It spread out around her like rays from the sun.

Reluctantly Remy grinned back. "Well, I do my best."

After a moment, she sobered again. "Do you think her death is connected to our problem?"

Remy shook his head. "No way to know for sure, but I'll call my source in the NOPD. See what I can find out."

"Thanks. I think I'm getting paranoid. They were all here back then. It's like we've all come back to where we were. Even the same things are at stake again." She shivered slightly.

He held out his hand. "Let's walk and talk."

She took the hand he'd extended and let him pull her to his side. He looked down at her, enjoying the way movement made her hair lift and move. Like Dorothy the person, her hair was full of light and shadow and he was sure it would be soft against his hands if he ever got the chance to—

Okay, don't go there. Not if he wanted to finish the walk with any dignity.

"About Titus—"

"You shouldn't bait him," Dorothy said.

He gave himself a mental shake and added, "I didn't think you noticed."

"When Magus was alive, about all I had to do was watch and listen. I guess it turned into a habit."

"Then you've probably noticed he's a bit intense about you. It's not—" he hesitated.

"Good for either of us?"

"So you've noticed?"

Dorothy nodded. "When this is over, I'll talk to him, but I can't deny him his chance to find out what happened. He needs it, in his own way, as much as I do."

He nodded. He still thought it a mistake, but it wasn't any of his business.

"So, this aunt of yours, what's she like?"

He saw a stone bench and steered her toward it. Being with her was nice, but it was too damn hot to walk far. He wished now he'd paused to get something cool to drink.

Dorothy sank to the bench, her violet gaze studying him thoughtfully as she said, "What's she like? I think you should draw your own conclusions."

"Any chance she's not who she says she is?"

"If she were younger, we'd be twins."

"Okay, do you believe her story? It's pretty wild."

Dorothy stretched her legs out, studying her sandal-clad feet as if they held the answers to the mysteries of the cosmos. "I didn't at first."

"And now you do?"

"Let's just say, I'm not as skeptical as I was." She slanted a lazy look at him and a strand of her hair fell forward, near one of her eyes.

Without thinking, he smoothed the strand back in place. It took at least two, slow beats of his heart for him to register the feel of her hair against fingertips turned supersensitive. And then there was her skin. Silk would be jealous of her skin. Cashmere would wish it could be more like her. His breath stopped. His heart might have, too. Slowly, giving her time to pull back, he slid his hand into her hair and around to the back of her head.

She just watched him with her amazing eyes, their depths reflective, curious, and interested. But the pulse at the base of her neck doubled its pace. He adjusted his head, then the angle of hers, and brought their mouths within striking distance of each other.

"I've wanted to do this for days," he said huskily. Now he could smell her. Sweet, with just a hint of sass. "You smell good."

She trembled under his touch, starting a wildfire in his midsection. "So do you." She sounded breathless, a little amused, definitely interested. Still he waited.

"If we do this, we'll have crossed a line," he murmured, as longing assaulted his willpower. "We won't be able to go back."

"It's just a kiss, Remy Mistral," she said softly. Her violet eyes darkened to mysterious and sultry, as if she were feeling her power, exploring its depth and breadth.

"Really?" With a husky growl he closed the distance, not hard or driving. First he just danced across the silken surface of her mouth. Brushing, teasing, taking quick tastes and pulling back when she tried to cling. He could feel her fighting him, not against the kiss, but against being the one to surrender. The power struggle was brief and, when he realized there'd be no winner, he gave in, letting his mouth sink into hers.

For now the contact was limited to hands and mouths. She gripped his shoulders. He had one hand on the back of her neck, the other at her waist, while his mouth learned the secrets of hers. When they needed air, he eased back. The hot afternoon air felt surprisingly cool as it rushed into the small space between them.

"Only a kiss?" he asked her now.

She chuckled, the sound rich and sexy and slightly provocative. Even better, it made their bodies brush together. He started to close the distance again, but her hand at his chest stopped his drive.

"Would you like something cool to drink?" she asked.

"What?"

He realized she was looking over his shoulder. He turned and there stood a girl in a maid's uniform, her cheeks bright with embarrassment, a tray of something cool in her hands. He looked back at Dorothy.

She shrugged, biting back a grin. "Sorry, but I knew you'd be hot and thirsty when you arrived."

He slowly released her, letting his hands stay in contact with her as long as possible. That erased the grin. She shivered once, before contact ended. He smiled at her then.

"I am thirsty . . . and hot."

Her smile was a private one, just for him, before she reined it in and stood up.

"Thank you, Anne. You can set the tray here." She indicated the place she'd been sitting. As she poured him a drink, Remy noticed she looked rather wickedly amused, with no sign of embarrassment. As he took the glass from her, he realized how good she was at protecting her essential self. He knew she wanted him, but he had no idea how she felt about wanting him, or if it meant anything beyond simple physical gratification.

He'd assumed she didn't play sex games, just because there was an air of innocence, a purity about her, but the truth was he had no way of knowing anything. His head wasn't clear enough to clearly read her. All he knew, it had felt right to kiss her. And that it wouldn't take long for mere kissing to not be enough.

He watched her sip from her glass, the lips closing around the rim, starting up the heat inside him again. As if she felt his look, her lashes lifted. There was a question in the depths of her eyes, but he couldn't read it, then her gaze shifted past him again. Resigned and frustrated, he turned and saw a woman approaching who looked like a much older twin of Dorothy.

"Your aunt?" he asked. Dorothy nodded. "Interesting."

"That's what I thought," Dorothy said, with a grin.

Chapter Twelve

"Do you look like your sister?" Remy asked Kate as they walked back up to the house.

"People used to think we were twins," Kate said without looking at him, "until I started looking like the older sister."

Remy had never met Emma—he'd been, what, maybe eight when she left town—but he'd seen news footage of her with Magus. Like Dorothy, she wasn't a traditional beauty, but she could fool you into thinking she was by a force of personality that was clear even in those old newsreels. If Kate had a strong personality, she was keeping it well-hidden. Even her eyes had "no trespassing" signs posted. Despite this, there was something about her that drew the eye and demanded attention. It was as if her attempt to not be interesting somehow made her more interesting. Her still waters definitely ran deep, but what was down there in them?

Dorothy drew ahead of them to confer with one of her staff. Kate watched her, but what she thought about her niece, she kept to herself. Remy stopped, angling his body so she had to stop, too.

"Why are you really here?" He kept his tone neutral, but firm. Remy told himself he was just worried about Dorothy. She was surrounded by people, but none of them, not even Titus, were really concerned with her and what she needed. They all needed something from her. For Titus, Remy suspected it was absolution.

She studied him, her mildly curious expression so like

Dorothy's for a moment that it was eerie. It was like looking into her future. It wasn't, Remy conceded, half-bad. Kate had aged well and even had a hint of sex appeal when she let it peep out from behind her battlements.

"Why are you worried about it?" she asked, as if she were really puzzled.

Remy's gaze narrowed. "I care about her. And I know that the people in her family have pretty much let her down every time she's come close to them."

Pain flickered in her eyes and he felt a moment's remorse, before reminding himself that however hard, his words were true. Oddly enough, it reassured him that she could feel pain. She wasn't totally iced over.

"So you think I'm here to let her down?"

She was still answering his questions with questions, but he knew how to be patient, too.

"I think your timing is interesting."

She looked away from him, as if considering his words. "I suppose it is. I hadn't really thought about it in that context. I just knew I needed to see her." She hesitated, then added, more as if she were thinking aloud than talking to him, "My husband didn't want me to come." She looked at him again, a wry smile giving her face a fugitive charm. "He doesn't understand, either."

"I'd like to understand. That's why I asked."

Her expression gentled, but her voice was firm. "It's really none of your business, though. This is between Dorothy and me."

She left him then, walking back to the house without haste, but with unconscious grace. Dorothy watched her walk past. They exchanged words and Kate went inside the house. Only then did Dorothy look at him. He shoved his hands in the pockets of his slacks and walked up to her.

There was a question in her eyes.

Remy answered it. "She told me to mind my own business."

Dorothy grinned. "She obviously doesn't know who she is dealing with."

"Has she told you why she's really here?"

Dorothy looked down, fidgeting with the decorative button at the neck of her T-shirt. When she finally looked up, she looked rueful—and remarkably like her aunt had just looked.

"I haven't asked her." She moved restlessly. "I've had so many questions for so many years and now, finally, there is someone here who can at least answer some of them. And I haven't asked."

"What are you waiting for?"

She half-laughed. "A lightning strike, maybe?"

"The right moment never comes. *Carpe diem.* You need to seize the day. You don't know how long it will last." He wanted to seize the moment. He wanted to touch her so bad, the tips of his fingers hurt, but he also knew what would happen if he did. He'd start kissing her again and then he'd just be another person wanting something from her. Right now she needed someone to give her something.

"After your meeting with Bubba Joe, why don't you have her meet you in town, get some supper at one of those little fishing places along the bayou and just talk to her?"

She smiled slowly. "That's a good idea."

"What, you didn't think I had those?"

She laughed. "Oh, you have them. They just usually aren't so harmless or so sensible."

"Even I can't be amazing all the time." His grin was full of sass and he knew it. She knew it, too, but what almost made his heart stop right then was the realization that

183

she liked it. He could tell.

"I guess that depends on your definition of amazing." Her grin sassed him back.

If she didn't go, he was going to grab her and start kissing again. Maybe she knew that, too. She reached out, almost touched his arm, pulled her hand back, then turned and went into the house.

Remy stood staring at where she'd been until the feeling of being watched penetrated his absorption. He turned and found Titus staring at him. His cold, light gaze was a stone wall to his thoughts, but Remy still felt his hostility, even across the clearing. He hoped his thoughts were equally clear to the failed bodyguard. He hoped Titus knew that if Remy were in charge, his ass would be fired right now.

Maybe he got it. He turned abruptly and strode off toward the garage, presumably to get the car.

He probably shouldn't antagonize him, but the chances of Titus ever taking a bullet for him were a million to one anyway.

Bubba Joe knew he had to play the scene carefully or his prey wouldn't play. They'd both be suspicious, on guard. He also knew that Dorothy wouldn't like the memento he had from his encounter with Emma, that once she saw it, she wouldn't want an audience for the rest of their discussion.

He'd made it clear to Juanita, that if she wanted to keep her job, Titus better have a drink with her. He'd taken the precaution of spiking with roofies anything they were likely to drink. He didn't want her hearing any cries for help, either.

Then he and Dorothy would have a heart-to-heart about her slut of a mother. And that the whole world would know

Emma was a slut, unless she handed over the evidence against him.

He'd wondered sometimes whether he should get rid of his mementos from his encounters, but part of him had always known he might need them someday, to persuade or dissuade his partners from being unwise. They were cold, hard proof, both the bits of clothing *and* the pictures he'd secretly taken.

Dorothy would be more malleable, once she realized what was at stake. More malleable than her mother? Maybe. Emma had been good. He liked it when they fought him, but he couldn't always afford the pleasure. Maybe if Suzanne had had some spunk, he wouldn't have hated her so much. She'd been too cold even to enjoy it.

He should have killed her this afternoon when he felt like it. Then she wouldn't have gotten away from him. She'd been *his* to keep or kill. Instead, she'd eluded him. Not only that, she'd betrayed him. With another woman. A prostitute. He'd been with Cassandra himself a time or two. Darius had introduced him to her. It made him sick to think of it.

Then another thought occurred to him. What if Darius had introduced Suzanne to Cassandra? Be just like him. He'd think it was funny. He silently cursed Darius, Suzanne and Cassandra, only stopping when he'd run out of expletives.

He stared broodingly at the phone, then snatched it up and dialed Darius's number.

"I know what you did, you," he let loose again, cursing Darius with every word he could think of.

When he was tired and panting, he heard Darius ask, "Who is this?"

It was gas to a fire. "You introduced Suzanne to Cas-

185

sandra. Maybe you even had something to do with her death. You can bet I'll be talking to the cops, Darius. I won't take this lying down."

He slammed the phone down. He'd fix him and his little protégé, too. No one messed with him or anything that belonged to him. He jumped up, pacing and cursing.

Tonight there was no one to vent his rage on but Dorothy. Her father had been a fool and she was, too. Kind of nice she looked a bit like Emma. Once he found out where she'd put the evidence, they'd replay her family history. If daughter was like mother, he was in for a good time tonight. And when he was done? Well, he still needed someone to play Suzanne's role in his life.

He'd considered slipping her a roofie, too, but he wanted her awake. He wanted her to know who was in charge, he needed her to feel his power over her. Her mother hadn't talked and she wouldn't, either. Not if she didn't want the word out on what her mother had been. He knew he hadn't been the only one. He'd give little Dorothy chapter and verse on her mama. Chapter and verse.

He thought he heard a sound outside, so he went to the patio doors and looked out, but didn't see anything. He walked out and leaned against the wall, looking out over the garden. He'd need to hire a housekeeper now that Suzanne was gone. He couldn't be expected to take care of everything. He'd better start a list. He turned purposefully and went back inside. He sat down, picked up the black bra that had been Emma's and fingered it with a reflective smile, then tossed it aside and picked up his pen. What was it he needed? Oh, yeah. A housekeeper. A campaign manager. What he really needed was a new wife. Maybe Dorothy would oblige? He laughed and wrote her name at the top of the page.

He looked up and his jaw dropped. "You!"

"No matter what he says or does, don't send me away," Titus cautioned, as he reached around Dorothy to ring the bell. "I've heard . . . things about him. Rumors he's not beyond using force with women."

Dorothy nodded, her stomach tightening with tension. There was the sound of someone fumbling with the door and it swung open to reveal a scared maid. She looked like she'd been crying—a reminder that the mistress of the house was dead. What am I doing here, Dorothy wondered. This was wrong. What was Bubba Joe up to?

If her mother had had an affair with this sleazeball, she wasn't sure what she'd do. It made her skin crawl to even think about it. She felt like she was losing her mother. With each new impression, the mother she'd known grew fainter and fainter. I'm going to lose her and I came back to Louisiana hoping to find her, Dorothy thought bleakly.

"Mr. Henry is expecting me," Dorothy said, her voice husky with growing dread.

As if he sensed her hesitation, Titus said, "You don't have to do this. Let me talk to him—"

Dorothy shook her head sharply. "You know he won't talk to you."

"He'll talk to me," Titus said grimly.

The maid looked from one to the other, clearly puzzled. Dorothy had a feeling she didn't speak much English. She was probably lucky she didn't. Dorothy tried to smile at her.

"I'm so sorry about Mrs. Henry."

The girl's eyes filled up with tears. "*Señor* in library." She pointed down the hall to a closed door. "He say, go in."

"Gracias," Dorothy said, expending the sum of her Spanish.

The girl smiled shyly at Titus. "You like drink, *señor?*"

Titus recoiled slightly. "No, thanks." He stepped forward, grasping the doorknob, turning it and pushing the door open. Almost immediately, he recoiled with a muttered curse. He turned, blocking Dorothy and the maid from seeing into the room. "Call the police. *Policia,*" he told the maid.

"What—" Dorothy looked at him.

"He's dead and it's not pretty." Titus's face was grim and hard. "Get her to call the police. I'll look around, see what I can see."

"You can't mess a crime scene," she objected softly.

"I won't. I'll just look at it."

She nodded, then asked, "Was he . . . murdered?"

Titus shrugged. "It looks like he took his own life. I saw the gun in his hand."

Dorothy straightened. "I want to look, too."

"The back of his head is blown away." He pulled out the car keys. "Go meet your aunt. You didn't see anything. You don't know anything."

"You have to tell them I was here—"

"I'll take care of it."

Dorothy hesitated. "You'll tell me what you find?"

"If I have time to look." He arched his brows pointedly.

She nodded, started to leave, but stopped to say in a low voice, "Thanks."

She felt him lightly touch her shoulder, his face softening. "We'll get this figured out. I promise."

She managed a smile of thanks for him and then slipped out the door. It was nice that things were back to normal with Titus, but it made her feel guilty. She was using him, his guilt, even when she knew it needed to stop. As she drove away, she dialed Remy's cell phone with the feeling she was betraying Titus again.

Bozo saw Dorothy leave Bubba Joe's house without her faithful pit bull, Titus. He considered for a moment before deciding to follow her. He'd hoped to play rescuer and build a bond, but it wasn't to be. If he turned up now, Bubba Joe would suspect he'd been manipulated. That would be a pity. No one liked to see the strings they were dancing to. What had cut their meeting so short? It couldn't be Suzanne's murder. Bubba Joe already knew about that. As he followed her onto the highway, he saw police lights flashing in the distance, but getting steadily closer. He slowed enough to see them turn into Bubba Joe's lane. Now that was interesting. It was, however, less than satisfying. He needed to know what had actually happened. Had she found out he was behind her father's death? How pedestrian to call in the cops. She lacked her father's flair.

Now she stopped. He watched her enter Pat's, a rustic-looking seafood place. It was too dark for him to see her face, but she moved with the unhurried grace of her mother. She was so like Emma, it made him almost nostalgic. A pity he didn't have time to wallow in it. If she wasn't meeting Mistral, who his source told him had only just left Oz, maybe they could have their little talk about her paternity now.

He slipped inside and peered over the divider into the small dining room. Yes, there she was. She wasn't alone, though. They both had menus in front of their faces. He waited until the waitress approached. Almost, yes, the menus were coming down—

No, it couldn't be. Emma was dead. She was older and

189

her hair was gray instead of red, but it was definitely Emma. As if in a trance, he headed for the table. He wanted to tell her . . . what? That he'd missed her? Well, it was a start.

He stopped by the table. Emma looked up. Violet eyes in a well-remembered face studied him without recognition. She couldn't have forgotten him. That just wasn't possible.

"Emma?" he said, playfully rebuking her with look and tone.

Emma looked at Dorothy, clearly puzzled. Dorothy hid a smile.

"This is my Aunt Kate," Dorothy said. "My mother's sister."

He felt both shock and relief. He'd think about why later. For now he smiled widely, took her hand and kissed the back of it.

"You are most like your sister. Bozo Luc. I am enchanted to make your acquaintance, mademoiselle?"

"Madame," Dorothy said dryly. "Very madame."

He smiled at Kate, still holding her hand. "A very great pity, madame."

She smiled at him, of course. All women did. He reluctantly released her hand and turned to Dorothy. From the inside pocket of his jacket, he pulled the envelope with the faked paternity test.

"Perhaps later you'll peruse this and call me, chere." He held her gaze with his for as long as she would allow, going for a gentle, paternal look. He could tell he had puzzled her. Good. That was the first step in what he hoped would be an interesting little dance. And a change of partners for her.

She took the letter, appeared to weigh it for a moment before tucking it in her purse. Her gaze considered him, as if she weren't sure she should tell him something. Then she said, "Did you hear about Suzanne Henry?"

"Such a tragedy. I wonder how Bubba Joe is taking it?"

"Not . . . well," Dorothy said. She exchanged a quick look with Kate. "He's dead."

Bozo stared at her. His heart may have stopped. He reached for and found the edge of a chair. Dorothy jumped to her feet and grabbed his arm, helping him to sit down.

"I'm sorry, sir. I didn't mean to startle you."

What she meant was that she didn't know it would startle him. He didn't blame her. He didn't know it would, either. So Bubba Joe was dead? He was grateful for the seat and the glass of water she handed him. He took a drink. "Do you know how . . ."

"Titus found him. He said it looked like a suicide."

She didn't believe that any more than he did.

"I think I shall miss him," Bozo said, surprised. "We've been adversaries a long time." He'd had no idea his goading of Bubba Joe would work so well. Of course, he hadn't known Suzanne would be murdered. Maybe it really was the pressure, but even as the thought formed in his head, he discarded it. Bubba Joe was entirely too selfish to take his own life. No, someone had ended it. It was the only thing that made any sense. Which begged the next question: why? And of course, who?

He looked at Dorothy, sitting so calmly at the table. If he hadn't seen her arrive and leave, he'd suspect she had something to do with it. Was there, as Darius suspected, another player in the game? Whoever it was, they clearly knew something, but what did they know and what were they after?

If Bubba had hired Vance, then what secret was there left to find out? There was the money, but he didn't see how Bubba Joe could have afforded to pay enough to make it that interesting a figure. It was possible that Bubba Joe had been killed for his romantic excesses, but the timing was definitely interesting if that were the case. Perhaps a coincidence, though Bubba Joe usually took care of his problems before they reached a serious level. A cockroach had been eliminated, but an entertaining one. Yes, he would miss him.

He stood up abruptly. "I must be off. You've given me much to think about, chere. You know where to reach me when you're ready to talk." His motto was, if he couldn't leave them happy, why, then leave them puzzled. After gallantly kissing the hands of both women, he made his way out, comforted by the certain knowledge that both of them watched him leave. Ah, he still had it.

Dorothy looked at Kate. "Well, that was interesting. Weird, but interesting."

"Do you want to look at what he left you?" Kate asked Dorothy.

Dorothy hesitated. "That's what he wants me to do. I'm tired of doing what people want me to do. What *I* want to do is talk to you. You said you might be able to answer some of my questions. Is now a good time for you?"

"Of course. If you're sure you're up to it. It's been a rather challenging day."

Dorothy smiled ruefully. "That's an understatement of massive proportions." She hesitated. Where to begin? Remy was driving out to join them, as was Titus, when the cops let him go. It was clear they needed to put their heads together and figure out if they knew anything or had made any progress. It didn't help that her time was short. She should just get on with it.

"I guess the big question is, when they broke up, why didn't Magus keep in touch with me?" She tried to keep her tone neutral, but some of the pain she still felt about that slipped in anyway.

Kate's face whitened visibly. "Your mother, she didn't tell you anything?"

"I didn't know Magus existed until he showed up the day my mother died," Dorothy said flatly. "He asked me to take a paternity test, and then he asked me to come live with him. But he made it clear he didn't feel guilt and never explained anything. I sometimes thought that later, when we were more comfortable together, he wanted to talk to me about that time, but he died."

Kate covered Dorothy's hand with hers. "Neither of your parents served you particularly well, did they?"

Dorothy didn't look at her. "Oddly enough, I loved them both, but it's like I can't see them clearly because of all the questions that I never thought would be answered. There's all this stuff in between my memories of them. I feel like they're slipping away from me because of it."

Kate nodded. She looked down, considering, and then said slowly, "Your paternity is the answer to your question. Emma, well, Emma wasn't faithful to Magus."

Dorothy had expected this. The clues were rather obvious since she'd come back, but it still was painful to hear. "It seems so not like her."

"Emma loved Magus, Dorothy. But Magus," she appeared to struggle for the right words before finally saying, "he liked pursuing things more than having them. I think he truly loved Emma, but he didn't . . . nurture the relationship. She . . . did outrageous things trying to get his attention. Then she got pregnant. She could have kept her indiscretions from him, but I think she felt like she had to be honest if they were going to have a chance of making things work. And she thought it would finally get his attention. And she did. He was furious. He didn't believe her when she said you were his. They had a terrible fight and he told her to get out, so she did."

"So he didn't wait to find out? He just threw her out?" She could see Magus doing that. He'd had a lot of pride, but still. Why wait for eighteen years to find out if she was his daughter? Was he never curious? It hurt, she realized, more than she'd expected. Knowledge didn't always heal.

"Magus prized loyalty above all else." Kate's gaze pleaded with her not to pursue it, but it was too late for that now. "And the men she chose were supposedly his friends."

Dorothy rubbed her face and braced herself before saying, "Darius Smith." It wasn't a question, but Kate nodded. "Bozo Luc?" Another nod. "Please tell me she didn't sleep with Bubba Joe?"

Kate's face twitched and her grip on Dorothy's hand tightened painfully. "She intended to, but found she couldn't. Only he wouldn't let her . . . stop. He . . . forced her. He knew she wouldn't charge him with anything because she sought him out. He kept her bra. And he claimed he had pictures."

"So that's what he intended to tell me tonight." Dorothy covered her face with her hands. Had he hoped to replay family history? She couldn't think of a word bad enough to describe him.

"That's why I didn't want you to go when you told me where you were going. I wouldn't have put it past him to try the same trick on you. He really was a cockroach."

"No wonder Mom didn't like men." It explained how the mother she knew could be so different from what everyone else remembered. "Why didn't she tell Magus?"

Kate shook her head. "She felt a lot of guilt for what happened. I think she felt she deserved to be punished.

Thirty years ago, people still had a lot of misconceptions about rape, particularly date rape. She had sought him out intending to seduce him. When it all came apart you weren't real to her yet. You were just a consequence of her actions. A reminder of what she'd done."

"So she never knew which one was my father?"

Kate shook her head. "She knew. I think at first she couldn't forgive Magus and then later, she was afraid he'd take you away from her. He could have given you so much more than she could."

"And then she got sick."

"We weren't in touch then, but I'm sure she felt she couldn't leave you without anyone. Who knows? Maybe at the end she forgave him and wanted you both to have a chance to be together."

"Why . . . didn't you ever contact us? Why didn't she talk about you, either?"

Kate looked sad. "It all seems so silly now. I thought she should contact Magus and she wouldn't. She couldn't. I can see that now, but then . . . it seemed to matter. I wasn't . . . the best person, either. I wasn't making good decisions. She . . . wanted you to have a good life. That was more important to her than anything."

Dorothy felt there was much Kate wasn't telling her, but maybe it was just as well. Old quarrels needed to stay in the past. "It was a good life. It was hard sometimes, but that's a good thing. I'd never have survived Magus's world if I hadn't had that solid start."

Kate's smile was teary, but brilliant, too. It gave Dorothy a glimpse of the charm that her mother probably had.

"I wonder what made Magus come? I wonder what she told him."

Kate shook her head. "That I can't answer, Dorothy, but

maybe it's enough to know he did come. I . . . know he was very proud of you."

Dorothy was surprised. "You remember speaking with him?"

She nodded. "It's been coming back to me, faster now that I'm here." She looked down, the lines of her face both tense and sad. "I needed money. I thought he might help me, for old times' sake."

"Did he?"

"I don't know. He didn't want me there, didn't want me to talk to you. I don't blame him. He wanted to protect you from what I was. And then I had my little, ten-year break-down." She smiled wryly. "I'm grateful for the chance to change my life, but I'll always regret that I wasn't there for you."

"It's nice to have you here now." Dorothy smiled at Kate, but was aware she was still holding part of herself back. She hadn't heard deception in Kate's voice, but she still felt she was holding something back. What Dorothy didn't know was if it mattered. It could just be the awful truth about who and what she'd been. Or maybe she knew something about Magus's death. She sensed so much guilt from her aunt, it was hard to sort it all out. She pushed it aside.

"Yes?" Kate said.

"There's one thing that really bugs me. Were you ever to Oz when Mom was there? Because it's like she was never there. I don't even know what room she slept in or where she spent her time. If anything there was something she bought or liked. I can still feel Magus there, but not her."

Kate looked like she wanted to say something, but instead she slowly shook her head. "No, I was never there then. She had a maid, though. I'll bet Titus would remember her name. If she's still around, still alive, she'd know."

Dorothy smiled. "Yeah. I don't know why I didn't think of that. Magus's housekeeper lives in town in a little house Magus bought for her. I'll bet she'd know."

"It's not Helene Tierry, is it?"

"You knew her?"

Kate appeared to pause before she said, "Emma told me about her. That she was very kind to her. Our mother died when we were young, you know. I think Helene tried to help Emma cope with things. Emma realized it later and was grateful. I'd like to see her, thank her on Emma's behalf."

"She'd like that. I stopped in and saw her the first day I was back. She helped me, too, but she never talked about my mother. And I never asked her. It never occurred to me she was there then. I wonder why she never said anything."

"Probably because she knew too much," Kate said dryly.

"Poor Mom. Poor Helene," Dorothy said softly. She smiled at Kate. "Thank you."

Kate's answering smile was a bit dewy, but her face closed again as she looked past Dorothy.

"Here's your friend and Titus now." Kate looked quizzically at Dorothy. "Do you like him, your Remy?"

Dorothy felt color surge into her cheeks. "Yes, I do." It was both a lie and the truth. Weird. But then, her life hadn't been normal for a long time.

She waved at them, feeling her heart leap in her throat at Remy's approach. It was going to have to stop doing that. It wasn't good for it. Remy smiled at her and it leapt again. The heedless thing. Did it have no sense of survival?

Remy and Titus pulled out chairs and sat down. The waitress rushed over and took their orders and brought their drinks before bustling away and finally leaving them alone.

"What did you find out?" Dorothy asked. "Was it suicide?"

"The cops aren't sure," Remy said. "He had good reason to take his life."

"What do you mean?" Dorothy looked from him to Titus.

"There was a photocopy of a contract on his desk," Titus said.

"Contract?" Dorothy's throat went dry.

"Between him and Verrol Vance for the death of Magus Merlinn," Remy said.

Dorothy sagged back in her chair. "So he's the one." Something in Remy's face told her there was more, though. "What?"

"In the contract, it spelled out the consequences to Bubba Joe if anything happened to Vonda."

Dorothy stared at Remy. "So, someone else killed her? But why?"

Titus shrugged. "Someone else could have found out and killed her to bring him down. Someone who hated him. Or maybe someone was afraid of something else that Vance might have told her, something unrelated. Vance *was* a hired killer."

Dorothy exchanged a troubled look with Remy. It was hard for her to believe it was all some awful, yet fortuitous, coincidence that Bubba Joe had been exposed. "What do you think?" she asked Remy.

"I find it hard to believe Bubba Joe had enough money to keep Vance quietly in jail until he could pardon him."

"Do you think he was framed?" Kate asked.

"No," Remy shook his head. "He was in it up to his eyeballs. But was he in it alone?"

Titus snorted derisively. "So, what, you think it was some big conspiracy?"

Remy shook his head again. "No, but what if it were a small one? Darius Smith, Bozo Luc and Bubba Joe Henry all had good reason to want Magus out of the way."

"They'd never work together," Titus scoffed, but Dorothy could see he was intrigued by the idea.

"What if they didn't know about each other? What if Vance approached them? Or they each approached him on their own? If he had people throwing money at him to kill the same person, I'll bet he'd take it and think it was funny." He leaned forward. "In the agreement he had with Bubba Joe, there was a timer that kicked in if Vonda died. Now we find that agreement on his desk and he's dead. Do I think he killed himself? No."

"You think someone has," Dorothy hesitated, looking for the right word, "executed the consequences in the agreement with Bubba Joe?"

"Yeah, I do," Remy said.

Titus looked troubled.

"But, let's say you're right, then wouldn't that mean that the other men were in danger, too? Because if that's the case, then we can just sit back and let events unfold, can't we?" Dorothy said.

"There's just one problem," Remy said, his gaze sober and worried.

"What?"

"They're all likely to think *you're* the one behind this. That's probably why Bubba Joe wanted to talk to you this evening."

Unfortunately, he made a lot of sense. Who else had as much to gain from the situation as she did? "But I couldn't have killed him. I was with Titus."

"I know you didn't do it. I'm telling you what they might think. They'd know you have the resources to hire someone to take care of things for you. It's what they'd do in your place." Remy's face was grim, his body tense. "And if they feel threatened, they're likely to strike first."

Dorothy looked at Kate, her eyes widening. Then she turned and pulled the letter out of her purse.

"What's that?" Remy asked.

"Bozo dropped it off a few minutes ago. Maybe it's his first strike." Dorothy looked at it. *Call me,* he'd said, confident she would. She bit her lip, then slowly slid her finger under the flap and loosened it. She removed the sheet of paper inside and unfolded it. She had to read it twice before it sunk in what it was. She could feel her eyes widen and then narrow.

"What is it?" Kate asked, sounding worried.

"It's my paternity test." She looked up. "According to this, Magus wasn't my father."

Chapter Thirteen

Darius felt uncharacteristically relaxed. He was even re-
clining. He couldn't remember the last time he'd used his
recliner the way it was intended to be used. Oh, he felt mild
regret that he'd had to kill Cassandra, too, but it was overshadowed by the deep contentment both deaths had given
him.

Now he felt satisfied.

He sighed and stretched. He didn't need Emma's
memory anymore. He had something better, something im-
mediate that he could use to fill that void. Idly he wondered
how long the feeling would last before he would have to kill
again. Because he would kill again. He knew that now. It
was, at the moment, the only thing he knew for sure.

He needed to consider what he would tell the police.
They'd been seen together at lunch. That was certain. He'd
already made sure there was no video of him entering the
hotel room. Only Cassandra would be on the tape. She'd be
seen leaving and then returning. He'd left the pictures of
them together, but had been careful to remove any with him
in them and destroy them. It would have been nice to keep
one, as a memento of his first real kill, but it would also be
incredibly foolish. It wasn't like he was some demented serial killer. He was just a man who liked to kill.

For so many years he'd sought power, but always out of
sight, always indirectly. This was very direct and completely
urgent. What could be more fulfilling than power of life and
death? Yes, life was part of it. Each time, the first thrill

would be in the choosing. Would he let her live? And then there would be the building anticipation for that moment when he decided death must come. Then the sublime rush as life ebbed and flowed between his hands, contentment when it slowly faded away. It was much better than sex. Sex was so untidy and messy. Death was clean and swift and sure.

There was, of course, great risk, but if properly managed, risk could be reduced. And, he had to admit, the risk was part of the thrill.

He and the grim reaper had gone into business together and it wasn't costing him a thing. He smiled to himself. Not even his sleep. He breathed deeply and then reluctantly sat up. As good as this was, it didn't solve the puzzle of Dorothy.

He'd told Suzanne she might be involved as a way to toy with her, but the idea, once planted in his mind, had taken root. What if she was the timer or the recipient of the information? What if she had also hired Vance and he'd told her about the other partners? She'd be sitting pretty if any one of them went down for the murder. Just the sympathy alone would help propel Mistral into the mansion, particularly if they married.

For a moment he toyed with the idea of Dorothy as his next victim, but she was too like Emma. Even in his imagination, he couldn't do it. Unless she became unreasonable. The ideal, the most expedient plan would be for them to become allies.

His gaze narrowed. What did he mean by that? He closed his eyes, trying to picture Dorothy. Where would she be if they were aligned? Suzanne had used her body to build a pact with him. He saw her again in the bed, her arms reaching for him. Then the picture shifted and it was Dorothy in bed, reaching for him.

Well, why not? Her mother had come to him. She wasn't his daughter. It wasn't illegal. It would take some persuading. She'd have to realize it was the expedient thing to do. She seemed to have attached herself to Mistral. And if he were eliminated? He couldn't do it himself, of course. He didn't want to. There'd be precious little pleasure to be had in any encounter with Mistral. The man was a cretin. A fool.

It must be done quickly, before she could become any more attached to him. Her period of mourning must be, of necessity, short. Last time, she'd gone into seclusion. That would work for him, only this time, he'd arrange her seclusion. She might be angry at first, but over time, she'd come around. It would be just recompense for her mother's abandonment of him. Emma owed him. He realized that now. She'd used him to get back at Magus. Her daughter must pay her debt for her. It was only right and proper. In time, she'd understand that and, eventually, come to welcome the opportunity he was providing her. It was better than being dead.

The phone rang, breaking into his thoughts. He frowned, waiting for the caller ID to show up. Bozo? He picked up the receiver.

"Yes?"

"Did you hear about Bubba Joe?" Bozo asked him, his voice veering between excitement and worry.

"What about him?" Darius wasn't really interested in Bubba Joe right now. His mind was filled with thoughts of Dorothy, in his house, in his bed. He'd have the best of both worlds. Death and life.

"He's dead."

That got his attention. "How?"

"It looked like suicide, but the cops aren't sure yet. He was found with documents that tied him to Vance. He hired Vance to kill Magus, or at least that's what the documents indicate."

Darius already knew that part, but his death was . . . troubling. "Why do they suspect foul play? If he was going to be revealed, coupled with his wife's murder today, suicide seems almost logical, even for a selfish bastard like Bubba Joe."

"They aren't saying, but if he was murdered, there's only one person with a real motive."

Darius stiffened. "Dorothy."

The police were waiting for Dorothy when she and Remy arrived back at Oz. They were ahead of Titus and Kate. Both had errands to run. Dorothy was exhausted, frustrated and worried about the paternity test, but she greeted them calmly and ushered them into the front parlor. She offered seats and refreshment. Both were accepted. The niceties were observed and then the gloves came off.

The lead detective, who had identified himself as Burrows, said, "I'm afraid I'm going to need you to account for your movements this evening, from about five o'clock on."

Dorothy nodded. She'd expected this. If the bad guys suspected her, of course the cops would. "Let's see. I think I left here with Titus around five-thirty. We have security tapes that should verify the exact time. I know my appointment with Mr. Henry was for six o'clock. We drove straight to his house and found him . . . deceased. I left to meet my aunt in town and Titus stayed to speak with you."

"Titus is . . . ?"

"My bodyguard."

"You shouldn't have left the scene, ma'am," his partner

said severely.

"It's not like I left the country, Detective Kyle," Dorothy said calmly. "You knew right where to find me. And I didn't see anything. Titus wouldn't let me. He said it wasn't pretty."

"What was your meeting with the deceased concerning?" Burrows asked.

"Mr. Henry said he had something of my mother's that he thought I'd like to have."

"What was it?" Kyle asked.

"I don't know. He never said, and since the meeting never took place . . ." Dorothy shrugged, letting the sentence trail off into silence.

"Did you suspect him of involvement in your father's death?" Burrows asked.

"Yes." Dorothy tilted her head slightly to the side, enjoying the effect of her simple declaration on the two men. Clearly, they'd expected her to dissemble.

"Why did you suspect him?" Kyle asked this question.

"Because I didn't like him. He was rather . . . icky."

Both men nodded like they understood, but their eyes told a different story. She thought Kyle wrote down "icky." She exchanged a quick grin with Remy, assuming serious again before they looked up.

"You offered a lot of money for information about your father's death," Burrows said.

"I offered *Vance* a lot of money," Dorothy corrected him.

Burrows nodded. "This is a list of items we found at the scene. Do any of them look like they could have been your mother's?"

Dorothy took the list and studied it carefully before slowly shaking her head. "To be honest, detective, I wouldn't know what I was looking for anyway. As I said, he never told me what it was."

"And Titus will verify your story, I'm sure." Burrows sounded resigned.

"I'm afraid so."

"And your aunt . . . ?"

". . . should be along soon. And I'm sure Titus will be, too. Though separately. She'll confirm that I did, indeed, meet her for supper."

Burrows looked unsatisfied, but he nodded and stood up. "If we have any further questions, we can contact you?"

"Of course, detective." Dorothy stood, too. She wanted to ask about the contract, but that would reveal too much knowledge. The maid ushered them out, leaving her and Remy alone. She wanted to go to his arms. It was like an ache in her midsection. She didn't. She straightened her back an inch more and asked, "Do you think that contract was real?"

Remy rubbed his face tiredly. "I'm not sure what's real and what isn't anymore."

Dorothy sat down, information swirling in her head like patterns in a lava lamp. Patterns formed, then disintegrated, re-forming into new ones before she had time to process anything.

"What do we know for sure?" she asked. "Isn't that how detectives do this?"

Remy sat down opposite her. "That you're Magus's daughter." He held her gaze with his as he said the words with reassuring conviction.

"How can you be so sure?" she asked, feeling again the sense of the ground under her feet shifting and giving way.

"Because Magus would never have brought you into his life if he hadn't been sure."

"Kate says he loved my mother. Maybe he felt sorry for what he did." He'd never wanted her to call him anything but Magus.

Remy arched his brows. "Was there anything in what you remember to give you that impression?"

Dorothy smiled wryly and shook her head. And Magus could have helped her without bringing her into his life or leaving her his money. Remy was right. Magus would never have done that if he'd had any doubts about her paternity. So what was Bozo hoping to accomplish with this play?

"Does he think I'm so gullible I'll just believe him?"

"Possibly. Bozo's besetting weakness is his belief in his cleverness. He thinks he's mysterious and deep."

"If he releases those results, whether I am his daughter or not, it will nullify a lot of my ability to give you political support. Particularly since I don't have the real results to put on display."

"Which is exactly why he did it." Remy frowned. "You never saw the results, I take it?"

She shrugged. "I didn't want to see them. It was all so weird and uncomfortable anyway. I scarcely knew Magus and he didn't even seem to like me. I think he was disappointed. He wanted someone more like my mother, not some scared, grieving, angry kid without polish or charm. Helene helped me acquire some polish and taught me how to hide my feelings."

"That's Magus's housekeeper?"

Dorothy nodded. "She was great. I was disappointed when she didn't come with me to the Dallas house, but I understood. I think she was just tired. I sometimes wondered if she'd been in love with Magus herself. After he died, it was as if a light went out inside her."

"It's possible. We probably need to talk to her. She may

remember some things that you wouldn't.'"

"I don't know if she'll talk about that time. When I visit her, it's the elephant in the room with us."

"Well," Remy said, "she may know a bit about the paternity issue. I'm sure she'd help you with that."

Dorothy nodded, leaning back in the chair and closing her eyes. Bits and pieces of information drifted past her mind's eye, like paper in a soft breeze. As one piece swirled close, her relaxed mind studied it indifferently, letting it dance closer, as if wooing attention.

"What," she said dreamily, "if the book *was* the clue Vance left Vonda?"

"What do you mean?" he asked, sounding as sleepy as she did.

She opened her eyes. "What if he hid something here?" Almost immediately she frowned and shook her head. "That's nutty, isn't it? How could he get in here?"

Remy sat up, his face thoughtful. "I know everyone thought he was a political operative at the time. In that capacity, he may have come here to deliver information to your father. At the time, Smith, Henry and Luc weren't in open opposition to your father. On the surface, they were working together for the good of the party."

"So he could have been here?"

"Helene might remember if he was ever here. It's a place to start, anyway."

He smiled at her. If she hadn't been so tired, she might have closed the distance. Instead she smiled back, and then sighed. It was so weird, being suspected of all sorts of nefarious dealings by her suspects. And kind of funny, really. Mata Hari, she wasn't.

A niggling voice in her head asked, but you could be, couldn't you?

"What," she said, her voice still lazy, "if we upped the stakes a bit?"

He opened one eye, his expression wary. "We are. With the party."

"I mean more than that. They think I'm doing all this. Why shouldn't I confirm their suspicions? I'm tired of being on the defensive. It's time to attack."

"I'm supposed to be their target, not you," Remy said, sitting up and rubbing his face. "Besides, what would your play be? No, I think we should just continue the way we planned."

"It's too slow. And the killer is moving too fast. We could be in it together," she added, tempting him with a smile and participation. "They think I'm in it for revenge. What if we tried a spot of blackmail? After Bubba Joe's death, they'll believe we have proof of their involvement. It's possible that by the dinner party, we will have that proof."

"Give me time to try one more thing," Remy said.

"What? We've exhausted all our leads, or they're dead."

"Not all of them," Remy said. "Do you remember in the letter Vance wrote, he mentioned his mother?" Dorothy nodded. "Well, I researched him down to his toenails back then and I didn't find any info about his mother. And no mother ever visited him in prison."

"You think he didn't have a mother?"

"I think it was one of the clues for Vonda."

"I don't see how," Dorothy said. "If she doesn't exist."

"Vonda had a mother. And it's possible Vance has a mother, but we just don't know who she is."

"Or where she is." Dorothy considered his ideas. "It could work. But my way is faster." She grinned at him.

"My way is safer," Remy shot back.

Dorothy sobered. "Maybe."

He got up and sat down next to her, putting his arm around her and pulling her comfortingly close. It was lovely to relax into his embrace. It was the first time today she'd felt safe.

"It's going to be all right," he murmured to the top of her head.

At the moment, she almost believed him. She had been known to believe as many as six impossible things a day, after all.

Bozo was surprised that Dorothy hadn't called him. He pushed back from his desk impatiently and started to pace the length of his elegant library. He loved this room. It not only proclaimed his importance and his status, but it connected him with his history. The books that lined the walls were the same books his great-grandfather had paced beside. He was pretty sure none of his ancestors had actually read them. What he knew had been imparted to him by his father. Books were already old news by the time they were published. And life was too short to bother with old news.

He stopped at the tray of drinks at the end of his desk and poured himself a stiff one. Dorothy was proving to be a challenge almost worthy of her father. A pity her mother had lacked their cunning. She might still be alive. He lifted his glass and said, half-mockingly, "To Emma. May she rest in peace."

"I don't think I can," Emma said from the terrace doors.

Bozo whirled around, splashing himself with whiskey in the process. He could feel the blood drain from his face and his heart sped up dangerously. In the muted light from his desk lamp, he wasn't sure if she were corporeal or not. She was too much in the shadows. All he saw for sure were her eyes, violet and dangerous.

"Emma?" His voice was a hoarse croak.

She stepped deeper into the room. As light fell around her, she resolved into a living, breathing human being. Kate. She said her name was Kate . . .

"Clever girl," Bozo said. "I'm guessing that the real Kate lies in your grave?"

"That's right." She appropriated his chair, crossing her legs in one smoothly elegant motion. The clothes were modest, but the essence was all Emma.

"And you, not Dorothy, are behind the various . . . demises?"

"You give me too much credit. I was never that clever, was I?"

It was almost as if she'd heard his thoughts.

"Why did you come back?" He was truly curious. He sat down opposite her and smiled. This evening was turning out better than he'd expected.

"To see my daughter, of course."

"That would be the daughter who thinks you're her aunt and her mother is dead?" Bozo shook his head. "Have you forgotten who you're talking to, Emma? I know you. Why are you really here?"

She laughed lightly. "I see I could never fool you, Bozo." She leaned forward, resting her elbows on his desk and her chin on her hands. "Naturally I'm after money. Magus cut me off without a penny, you know."

"You don't think Dorothy would be so delighted she would share the wealth with you?"

"Not that money. The money that was paid Vance to kill

Magus. It's quite a sizable sum. More than enough to keep me happy. And quiet."

He leaned back. So that was it. "How did you get your hands on it?"

"Vance was . . . very sweet . . . in a lethal sort of way."

Bozo stared at her for a long moment, and then gave a short, sharp laugh. "I always said you were something, chere." He hesitated. "If you have Vance's evidence, then you know I'm probably the only one who didn't pay Vance to whack Magus. Which makes me wonder if you do have it. Unless there is some other reason you're here?"

Her smile was amused and very sexy. Her hair might be gray, but she still had it.

"I'm here because of that little item you gave Dorothy tonight."

"The paternity test?" He arched his brows in surprise. "Why do you care?"

"Magus had some distant relatives, annoying people, who might contest her inheritance if they thought she wasn't a proper DNA carrier—which we both know she is."

He shrugged. "Again, why do you care?"

"Aunt Kate might need a loan someday. She has a . . . tendency . . . to go through money rather quickly."

He laughed again, longer this time. "You always were a fast piece, Emma. And if I won't play? It seems like you have as much to hide now as I do."

She smiled again. "Do you really think Dorothy will believe anything you have to say now? She *knows* she passed that test. It's not like you to stumble like that, Bozo."

He shrugged. "It was a calculated risk." He was quiet for a moment. "All right. You win, chere. I'll back off Dorothy, but I should get something for my trouble." He let his gaze slide down her body, then up. Who had said it was best to make love to older women because they were so grateful? It would certainly be a novelty. Sometimes he wearied of his energetic young women. He arched a brow in inquiry. "How about a ride for old times' sake? You were the best, you know."

She sat back and laughed. It was a lovely sound. "Don't you know that trips down memory lane are always disappointing?"

That only made him want her more. "I have more money than God, Emma. You please me and I'll make it worth your while."

The smile faded to polite. "When I need to go into the oldest profession, I'll let you know."

He was puzzled. "Money is money, Emma."

"No, Bozo, it's not. Not when you owe someone something for every dollar. I want my money without strings." She stood up. "You treated me decently back then. Don't spoil it now. I might forget I'm a lady."

"You never did do what anyone expected you to do," he said, rising to face her. "No hard feelings?"

"If you stay out of my way, we're freaking best friends." Her smile held a warning.

He frowned, asked slowly, "Where . . . were you when Bubba Joe died, Emma?"

Her brows arched. Her smile was sweet. "Why, Bozo, I'm crushed that you even asked."

She came around the desk, the sassy sway of her hips igniting another round of regret. She trailed a finger down his arm, leaned over and kissed him on the cheek, the movement enveloping him in her heady scent. Only then did she turn and leave the way she arrived, through the terrace doors.

He stood there for a long time, touching the place her lips had so briefly been.

"I think, Emma darling, that you didn't protest enough."

He sank back into his chair. He could believe Emma had killed Bubba Joe. He just couldn't figure out why.

Chapter Fourteen

Dorothy was so tired, her eyes were crossing. What she'd wanted to do was fall on her face onto the bed. Only habit and discipline got her through her nighttime ablutions and into a nightgown. She was just untying her bathrobe for that blissful fall to the sheets, when she heard a gentle knock at her door.

She didn't want to answer, but her light was probably visible under the door. "Come in." The end of her sentence almost got swallowed up in a huge yawn. She tried to get her mouth back to normal before she could be seen.

"Can I talk to you for a minute?" Kate asked.

"Sure." Dorothy led her to a small sitting area and sat down across from her, holding back another yawn. This could get embarrassing. "I was starting to worry that your memory went out again." It was very late. It was hard not to wonder what she'd been doing all this time, even stupid with tiredness.

"I have a confession to make," Kate said, looking a little worried. "I know I probably shouldn't have interfered, but he made me so angry and, well, *he* gave me the idea."

Dorothy shook her head slightly. "What idea? He who?"

"Bozo Luc. I remember Emma talking about him," she said.

"What did you do, Kate?" Dorothy straightened in apprehension. That cleared the yawns out.

"I went to see him. I thought I might be able to get him to back off you."

"Why would he care what you think?" Dorothy couldn't figure out where she was going with this. She was still too tired, even with the minor adrenaline surge from panic.

Kate looked down at her hands, twisting in her lap, then up again, her eyes a potent plea for forgiveness. "I pretended I was Emma."

Dorothy's eyes got so wide, they almost sprang their lids. "You what?"

"I pretended I was Emma. I told you, he gave me the idea. I knew enough to bluff and it's been so long, almost thirty years, you know." She frowned slightly. "I didn't count on him hitting on me, though."

Dorothy sagged back against the chair. Then she started to laugh. "You mean he bought it?"

"Hook, line and T-shirt." She leaned forward. "But that wasn't the most interesting part. I . . . kind of let him think that I had the info exposing who was involved with Vance. He said that then I must know he wasn't involved. Obviously I don't know him that well, but it seemed to me he was telling the truth."

"But what did you do?" Dorothy leaned forward. It was a brilliant move, but dangerous. What if he had been involved? "You took a big risk."

"I didn't want him messing with you." She smiled a bit shakily. "I can't believe it worked. I told him that I might want a loan someday." She grinned at Dorothy.

Dorothy laughed, then sobered. "Do you think that's what my mother would have done? Was that how she was?"

Kate stiffened, leaning forward. "No! I just thought that's what he'd believe. If he'd guessed I cared about you, he'd have used it against us."

Her eyes entreated Dorothy to believe and she mostly did. Then Kate started looking guilty again.

"What?" Dorothy asked, wondering what more she could have done.

"I kind of, sort of, implied that I killed Bubba Joe."

"You what? What if he tells the police?"

"He won't tell anyone anything. There's too much he has to hide. And he got beat by a woman, not to mention turned down."

Dorothy laughed. "You're really something, Aunt Kate."

"I don't know about that." Kate stood up. "Well, I should let you sleep. You must be exhausted."

Dorothy stood up, too, fatigue creeping in to turn her clumsy. She wanted to hug Kate, but it was too soon, there were still too many unanswered questions between them.

She smiled instead. "I'm glad you're here."

Kate's smile was a bit teary. "Thanks." She stepped back. "I wouldn't have disturbed you, but I didn't want Bozo Luc disturbing your sleep."

Dorothy smiled. "Well, he won't now." She teetered on the edge of a hug again, but Kate stepped back from her.

"Good night," Kate said. "Sleep well."

Dorothy echoed the wish, watching her leave. It was only when the door closed that she sobered. It was hard to forget the look in Kate's eyes when she talked about his rape of Emma. But the killer had had Bubba Joe's contract with Vance. If Kate had that info, where would it have come from? She had been here when Magus was killed, Dorothy recalled. That's when her memory went bust.

She gave herself a shake. It was crazy. If Kate knew Vance, it would mean she'd conspired to kill Magus. Or at the very least was complicit in it. What reason would she have to do something like that?

Kate gave a relieved sigh when the door was closed between her and Dorothy. That had gone far better than she'd expected. Still, she wasn't out of the woods yet. Dorothy was tired. If she started thinking, she might start to wonder. And if she told Remy, he wouldn't just wonder. He'd start digging. Kate couldn't remember everything he'd find. Her memory was still coming to her in painful chunks.

It had been a calculated risk, telling her about her encounter with Bozo. But she wouldn't put it past Bozo to call and try to introduce some conflict into the situation. Divide and conquer had always been his modus operandi. Interesting that he was still interested in Emma, though it was clear Dorothy, and Magus's political clout, were what interested him the most. He might have retreated temporarily, but he wasn't out yet.

She so wanted to tell Dorothy the truth, but she didn't know the whole truth yet. There were still two men she needed to talk to. Hopefully then she'd achieve complete clarity about ten years ago and her role in it all.

She went down the hall to her room; once inside, she shut the door and reached for the light. She didn't find it. Someone grabbed her by the throat and turned her around, pressing her against the wall with bruising force. Even as panic surged, she recognized his scent.

"Who the hell are you?" Titus hissed in her ear. "And don't lie to me!"

His hold on her throat tightened. She couldn't breathe or speak.

I'm going to faint, she thought. And did.

Bozo wasn't quite sure what made him call Darius. He'd always sensed that Darius cared more about Emma than had been apparent, but he had no proof. Still, if there was an off chance he could shake his tree, it would be entertaining. It wasn't until the phone was ringing that he realized how late it was. Still, the deed was done. If he hung up now, Darius would still see his number on the caller ID.

"What." Darius sounded awake, but not happy.

He didn't state the obvious. He wouldn't. There was something in his voice, though, a hint of menace that made Bozo glad he had real news for Darius. Was this something new, he wondered, or had he just missed it before?

"Did you know Emma had a sister, Darius?" he asked, cutting out the preliminaries he'd had planned initially.

Silence. Bozo counted ten heart beats before Darius said, "No."

Bozo hesitated. If he told him Emma was alive, would that give him an edge or lose him one?

"She's staying with Dorothy. Emma must have talked pretty freely. She knows a lot." That seemed safe, though why he was thinking that baffled him. He'd never been afraid of Darius before.

"Really."

"Her name is Kate." He hesitated again. "She looks a lot like Emma. I thought she was Emma first time I saw her."

"Really," Darius said again.

Why did he feel more threatened with each word? Bozo realized he didn't want to be the one to tell Darius Emma was still alive. Not now, not ever.

"Is there more?"

"No!" He sounded too bright, he realized immediately. Maybe Darius wouldn't notice.

"Yes, there is." The voice was flat and deadly.

Bozo ran a finger around the inside of his collar, wishing he'd never made the call. What had set Darius off?

"She came to see me tonight. K-Kate did." Why had he stumbled over her name? He might as well tell him if he was going to be an idiot. "I was trying something on Dorothy and she warned me to back off. She said—" He stopped. If Darius was involved with Vance, he was imposing a death sentence on Emma.

"What did she say?" The flat voice compelled him to answer.

"She said she had it. That she and Vance had been lovers. That he had trusted her."

Another period of silence. The sense of menace flowed out of the phone. The feeling was so strong, Bozo actually looked around, then went and locked his terrace doors. No more surprises tonight, he decided. And he was done. Darius can figure the rest out himself.

"Did you believe her?"

"I don't know," he admitted. "Since I wasn't involved, it didn't seem to matter." He realized he'd made a mistake there.

"So you think I am involved?"

"No!" Again it was too much. "I just know you like . . . information."

"I don't like it when people hold out on me, however."

"That's all I *know*," Bozo insisted. This time he hit the right note, he thought with relief. "Look, I'm whacked. I'm going to bed. Just thought you'd want to know."

"I appreciate it." Was that irony in his voice, Bozo wondered uneasily. Maybe he wouldn't go to sleep. Maybe he'd take a little trip. Just until the air cleared. The phone went dead without further comment from Darius, but the feeling of danger lingered.

He hung up the phone, thought for a moment, and then headed for the stairs. He really did need a vacation. With his foot on the stairs, he wondered, should he warn Emma? Why should he involve himself further? If she did have the evidence, then she already knew what she was dealing with. She was a big girl. She could take care of herself.

Kate opened her eyes slowly. There was that feeling she'd forgotten something important again. She was lying on her back. In her room at Oz. Yeah, she was at Oz. She'd talked to Dorothy and then come here and—

She turned her head sharply. She wasn't alone. Titus sat on a chair next to her bed, studying her expressionlessly. She looked away. She wasn't ready for this, for him. With consciousness had come another chunk of memory. Would have been nice to have remembered this part a little sooner.

"Who are you?" he asked again, his voice flatly determined.

She struggled upright. He didn't jump to help her. She noticed he had his gun out. It wasn't pointed at her, but it easily could be. She settled her feet on the floor so that she faced him, and looked at him. He'd aged a bit, no surprise there, but the real change in him was in his eyes, in the way he looked at her now. It was very different from the way he used to look at her.

She licked her lips. "You know who I am."

"Emma?" The name came out on a current of pain.

It hurt her to hear it. She couldn't look at him, but she had to. She owed him that. She nodded.

"What have you done?" he asked. "What have you done?"

She looked away. "Nothing I'm proud of."

The tempo of events was quickening. Darius could feel the acceleration as he sat staring at the phone. Bozo hadn't told him everything he knew, not by half. But he would. In the meantime, he needed to consider what he had seen fit to share.

First, of course, was this Kate, sister to Emma. She looked like Emma, he'd said. And she had information on who had hired Vance to kill Magus. If that were true, why hadn't she contacted him? Most likely, she'd been bluffing, but he'd have to talk to her himself to be sure. He hadn't stayed in the game by taking unnecessary risks.

Clearly something about her visit had disturbed Bozo considerably. She'd told him something that had set him back on his heels. So he'd called Darius to strike back. The fact that Bozo wanted Darius to do his dirty work for him was typical. He was more a pot stirrer than a soup maker. He'd stirred this Kate into the mix for a reason.

"I was trying something on," he'd said. Bozo clearly wanted Mistral out of the governor's race. That was a given, but what card would he have had to play that Kate could have nixed so neatly?

Bozo knew about his affair with Emma. Was it possible he'd tried to play a paternity card? But what could Kate have said to him that made him back off? He definitely needed to speak with Bozo. He could feel the answer, just out of his reach. He could also sense that Bozo was going to make a run for it. He had a canny sense of when the boom was about to drop on him.

He picked up the phone, spoke a few words into it and hung up.

His thoughts cleared of Bozo for the moment, they turned back to the issue of Kate and any information she might, or might not, have. If she did, then of course she had to deliver it to him. Why, he wondered, hadn't she given it to Dorothy already? If she were after money, Dorothy was the golden goose.

The landscape was becoming rather crowded, he decided. He knew who he'd killed, but there was still the faceless person behind the deaths of Vance, his lawyer, and Bubba Joe. Someone had an agenda, but what? Was this Kate behind it? The trouble with this hypothesis, it made no sense. He could create a scenario where Dorothy was involved. Most of the deaths made sense with her as a central player. Even Bubba Joe's death fit the pattern.

He knew why Suzanne was dead and he knew his part in it. He had a pretty good idea of how much Bozo was involved and would soon know more.

He had his plan in place to bring Dorothy to a more expedient frame of mind and the elimination of the problem of Mistral. He'd be dead and the Wizard's daughter would be his to control, in life and death.

He needed to figure out who Vance had made his timer, who had the information on who was involved. Surely that was the key to the mystery player?

He pulled out his copy of the letter that Vance had written for his wife and studied it again. It held precious few clues, but one thing struck him this reading.

Vance didn't have a mother, did he? He needed to study the information in his file again. Perhaps somewhere in his visitor list at prison, or the people he wrote to, was the clue to who he called mom.

He looked at his watch. He had a few minutes before Bozo's arrival to review the file. He pulled it out of the drawer, but before he opened it, he found himself thinking instead about Kate. Sister to Emma.

Emma stared at Titus with his blank face and his disillusioned eyes. It hurt to look into them. Her whole body hurt with the storm of emotion from returned memories. She needed a break to process it all. The things she remembered, the things she'd done, both then and now. But he wasn't leaving. That was clear.

"That's your story? That your memory shorted out for ten years?" His voice was flat, devoid of emotion.

She nodded.

"Were you involved in Magus's murder?" he asked.

"How could I be? I had no money to hire anyone. I came to beg for money from Magus," she said.

"Not to see Dorothy?"

She shifted impatiently. "I don't know. I know I was angry at Magus, but not enough to do anything." She heard the uncertainty in her voice and saw the disbelief in his eyes. "I was a mess, but I've changed. Remembering what I did . . . it horrifies me."

"What we did. That horrifies you, too?" For the first time, anger flickered in his face, in his eyes.

She chose her words with care. "It horrifies me that I used you, my friend, in that way. I cheapened us both by betraying my wedding vows. I'm so sorry!"

"Does Dorothy know you're alive? That you gave her away because you couldn't be bothered with her?"

Emma flinched as if he'd slapped her. "No. But I'm going to tell her the truth!"

"When?"

"When the time is right. She's dealing with so much right now. It would be selfish of me to add to it. Wouldn't it?"

"You're scared she'll throw you out," he said, but for the first time, she saw a hint of softening in his face. He looked down, as if he couldn't bear looking at her.

"I'm so scared of so much. This is so dangerous, what she's doing. She's going to get hurt again. Can't we do something? Can't we help her?" She leaned toward him, her eyes pleading with him. "I don't expect you to forgive me, Titus, but can't we help our Dorothy?"

His head lifted, his eyes widening. "What are you saying, Emma?"

She dropped to her knees in front of him and hesitantly rested her hands on his. "Haven't you ever wondered if she was our daughter?"

His body shuddered. His face convulsed for a moment, before he got himself back in control. He pulled his hands away from hers and she thought she'd lost. He grabbed her shoulders, his expression hungry as he searched her face. Then he pulled her into his arms, burying his face in her hair, as sobs shook his body.

"I thought you were dead."

She smoothed his hair like he was her child. "I know. I'm sorry."

"I've tried to watch out for our girl."

"You were wonderful. I don't know how to thank you."

He looked up at her, his face ravaged. "I never stopped loving you."

He bent toward her, his intentions clear. His mouth covered hers; for a moment she hesitated, before relaxing into his embrace. Henry might not approve, but he would understand. As his hands pulled at her clothing, she stared at the ceiling, trying not to think about it. It wouldn't be the first time she'd used her body to get something. At least this time she was doing it for her daughter.

Chapter Fifteen

Dorothy ran into Remy in the hallway as she was heading down for breakfast. He smiled like he was glad to see her, despite their lack of an audience. And he offered his arm. She took it, liking the feeling of warmth and safety it gave her as they went down the stairs, their bodies occasionally brushing together.

"We need to walk and talk," she said, slanting him a quick glance. She didn't feel comfortable just looking at him. She was afraid her eyes would give away how happy she was to be with him. Had she picked him for her dance simply to revenge her father or because she wanted to spend time with him? It was getting harder and harder for her to remember the whys and wherefores. Or sort through her feelings with any precision.

His bright, curious gaze studied her. She found a neutral place inside herself and met it calmly enough, though it was getting harder and harder to find that place now that she knew him better. His looks had attracted her in the past, when she was a more shallow pool of a person. She still liked the way he looked, but the kind of person he was interested her more, now that she was older. True safety could only be found with someone of steady character, her mother had taught her. Now she understood what her mother had meant.

He nodded, clearly wanting to find out more, but restraining himself.

"How's your speech coming? Friday is coming so

quickly," she said, as they approached the dining room door. The party elders had sprung the speech on them, probably hoping to knock them out early.

"I'll admit I'm a little nervous." He looked rueful and a bit surprised.

"It's a different venue from your radio show," she pointed out. "It's one thing to have ratings on the line, but another to be on that line yourself. And politics are tricky. What you hope to accomplish and what you can . . ."

She trailed off, with a rueful shrug.

Remy nodded. "I'm trying to stay grounded in reality, but I've been thinking about what needs to be done for so long, I don't know. It's harder than I expected it to be."

"Magus always used to say that in politics, you should aim high and keep your expectations low."

Remy laughed, pushing open the dining room door for her. "That sounds like Magus."

"It does indeed," Kate said, from her spot near the middle of the table. Across from her Titus sat with a plate of eggs and bacon.

It felt like they were interrupting something, though there was no overt sign of it on their faces. There was a tension in the room, despite the fact that Titus was his usual stone-face and Kate looked pleasantly aloof. It was hard for Dorothy to process what Kate had done last night, looking at her this morning. Had she really gone to Bozo and pretended to be Emma? And basically admitted to murder?

"Good morning." Dorothy walked around them both, to the buffet where covered plates of food awaited her attention.

Kate looked up, with a quick, though strained smile, before readdressing herself to her coffee and toast. Titus just nodded, but she had the distinct feeling he was pleased about something. It was a rare enough state of being for him, it was hard to miss. He looked at Remy and appeared to withdraw a bit. His antagonism was getting out of hand. Maybe she needed to send him away for a few days. Give him time to distance himself. And get him out of the way for the announcement of their engagement. He was going to hate that. With all of Magus's holdings, it would be easy to get him out of the way without him suspecting anything.

"Do you think the security staff is up to speed now?" she asked, sweetly laying the trap for him.

He straightened. "Of course."

"Then you'd be able to take a little trip for me? I need some papers hand-delivered and you're the only one I can trust to do it for me." She kept her smile sweet and slightly anxious. What was interesting, he looked at Kate first, as if he couldn't help it. He realized what he'd done and adjusted his attention quickly, but it was too late for her not to notice. Kate, Dorothy noticed, kept her attention on the task of spreading jelly on her toast, as if the fate of the world depended on how well she did it.

"Certainly. When did you need me to leave?" He'd managed to keep his face impassive, but he sounded unhappy. If they hadn't had an audience, he would have argued with her, she knew.

"Right away, actually. I'll get the envelope for you right after breakfast. You can take the company jet. I'll call and set it up. Thank you." She smiled at him more gently than normal because of guilt at her relief. When had he stopped being her support and become an oppressive presence?

"Right." He stood up. "I'd better get ready then."

She smiled at him again. "You can finish your breakfast."

"I'm not hungry." He didn't stalk out—he had too much

self-control—but it still felt like he did.

She exchanged a quick look with Remy, who was trying not to grin. He picked up the orange juice.

"Can I pour you some?"

She nodded, but looked at Kate. "You all right this morning?"

Kate jumped slightly, as if her thoughts were far away. But she smiled with her usual calm.

"I'm fine. Was just thinking about all the things I need to do today. If you'll excuse me, I think I'll head into town. Unless you need me for something?" Her eyes twinkled with her awareness of Dorothy's subterfuge. Was there also relief in them?

"Titus hasn't been giving you a hard time, too, has he?" Dorothy asked, with a slight frown. He had no right to be rude to her guests. If he pushed her too hard, she'd have to do something about him for sure.

Kate quickly shook her head. "No, of course not."

"He broods," Remy said. "He smolders."

Kate laughed. "Well, he does do that. But we are old friends."

Did she hesitate before that last word? Had they been more than friends? It was an intriguing thought. Once again she was reminded of how much she didn't know about the past.

Kate stood up. "Is there anything I can do for you before I go?"

Dorothy thanked her, but being alone with Remy was what she'd been hoping for. Though she was anxious to tell Remy about last night, she still waited until they were walking away from the house. Titus had assured her he'd thoroughly swept the house for bugs, but it was hard to relax there after everything that had happened. And there were many more staff wandering around. She did not want to be overheard. She wrote a note to her personal assistant, asking him to keep Titus busy for a few days, then sealed it in an envelope with some important-looking sheets of paper and handed it to Titus.

He took it, but now that they were alone, he made his pitch, as she'd expected. "I'm your bodyguard. I should be here."

"No one has done anything to threaten me. And I promise I'll be careful." He didn't move. She stifled a sigh of impatience. "It's only for a couple of days. And I need you to do this for me. Please?"

He did sigh. "Fine. Just . . . be careful." He started toward the door, then stopped and looked back. "Do you trust Kate?"

Dorothy arched her brows. "I'm not sure."

He managed a slight smile for her. "Good. Go slow there."

"Do you know something, Titus?"

He hesitated. "I'm just chronically suspicious."

She nodded, but didn't believe him. Darn his hide for always treating her like a kid. She was definitely going to have to break him of that habit. But not right now. She met Remy in the hall, feeling the claustrophobia fall away from her as they stepped outside together. Once well clear of the house, she told him what Kate had told her last night.

"Clever," was his main comment. He stopped and looked at her. "Do you trust her?"

"That's what Titus just asked me." Dorothy frowned. "I told him I'm not sure. There's more going on inside her than she's sharing. I'm just not sure it matters in our current situation, though." She thought about telling him her feeling about Titus, but Remy had already moved on.

"And Titus? Why did you get him out of the way?"

Dorothy smiled. "I just needed a break from his brooding. And his hovering. In this life my father left me, sometimes it's hard to breathe for all the people around. They aren't bad people. Magus did a pretty good job of picking his employees, but they all still want or need something from me. I'm an introvert and it makes me tired." She shook her head ruefully. It was her fault she was surrounded, but it didn't make it any easier to endure. "Titus didn't used to press so close. I guess he's feeling threatened by everything. I don't want to lose his friendship, but he needs to let me go. He needs to realize I'm a grown-up now."

"He doesn't like me," Remy said, though clearly not overly concerned by it.

"I am sorry. I haven't told him we're pretending. Maybe I should?"

Remy considered this before slowly shaking his head. "I think it will just make it harder for him to see us acting intimate. He'll think I'm taking advantage of the situation. He doesn't bother me, other than a reflexive impulse to pull his chain." He looped an arm over her shoulder and they started walking again. He grinned at her. "I'm still working on controlling my baser self."

She laughed, liking the warm, sweet feeling that swept through her at his undemanding touch. He offered support without asking for anything in return, and all without words. Though she hoped he wouldn't try too hard to control that baser self. She rather liked that part of him, too.

She walked silently for a while, but finally sighed. They needed to get down to business.

"Kate thinks she neutralized the Bozo threat. And she believed him when he said he wasn't involved with Vance."

"Do you believe her?" Remy asked, lifting a branch out of her way.

"I believe she believes it—which isn't really an answer, is it? I'd be more comfortable with real proof. I wish we could figure out what Vance was trying to tell Vonda."

"I've actually been looking into that. There's no record of anyone claiming to be his mother, either visiting him or writing to him."

"I wonder why he asked her to contact his mother then?"

"There was one visitor to him right after he was first arrested that was . . . interesting," Remy said.

Dorothy stopped, turning to face him. "Who?"

"Your housekeeper, Helene Tierry."

Dorothy felt her jaw drop, but she couldn't help it. "Helene. Our housekeeper visited him in jail?"

"That's right. I think our first visit today ought to be to her, don't you?"

"Oh, yeah!"

Dorothy was so stunned by this, she didn't notice at first that they were still stopped, still facing each other and that Remy was looking at her intently.

"What?" she said, feeling warmth sweep through her again at the look in his eyes.

His grin was crooked and edged with wryness. "I'm trying to think of all the reasons why I shouldn't kiss you again. It's that baser self rearing its ugly head again."

"Oh." She looked away, then back at him. "I'm afraid I can't help you. I have my own baser self to deal with."

"Really?" Remy's smile turned satisfied as he stepped slightly closer to her. He touched her lightly at first, almost hesitantly, his fingers dancing up her arms, before connecting warmly with her shoulders. He pulled her close, but not touching. Perhaps he knew, as she did, that would take them too far. She met his gaze bravely as she waited for him to kiss her.

"How come I didn't see what you were ten years ago?"

She shrugged, fighting back the impulse to trace the line of his mouth with her tingling fingertips. "I didn't know who I was then. How could you?"

"You're too forgiving. I was an arrogant jerk."

"If you don't quit talking and kiss me, I'll be forced to agree."

He chuckled, sliding his hands up to cradle either side of her face. He bent her head to one side, his to the other, and slowly brought their mouths together.

Sweet heat spread out from the point of contact, turning her limbs fluid and making her head spin. She could feel her feet lift from the ground. It felt like she was floating, possibly soaring, but when he gently pulled back, her feet settled once more on terra firma. Her lips missed him, even as her brain understood the need for oxygen and self-control.

"That was very nice," she said softly. "How come I didn't know that about you ten years ago?"

He grinned. "I didn't know it, either. You have a strange effect on me."

"I'd love to pursue that," she said with a sigh, "but we should get going. I'm dying to talk to Helene."

Remy lightly traced the line of her cheek before stepping back from her. Her skin felt cold and a bit forlorn with the contact. More than anything, she wanted to turn back into his arms and stay there, but duty called. And she always did her duty.

Bozo Luc had eluded him and Darius wasn't happy about that. He'd anticipated that Bozo would run, but underestimated how quickly. His flight had been . . . precipitous. It was almost as if he'd sensed the threat Darius posed to him. Bozo hadn't been afraid of him in the past. Odd that he should start now. And annoying. He didn't know what information he was missing, but for now he needed time to consider what he did know.

The arrival of Emma's sister, Kate, interested him very much. He needed to meet her. She obviously had more information to share than Bozo had let on. As if his wish gave birth to reality, his intercom buzzed. A Ms. Kate Needham to see him.

How interesting.

His blood quickened in anticipation. It was an odd feeling and a new one for him. It had only started happening since he killed Suzanne. It was as if every woman he met became a potential victim. He'd even found himself studying the help, wondering how they'd look as they died. Now two of his maids had given notice. He should probably modify his behavior, but it was so new and fascinating to him, he didn't want to stop. Maybe if it cost him his housekeeper.

Darius found Kate waiting in his living room. He stopped in the doorway, studying her. The room didn't suit her. It was all black and white and very cool. Despite her gray hair, she was warm and vibrant. Very much alive. Just feeling the pulse of her blood through her veins ignited that part of him that wanted to stamp out life.

She had her back to him, but she had a straight, graceful figure. Was she the older or younger sister? To his knowledge, Emma had never mentioned a sister. It had been twenty-eight years since he'd parted with Emma, but with Dorothy's arrival on the scene, it seemed like yesterday. Had he hoped this Kate would be Emma? It was possible, he supposed.

As if she sensed his scrutiny, she turned slowly to face him.

"Hello, Darius." Her violet eyes were calm and curious.

Emma's eyes. So that's what Bozo hadn't told him. There was no Kate, there was only Emma. Inside, he absorbed the shock of it. It rocked him to his core. Outside, he refused to even blink as she studied him, perhaps surprised by what time had wrought on his aspect.

With her hand, she lightly brushed the cold leather of his dark couch. "Interesting place you have here. A bit chilly. Not how I remember you."

Her eyes reminded him of what they'd shared—how very far from chilly he'd been that night she came to him. For the first time since he strangled Suzanne, he found himself looking at a woman and not thinking about killing her. His gaze probed her face, her eyes, searching for the woman he remembered, trying to find the passion that had obsessed him for twenty-eight years.

And failing.

He strolled toward her, but stopped when each step closer revealed her age more clearly. He didn't want to remember her this way. She should have stayed dead.

"You're not exactly how I remember, either . . . Emma."

She shrugged. "Time. It's a bitch, isn't it?"

Had she always been this hard? He turned toward the bar. "Can I offer you something? We should toast our reunion, don't you think?" He looked at her, one brow arched.

The way she walked toward him was as graceful as he remembered. He could almost forget she was old. Almost.

"I'll have tonic water, if you have it."

She kept her distance and the bar between them. The morning light wasn't kind. Time hadn't been, either. Who she was now threatened to blur who she'd been inside his head. If he didn't have Dorothy to hold on to, he might have lost her completely.

Now he found himself wondering what death would do to her—if he could bring himself to wrap his hands around her sagging throat. He supposed she was fairly well-preserved . . . for her age, but it wasn't enough for him. He expected better from the women in his life. She was hardly worth killing now.

He handed her a glass, then lightly clicked his against it before lifting it to his lips. He watched her lift hers, watched her lips close around the rim, then the movement of her throat as she swallowed.

And felt nothing. Not even the urge to kill her.

Though he'd force himself to do it if he felt any threat from her. But neither of them would get any pleasure from it. It was a pity, but also a relief. It was, he realized, Dorothy he wanted now. From Emma all he needed was the truth.

Thankfully, she didn't come on to him, just studied him as dispassionately as he was studying her. That amused him. If he didn't know for sure she was a woman, he'd say she had balls.

He gestured for her to take a seat, and then sat down opposite her. "I guess the rumors of your death were a bit exaggerated."

"When Magus threw me out, I went to my sister's. That's where Dorothy was born. When she offered to keep her, raise her as her own, I was grateful to agree. I didn't need a kid slowing me down. We switched identities because we didn't have the money to do it legally. I became Kate. She became Emma."

"And presented me with a puzzle."

She arched a brow in a mute question. It was a sad shadow of how she'd looked that night, an echo of the way she'd offered herself to him.

"Of how you could have changed so drastically from sex kitten to domesticated mommy."

She laughed and that was the same. For a moment he felt a stirring in his loins, but he made the mistake of looking at her and the impulse died. He hadn't expected this, that his passion for her would be so tied to how she looked. Was it a reflection on him or her? Probably both, he decided wryly.

"And were you Kate or Emma when you had your liaison with Verrol Vance?"

Both brows arched this time. "So Bozo called you. He's such a little weasel." She leaned back, stretching slightly in a sad mimicry of the past. "Actually, I never knew Vance at all. I just told him that to pull his chain."

He smiled slightly. "I'm sure he deserved it." He hesitated, before saying as if it didn't matter, "So you don't have anything from Vance?"

Her lashes lifted, as did her shoulders. Again, the movements were both familiar and alien.

"Is it likely I would have, even if we had done the deed?"

He lifted his glass, took a drink, and said, "No, it's not likely."

She leaned forward, her head slightly tilted to one side. "So you're curious, too?"

"Am I? About what?" This was pure Emma. It almost made him forget her age.

"About who hired Vance, of course. You always did like knowing things."

So she didn't suspect him. That was a relief, he realized. Beyond his distaste about touching her, he really didn't want to kill her. For old times' sake? Or just because he once loved her. If it was love. It was all mixed up inside his head now, the past and the present. And in the middle of it all, there was Dorothy, who looked so much like the Emma of the past.

He didn't like feeling confused. He didn't just like clarity. He needed it. He needed to know what was expedient and what wasn't.

Her eyes watched him as she added, "That's not to say I wouldn't have, if I had met him. I was doing anything and everything to get Magus's attention. I was such a fool."

"Is that what I was to you?" It was a kick in the gut. He was over her, but she wasn't supposed to be over him. He could see her considering what answer to give.

"The truth, Emma. I can take it." But could he? He didn't know.

"Okay, that's all you were. That's all any of you were. I'm sorry, but that's the way it was."

Others. There'd been others? How many, he wondered. And why didn't he know? "What others?"

Her brows arched. "Surely you knew? Bozo, Bubba Joe, the milkman. I think I even did it with the pool boy. And Magus never noticed."

He saw the hurt in the back of her eyes and it pleased him. Good, he thought, you should suffer for your sins. How dare she use him like that? Suddenly the idea of squeezing her throat until her eyes went blank wasn't as unappealing.

"Why did you tell him when you got pregnant? That was stupid."

"I may have been a slut, but I was an honest one." She shrugged and tossed back the rest of her drink and got to her feet.

He stood up, too. "Why didn't you come back when Magus died?"

He found he really was curious. He'd never known her, not really. He'd created her, made her what he wanted her to be. Was he in danger of doing the same thing with Dorothy? For just an instant, he wondered if he should proceed, but then he realized he had the power to shape her. She was young and, unlike Emma, she wouldn't be leaving him. She would become what he wanted or die. It was as simple as that.

She looked down for the first time since she'd walked in. "I met someone. We got married. It was better if my past stayed in the past."

"And why are you here now?"

She hesitated and finally shrugged. "I'm getting old. I found I was curious about this person Magus and I created out of our angry passion."

"It's not because you need money, then?"

The edges of her mouth turned up. "Well, there is that, too." Her mouth curved into a real smile. "You always did see through me, didn't you?"

He felt a rush of relief. She hadn't known. He'd been a fool only to himself. For that, he'd let her live and walk out the door. Now he was curious.

"What exactly did Bozo try to do?"

"He didn't tell you." She shook her head. "He had a faked paternity test. As if Magus would ever have taken her in if she hadn't been his. So I made him back off."

"Why did you care?"

Emma's brows rose as if to say, isn't that obvious. "If she's not Magus's DNA, her inheritance could be challenged."

"And you can't have that, can you?" He lifted his brows

in mock amusement, while considering whether he believed her. If she'd fooled him before, she could fool him now, he supposed, though what power she'd have to do him any damage was debatable.

"Does Dorothy know you're alive?"

Her lashes dropped like walls. "Now that wouldn't be too smart of me, would it?"

And she'd just handed him a weapon. No, she was no threat to him anymore.

"No, I don't suppose it would. And you were always smart, weren't you, Emma?" Did she notice how ironic he sounded? If she did, there was no sign of it. She merely looked satisfied.

"So, you won't mess with her, either, right?"

"I'm afraid I'm going to have to, Emma. She and Mistral are getting in my way."

Her lips thinned. "What if I can talk her into getting out of your way?"

He pretended to consider this. She didn't, she couldn't know, that Dorothy had a larger purpose to serve. They'd come full circle, or were almost there. Dorothy would complete the link between the past and the present, making all whole again. She would finish what her mother had started. It had to be.

"Do you really think you have that much influence?" A so-called aunt who'd been missing in Dorothy's life until now? She was delusional.

"I'm the only family she has left. She wants to trust me. She needs to trust me. I think I can deliver."

"If you can, then we have no problem at all." He smiled at her.

After a moment, she smiled back. She looked at her watch.

"I've got an appointment. This was fun, though. We should do it again in thirty years."

The flash of anger he felt surprised him, but he managed to keep it below the surface. He nodded and smiled, wondering if she knew how close he came to grabbing her by the throat and shaking her like the bitch she was.

She walked out without looking back, the same way she left him before. He probably couldn't afford to let her live. She might be able to figure out that he'd been the one to take Dorothy. He almost went after her, but there'd been so many deaths. And who might she have told she was coming here? No, he needed to be cautious with his newfound power, if he hoped to keep wielding it. When it was expedient, he'd take care of Emma.

He bent and picked up her discarded glass, realizing this was as close as they'd come to touching. Not a handshake or even a polite brushing of cheeks. Had she been afraid to touch him? Or afraid of what he'd learn if he touched her? No matter. He'd find out later.

Helene Tierry lived in a small cottage that Dorothy had deeded to her ten years ago, when Helene told her she was retiring. Dorothy remembered she'd thought, at the time, that Helene must be very shaken about Magus's death to retire so young. How hard must it have been to be on both sides of the equation?

Dorothy had always liked the cottage, and had often wished she could live there instead of Oz. It looked like something out of a fairy tale, with its white picket fence and wild tangle of flowers and vines. The gate squeaked a welcome as Remy pushed it open. He waited for Dorothy to precede him up the path before following her in. There was an air of abandonment about the house, so she wasn't surprised when their ringing of the bell netted no response.

"Let's try the neighbors," he said.

"She left, oh, about a year ago, I guess," said the lady across the street. "She missed her people. She was from the North, you know. She was that sad after the Wizard died. She had no heart for anything anymore."

If her son had killed him, it was understandable.

"Do you have an address for her?" Dorothy asked.

"Let me see if I can find it." After a time, the lady returned with a slip of paper, the spidery writing barely decipherable.

"Thank you." Dorothy smiled at the woman, who seemed pleased.

"We miss your dad around here, girl," she said. "You really think he'd be a good governor?" she asked, nodding toward Remy. Dorothy nodded, bemused by the question. "Then he's got my vote."

"Thank you," Remy said, sounding equally bemused and amused.

"You just do what you say you'll do. That'll be thank-you enough for me!" She shut the door then, leaving them to look at each other in abashed astonishment.

"You forget that all this affects real people, with real lives," Dorothy said, as they walked back to the car. She looked at the paper. "Darn it. I had to pick today to send the jet off with Titus. If I call it back today, he'll want to be on it. And you've got that event tomorrow. We could have Titus check it out."

Remy shook his head. "I was looking forward to a break from his scowling. Let me put a detective I know on locating her. Then we'll go talk to her ourselves after the rally."

"I could go, you know. She'd probably talk to me."

Remy shook his head. "I need you at the rally. You're the Wizard's daughter, remember? And there's our announcement. I just feel like we shouldn't wait. Besides, we're the only ones who have this." He waved the piece of paper with the address on it.

"For once we're ahead of the enemy," Dorothy said, with satisfaction. As Remy helped her into the car, she caught an odd look in his eyes. What was he thinking?

Remy was thinking, as he helped her into the car, about this morning and the kiss they'd shared. He was in deep and getting deeper all the time. He'd thought he could do this, but it was proving to be much harder than he'd ever imagined. How was he supposed to resist the irresistible? It was bad enough now, but what about when they were married and it was legal, if not ethical, to finish what they'd started with that kiss?

Their dance was proving to be dangerous on so many levels. He could feel the building menace from their unknown enemy. He was angry, whoever he was. And like a snake, he was poised to strike. Indeed, he already had. The shots fired at him had been shots fired across the bow, no question about that. Titus had indicated they'd found nothing but some shell casings. He wished he didn't feel like Titus would just as soon see him dead, as help him find out anything. It was a relief to have him out of the state for a while.

Just before he slid into the car, he found himself looking around. Was someone waiting out there to try again? If there was, he needed to be more alert. He didn't want anything happening to Dorothy. Not to mention, the last thing she needed was to see someone else shot in front of her.

"Where now?" Dorothy asked him, cheerfully.

"Lunch?"

"Just what I was thinking," she said with satisfaction.

As Remy put the car in gear, he looked toward the helpful neighbor's house. She was watching them out her window. What was that all about, he wondered? Or did he already know?

Emma didn't breathe easily until she was well clear of Darius's house. Had he always been like that and she just hadn't noticed? Had she been too stupid and too hell-bent on revenge to realize what kind of man she was playing with? She'd planned to make the same play to him that she'd made to Bozo, but the air of menace that had engulfed her when he entered the room put an end to it. She'd never have gotten out of there alive, of that she was sure. She was also convinced he was somehow involved in the plot against Magus. He'd been too relieved when she told him she'd never known Vance.

Would he leave Dorothy alone? She considered the question and had to conclude he wouldn't. There was some weird vibration she'd picked up every time Dorothy was mentioned. She hadn't a chance in hell of persuading her to back off and they'd both known it. So he was humoring her, but why would he? To keep her quiet? About what? She had no proof of anything. She just knew in the deepest part of her gut that Darius was dangerous. He wasn't going to step aside. He liked power, even if it was behind the scenes. He was determined to get it this time.

It was an interesting puzzle. None of the people who seemed to be involved had benefited much from Magus's death at the time. Had they been clever or just unlucky? There was much a candidate could do, but in the end, it still rested in the hands of the voters.

There had to be a way to stop him. Well, she knew a

way. Titus would probably be happy to help solve the problem, but she wasn't sure her soul could stand another payment. She'd never betrayed Henry until last night. It was as if, with her memory, her old values were returning, too. It sickened her, but at the same time, she didn't know any other way to do this. And in an odd way, she'd felt like she owed it to him for using him last time. At least now they were even. He'd used her very thoroughly last night.

As she drove away from Darius's huge and soulless house, she felt as if he watched her leave. There was something unhealthy about the man, something that reached out with unwholesome tentacles. All those years ago, she realized, she'd set in train events that were reaching into the present and spinning things out of control.

Somehow, something she did back then had made Darius interested in Dorothy now. Surely it wasn't sexual? He was so much older than her. Maybe he, like Titus, thought she was his daughter? That could be it.

And if his interest in Dorothy was sexual? She shuddered. What had she done? She longed for Henry with a deep-down ache. He'd kept her course true and steady for so many years. She should never have come here without him, but she'd been so afraid of him finding out the whole, awful truth about who she'd really been and what she'd really done.

He'd been so sweet about everything, more than she ever expected, but would he be able to forgive her again? Could he forgive her what she'd done here and now for Dorothy, let alone the things she'd done in the past? How could he, when she couldn't forgive herself.

And then there was Titus. She'd been able to control him last night, but if her husband showed up, she didn't know what he'd do. He was convinced that she loved him then and she still did. Amazing that he hadn't noticed her forced and faked response.

She was so grateful to Dorothy for sending him away. He'd have been back in her room tonight for sure, convinced of his welcome. What is with men, anyway? Not even Magus had been an unforgettable lover, for Pete's sake. She'd had her own reasons she had to go, all ready to present, but would he have believed her? It was as if he was demanding proof of her intentions through her willingness to go to bed with him. She'd used him in the past, and now they were even.

The only time she'd felt worse about something was the night Bubba Joe raped her. It was funny and sad that she didn't remember much from her encounters with Bozo and Darius. She did remember wondering if this was how prostitutes got through it, and she clearly remembered hating herself and Magus when it was over.

Titus, well, it was different with him. They'd known each other before, had been friends in high school. Clearly she was his first, and apparently his last, sexual partner, since his technique hadn't changed at all. She'd thought it sweet at the time. It wasn't anymore. Had he been nurturing the idea that Dorothy was his daughter all these years? She needed to find a way to wean him from Dorothy, though it looked like Dorothy had an inkling of how dependent he was on her and was trying to work it out on her own. She just didn't have all the information she needed to do it. And if Emma told her? She'd get tossed out on her ear.

At a stoplight, she leaned her head against the cool of the steering wheel. What a mess you wrought with your tantrums and your needs, Emma. Perhaps it was time to simply cut through all the cords.

She straightened up and put the car in gear. She would have liked to go home to Henry, but that didn't seem possible now. That old adage about not being able to go home was true on every level in her life right now. It would all take some planning. Then she'd write to Henry. The whole truth and nothing but the truth. She owed him that.

Chapter Sixteen

Friday dawned hazy and hot. There was the rally in the afternoon, then the dinner party in the evening, to be gotten through. At breakfast, Dorothy noticed Remy limited himself to coffee, though he did push some eggs around the plate for about ten minutes.

Dorothy couldn't think of anything even slightly comforting to say and her stomach felt like it had turned into a trampoline. Anything sent down would surely come right back up. She remembered these events with Magus. It had been like stepping into the midst of a storm. The whole purpose of them was to get people pumped up to vote for your candidate and Magus had been a master at turning up the emotional intensity. At the end, she always felt battered and storm-tossed, while he was super-charged.

Today, they'd find out if Remy had the same gift. He certainly knew how to turn it on when he was broadcasting, but as they'd both realized, this was different. This was, somehow, more real. For one thing, it would be face-to-face. And it all certainly mattered more to real people. They wanted, no, they needed, to believe in someone. And their need was both catalyst and curse, at least where Dorothy was concerned. All that energy passed through her like a hurricane heading for shore, leaving her beached and drained.

They should have planned the dinner party for another day, but the rally had been sprung on them by some of the party elders. Dorothy still wasn't sure of their motives.

Maybe they hoped to weed Remy out quickly and leave the field clear for their choice. Or maybe they hoped to capitalize on the momentum being built and get on the bandwagon early. Right now, everyone was the enemy as they took on those deeply entrenched in power.

Motives and desires were mostly hidden and constantly shifting in the world of politics. She realized that more now than she had back then. Of course, back then she'd been so green, the Jolly Green Giant would have looked pale next to her.

She was better prepared this time. In her head, she knew this was true, but her heart wasn't buying it. Back then, she'd basically been chum to the sharks. Today, well, she was one of the sharks, or at least swimming with them. It didn't make her any happier than being the chum, however.

She'd dressed for the weather and to impress and reassure, in a linen suit dress of a soft, off-white color. Her sandals were comfortable wisps of leather with just enough heel on them to be a tad sexy. She knew she looked cool and crisp and calm. She'd become a good actress. Today should earn her a freaking Oscar.

"Nervous?" Remy asked her, finally breaking the silence.

He looked dreamy in his lightweight suit and crisp, white shirt. The navy bumped up the brown in his eyes and made them, somehow, more sincere. The amazing part, *he* wasn't acting. This was who he was and that was why the party elders were so afraid of him. They didn't know how to deal with an honest man.

"A little," she admitted. "But I'll be all right. I bluff *good*." Her smile scraped across teeth turned dry with apprehension.

"I've seen you in action," Remy agreed, with a wry grin. He held out his arm with the elbow crooked. "Shall we go?"

Dorothy took a deep breath and nodded. "Let's do this."

Kate met them at the door, her smile wide, but just a bit sad. "I wish I were coming, but I think I'll be more use here, helping to get things ready." She gave Dorothy a hug, then Remy, too. He looked surprised and a bit touched. "Do I wish you good luck or broken legs?"

Remy grinned. "I have no idea, but I'll accept both, just to be on the safe side."

"You got it, then." Kate stepped back. "Good-bye."

Dorothy climbed in their limo and then Remy slid in beside her. As they pulled away, Kate waved again.

Dorothy frowned, looking back. "That good-bye felt awfully final, didn't it?"

Remy looked surprised. "Why would it be?"

"I don't know." Dorothy settled back, trying to quell the butterflies in her stomach. "No reason, I guess." Stress made it easy to feel paranoid and to read things that weren't there, she supposed.

Remy took her hand and gave it a squeeze. "We're going to be awesome." His grin invited her to share the small joke with him.

She laughed. "Awesome. *Right.* You're not going to use that word in your speech, are you?"

He grinned, but refused to answer. This was either going to be awesome, or a disaster of epic proportions, but she had a feeling it wouldn't be boring.

Darius arrived at the rally venue early. He had much to do before the arrival of the various candidates who would be speaking today. He'd already arranged for his protégé to be early on the schedule. He didn't want what happened later to keep his boy from speaking. The other thing he needed to arrange was for Dorothy to be seated at the very edge of the stand. That took some persuading. The party elders wanted her front and center, to help mitigate any sense that she was only there for Remy Mistral.

"If you marginalize her," Darius told them, "you'll be able to control her better. If you give her any more prominence, it will only encourage them both."

After some thought, they agreed with him. Satisfied with his arrangements, he stood on the platform and looked around, wondering which vantage point his hired shooter would choose. Security would be loose at the event. No one expected that much interest at this point in the campaign. Mistral was doing well in the polls, but he wasn't pulling ahead, though they all expected him to once he and Dorothy went public. At this point, any misstep could still change the equation drastically. They were all hoping he'd mess up, of course.

Later, when the field narrowed, then security would become more of a concern. It was one reason he'd decided to act now, rather than waiting for things to settle down after the various deaths. And he didn't trust Emma. She'd played the slut in his living room, but he wasn't a complete fool. She hadn't stopped by for old times' sake. She'd come with an agenda. He didn't know what it was or if she'd given up on it. Or had she merely postponed it?

Her comments were obviously designed to provoke him. Was she hoping emotion would cloud his thinking? She didn't know him then, if she ever had. He could believe she'd slept around back then, but not for the reasons she'd presented. When she came to him that night, he'd sensed a woman hungry for warmth and caring, not someone out for revenge. He might have been a fool to think it meant more than it did, but reading emotions, then using them against opponents, was his stock-in-trade.

For instance, he had no illusions about how Dorothy felt about him. He was also aware she felt quite strongly for Mistral. It would be both her strength and her weakness today. He also knew that emotions could change, either by choice or by force.

Today's play was risky, probably his riskiest play to date, but he'd calculated those risks and found them within the acceptable limits for a successful outcome. He'd laid his plans carefully. The odds were in his favor that by noon today, Mistral would be dead and Dorothy under his control.

He frowned into the distance. Would Emma be present today? It was hard to decide. He couldn't tell what she cared about, her daughter or her daughter's money. It was likely that Emma would suspect he was behind today's events, but he had a contingency plan for that, too. If she couldn't be persuaded to exit the field of battle, well, women disappeared all the time.

The band was playing, the crowd was clapping. Dorothy felt a bit of a sore thumb on the end of the row of chairs. She was so close to the edge, a misstep would tumble her down the stairs. Remy's lips had tightened when he saw where she was sitting, but after exchanging a quick look with her, he'd said nothing. In some ways, Dorothy didn't mind. It wasn't as tiring to be at the edge of the crowd as it was to be in the center of it. Prior to the start of the rally, they'd made a circuit through the crowds. It both touched, and intimidated, that so many people remembered Magus. The burden of carrying his banner for him weighed heavily on her shoulders when she was faced with the people he'd hoped to represent.

She'd been angry at him, she realized, since she found

out he threw her mother out when she was pregnant. Face-
to-face with all these people, she was reminded once again
that no one was all good or all bad. If I were to be judged
on a single act, she thought wryly, how would I fare? She'd
cold-bloodedly planned to make Remy a clay pigeon, and
for what? So that she could be free of this legacy Magus left
her? Oh, she'd talked a good talk about justice, but the
truth was she just wanted to go hide somewhere. As she
scanned the faces, turned up toward the stand, she wondered if she had the right. There were public and private re-
sponsibilities and sometimes they conflicted. And when that
happened, what was the right choice?

She stole a look at Remy. If he asked her to stay on with
him, would that make a difference? It wasn't quite as hard
to do all this when she had his support and understanding.
Magus had been fairly ruthless where she was concerned. It
was sink or swim, baby. Not feeling good, well, get over it.
Was that how he'd treated her mother? If he had, well, she
could understand—even if she didn't approve—what she'd
done back then, actions that had led to the issues currently
complicating Dorothy's life.

When she'd sought answers to past puzzles, she'd hoped
it would bring peace and understanding. She did understand more than she had, but peace still eluded her. It was
hard not to grieve for her parents' choices and what those
choices had cost them and her. But was she looking in the
wrong direction? Maybe it was time she quit worrying about
what might have been, and what had been, and figure out
what she wanted the future to be. If she never found out
who else might have hired Vance, would the world stop
turning? Would she curl up and die? Not bloody likely.
Magus might roll over in his grave, but after ten years, perhaps the change in position would do him good, too. Per-

haps it was time to cut the puppet strings and be a real girl.

Remy's hand closed over hers, out of sight of the watching crowd. "Almost show time."

Now would probably be a good time to start paying attention. Her stomach tightened. This was new territory for her. Magus had never let her get in front of a microphone. Distantly she could hear the flowery introduction, but the flow didn't separate itself into distinct words inside her head until she heard, "Let's welcome Miss Dorothy Merlinn."

He didn't mention Magus, Dorothy noted, finding she could be amused and terrified. Remy gave her hand one, last squeeze as she rose to her feet. She managed to make it to the podium without tripping or doing anything embarrassing.

"Good morning!" she said into the microphone. Her magnified voice surged out over the crowd.

"Good morning!" they shouted back. Flags waved as they started chanting, "Dor-o-thy! Dor-o-thy!"

It was rather heady stuff. Is this what Magus had craved? Or was this just a side benefit of doing the right thing?

"Thank you! Thank you!" The crowd gradually quieted down. "You've all been so kind to Magus's prodigal daughter. And I can't thank you enough for your kind words about my father as we visited earlier."

"Wi-zard!" they chanted now.

She could almost feel waves of unhappiness from the men behind her.

"He was amazing, wasn't he?" she called. "The last ten years have been spent trying to live without him." The crowd below her turned intent and serious. "As you know, I didn't have that many years with him. For a long time, I only knew what I didn't have, which was time with my father. Today, you have all helped me remember the time I did have with him and what an amazing person he was. Thank you so very much."

The clapping was different this time and their faces showed they were remembering, too.

"I'm not as politically savvy as Magus was," Dorothy continued, "but as I've gone through his papers and writings, one thing became clear to me: Magus had a lot of respect and admiration for the man I came here with today, Remy Mistral." She turned slightly to smile at him as the crowd broke into cheers and claps again. When they quieted, she went on, "Magus always enjoyed the people with lots of sass and class."

The crowd laughed and clapped.

"Remy Mistral isn't your typical candidate. He hasn't held any office, except the one at the radio station, and, trust me, I've seen it. It's pretty small and cramped." That got her some laughs. She could feel her insides starting to relax as she neared the end of her speech. "But he is a man who cares passionately about this state and the people who live here. He believes that government can do better and I believe him." More cheers. A few chants of "Rem-y!" Dorothy waited them out. "So, it is my privilege and my distinct pleasure to introduce the man I plan to vote for governor of this state, and the man I plan to marry. Remy Mistral!"

That brought the house down. Remy jumped to his feet and grabbed the hands she held out to him. He kissed her on both cheeks and turned to the crowd as if to ask them, isn't she wonderful?

"You can do better than that, Mistral!" someone in the crowd shouted.

He grinned and looked at them, as if to ask their permission. The crowd noisily gave it.

He drew her close, and then swept her down, Hollywood-style.

"You're no Al Gore," Dorothy taunted, so only he could hear. Then she couldn't say anything because he was kissing her and she was kissing him back. They probably could have continued indefinitely, but the crowd went wild, reminding them they weren't alone. Remy popped her upright again. She made a show of smoothing her clothes and hair, gave the crowd a bemused smile and went to her seat.

"Thank you, Dorothy," Remy said, looking at her with a very male, very satisfied smile.

The crowd hooted and hollered and laughed. He owned them now. The men lined up on chairs beside her knew it, too. She didn't grin, because they hadn't earned it yet, but they were going to, she vowed. They were going to.

As she listened to Remy give his speech, out of the corner of her eye, she noticed a long, dark limo pulled up under some trees not far from the stand. The driver clambered out of the front and walked toward her. He stopped, tipped his hat slightly and handed her a folded note.

Curious, Dorothy unfolded it.

My dear Dorothy,

Do not look up, to the right, or to the left. In fact, don't react at all. There is a sniper, with a gun aimed at Remy Mistral. If you react in any way or attempt to warn him, he will fire. If you want to save his life, do exactly as I say. At precisely eleven o'clock, stand up and walk toward the limousine with my driver. He will assist you inside. Once we're safely clear of the area, the sniper will be called off, but only if you continue to follow my instructions. If you don't get up, as instructed, the sniper will fire at will and Mistral's death will be on your head. If you understand these instructions, look at your wristwatch now.

Dorothy looked at her watch, not because she truly understood, but because she needed to see the time. Three minutes to eleven. Three minutes to try and figure out what to do.

As if her tormentor knew what she'd think, she read on. *There is nothing you can do but follow my instructions precisely. If you do as I say, everything will be fine.*

That couldn't be true. What did he hope to accomplish by this daylight abduction? Did he think no one would notice her leave? Or who she'd left with?

Without moving her head, Dorothy stole a look at Remy through her lowered lashes. He was lit up from within as he and the crowd played off each other. He was vibrantly alive. It was obscene that he might shortly be dead. Her gaze scanned the outside edges of the crowd as well as she could manage without moving. Inside her head, precious seconds ticked relentlessly away.

There. Was that a glint of something in the trees? Why did no one notice? Why? Because Remy was being so fascinating, that's why.

Okay. The threat appeared to be real. Was there some way to get to him? She assessed the distance and realized there was no way she could cross it before a bullet. Was this why she'd been seated here? A cry might save him. *Might.* She couldn't stand to see someone else die. Remy wasn't just "someone else." *She loved him.* He mattered. A lot. Too much. Bad time to realize it.

She felt something uncurl inside herself at the thought. She'd never been in love. Still without moving, she looked at him standing there in the sunlight. So sturdy, so strong, not perfect, but a good man. Someone who wanted to make a difference and who was willing to step into the fire and at least try, even if he failed. Even if he died. A sob tried to crawl up and out. Tears filled her eyes and dropped onto the note, smearing the words that said everything would be all right.

She glanced down at her watch again. She had one minute to decide. She could risk everything, by stepping down and walking away from the man she loved. It wasn't right. It couldn't be right.

He'd do it for me, she thought. He didn't love me, but he'd do it for me.

While there was life, there was hope.

She allowed herself one last look at Remy. He chose that moment to look her way. His smile was electric. She smiled back, desperately drinking in as much of him as she could. When he looked away, she looked down again. Ten seconds.

Nine . . . eight . . . seven . . . six . . . five . . .

A naked man suddenly burst from the trees and dashed in front of the bandstand. It was a clever diversion. All eyes followed him. No one was looking at her. She let the note flutter to the ground on the side of her chair away from the car and stood up. The chauffeur helped her down the stairs and walked beside her to the car. He opened the door, she climbed in and he closed it behind her, shutting her in with Darius Smith.

"Hello, Dorothy." His expression was so devoid of emotion, it was like looking into a dead man's eyes. Or her future.

"Make the call," she said as the car moved forward with a bumpy jerk. She was afraid to take her eyes off him, but also desperate for a last look at Remy. Her need to see Remy won. She looked back.

"Dorothy."

Darius recalled her attention, his voice without inflection, but with something in it that sent a chill down her back. She turned back to face him, her chin up.

"Make the call."

"I'm afraid it isn't expedient for me to do that."

As they turned the corner, she heard one shot, then another. And screams. So many screams. She tried to look back, but all she could see were people running, and then they'd turned a corner, leaving it all behind. She couldn't look at him. She couldn't bear to look at him. "I'll kill you if it's the last thing I ever do in this life."

He touched her shoulder lightly and she flinched away, pressing herself against the door, feeling for the handle.

"It won't open."

This time his hand gripped the back of her neck. She didn't cry out, but it took all her self-control not to. He forced her to turn around, then grabbed her chin and forced her to look at him. Despite the violence of his touch, he looked detached, almost indifferent.

"Whether you get a chance to fulfill your threat will depend on what you do right now, Dorothy." The hand on her chin slid down and circled her throat, tightening just enough to be unpleasant. "I can choose to kill you right now. Or I can let you live. You cared for Mistral. I understand that. I'll give you some time to get over it, but my patience isn't endless." His grip on her throat softened and his hand trailed down, stopping just above her breasts, while he let her feel his power over her. "You can submit, be broken and submit, or die."

He slid his hand over her right breast. He didn't squeeze

259

or even move. He just left it there to show her he could. She couldn't breathe, didn't dare move.

"It would be a pity if you choose death, and I'll regret the necessity, but I have rather burned my bridges, haven't I?"

As if her throat fascinated him, his hand slid up again, tightening, then releasing, again and again. Each time, the pressure was harder and longer. It made her stomach roil to touch him, but she had to touch him to survive. At her touch, his hand tensed, and then slowly eased away from her throat.

"As I said, my patience isn't endless."

"How long do I have to decide?" Her voice was raspy and thin as it pushed past the raw and sore places in her throat.

He thought for a moment. "I'm not an unreasonable man. I'll give you until tomorrow. Twenty-four hours." He looked at his watch. "I'll be generous. You have until noon tomorrow."

"And if I decide to . . . deal with the situation? How long do I have?"

He considered for the space of five heartbeats. "I should think a month is more than enough time to get over someone like Mistral."

He didn't touch her, but his gaze considered her. It was both cold and dispassionate and far worse than lascivious would have been.

"We'll put the word out that we eloped, overcome by unexpected feelings. And when I'm sure I can trust you, you'll have your freedom again."

She stared at him. Beyond the fear, she was truly amazed. He saw nothing weird or wrong about his behavior. This was what he wanted, so this is how it would be.

"Why me?" She clearly hadn't sparked some unholy passion in him. His interest seemed almost clinical, like a doctor with an interesting specimen he wanted to check out. It was more terrifying than passion would have been, because he truly didn't seem to mind if he killed her. He really was giving her this awful choice between death or hell.

He looked mildly surprised at the question, as if she should already know the answer.

"Because of your mother, of course."

"My mother? What's she got to do with this?"

For the first time he hesitated.

"What? Did she turn you down?"

"No." It was the first change in inflection he'd allowed himself. "She wanted to be intimate with me. I even wondered if you were my daughter."

His near squeamishness about sex was interesting, under the circumstances.

"And? I'm still not seeing where I come into this, since I'm clearly not your daughter."

He'd been looking off into the distance, but now his gaze homed in on her with disturbing, frigid intensity. "You look like her, you know."

Dorothy swallowed dryly and painfully. She wanted water as badly as she'd needed air, but there was no way she was going to ask him for it. "But I'm not her. I'm a different person."

His lips curved up in what should have been a slight smile, but somehow didn't quite manage it.

"I know that. That's actually a good thing. Your mother's a disappointment. And much too old to interest me now."

Okay, this was beyond weird. "My mother's dead."

His brows arched, and the edges of his lips edged into

cruel. "She still hasn't told you then? Interesting. Clearly she underestimated me."

Dorothy couldn't imagine what he was talking about, or why she should feel a growing dread about finding out.

"Actually, she's not dead at all. She's pretending to be your Aunt Kate."

"Right." Was that all? "Okay, I know she's been telling some of you guys that she's Emma—"

"Do you really think I wouldn't know Emma? After I knew every inch of her so . . . intimately." He licked his lips slowly. "You're the one who knows nothing. But you'll learn."

It was only pride that helped her absorb the blow without flinching, but she had the feeling he sensed it. It was worse than being stripped naked. Maybe. She was hoping she never found that one out.

Hope. While there's life, there's hope, she'd thought only moments ago. She was already learning how wrong she'd been. He'd baited the trap perfectly and she'd walked into it. She was going to learn from that, too.

He moved closer to her, his gaze suddenly changing. It was still cold, but there was a blankness to it, as if he were seeing her differently . . . as an object, maybe? Or not quite real. It felt like he was homing in on her pulse, drawing some kind of twisted pleasure from watching it speed up as he invaded what little personal space she had left.

The feeling in the car changed sharply. He wants to kill me, she realized. And she wasn't sure she wanted to stop him. Remy was dead. She couldn't stop the surge of despair that swept through her. She loved him and she never had the chance to tell him.

"I'd be better off dead." She didn't realize she'd said it aloud until she heard the words go into the cold, dead space that still separated her from him. His hands went almost lovingly around her throat, as his weight pressed her back against the seat.

His lips against her ear, his tongue probed the inside once, then again, before he whispered, "Would you, Dorothy? Would you really be better off dead?"

He eased back just enough so he could look into her eyes and then he slowly, ever so slowly, almost lovingly, began to cut off her air.

Chapter Seventeen

Remy didn't see the streaker burst from the bushes until he passed in front of him, so he didn't know why the crowd was laughing at first. Like everyone else, he watched the guy and his gear jog his way into the arms of a couple of cops, and then turned to look at Dorothy, wanting to share the joke with her. He only had time to register her absence before he felt the whistle of a bullet passing his head. He wouldn't have recognized it, or reacted as quickly, if he hadn't been shot at so recently.

"Shots fired!" he hollered, before dropping to his belly on the platform. All around him, people scattered or dove for the ground. The cops let go of the streaker and returned fire. Screams mingled with shots. Then an eerie silence settled over the scene.

Remy cautiously lifted his head and looked around. If it hadn't been so serious, it would have been funny the way heads gradually lifted from the ground and wide eyes scanned the area. All around him, as more people got up, the roar of outrage began to build. People started running around and he could hear sirens in the distance. Thankfully everyone seemed to be all right. Adrenaline subsiding, he got to his feet and peered at the podium. A line of bullet holes made a neat line from top to bottom.

His knees almost gave way again. Just because he'd asked for it, didn't mean he had to enjoy being a target. He steadied himself on the podium and then remembered Dorothy. Had she gone to the john and missed the action?

He eased through the frantic politicos on the stand to where Dorothy had been sitting and then looked around. He couldn't see her anywhere. He touched the shoulder of the woman who'd been sitting next to him.

"Have you seen Dorothy?"

She looked shocked and bewildered. "I thought she was right there. I know I saw her when the streaker came out."

She was just gone. He couldn't process it. She was just there. It had been only seconds between the streaker and the shooting. The streaker. Could he have been a distraction? But for what? The obvious answer was the shooting, but if the streaker hadn't come out and distracted him, he'd be dead. He'd turned to look at Dorothy and the shooter missed him.

He looked at her chair again, as if it might have the answer, and noticed her purse was still under her chair. He picked it up. A woman didn't walk off and leave her purse, at least no woman he'd ever met. He saw a piece of paper on the ground that had been hidden by the purse. With a growing feeling of foreboding, he picked it up and unfolded it. He had to read it twice before he could process it. Making sense of it wasn't possible. It was streaked with tears. He felt a chill as big as a freaking glacier slide down his back.

He grabbed a cop walking by. "Who's in charge?"

The cop opened his mouth to maybe argue, but something on Remy's face must have stopped him.

"Come with me," he said.

As he followed the cop, his thoughts turned into rats in a maze, chasing here and there, without getting anywhere. Who would force her to leave like that and why? What did they hope to accomplish? He tried to think clearly, but panic was rising on a flood of some other realization. Something he wasn't ready to deal with yet.

Dorothy. He was winded with it. His heart felt . . . gone. His heart? What did his heart have to do with this? It wasn't involved, was it? Okay, he liked her, but that was all.

He looked at the note again. It threatened him. She left to save him? And whoever it was had shot at him anyway. She was in the clutches of someone very ruthless and determined. But for what purpose? He should know, but he couldn't think. All he could see was Dorothy, alone and afraid with some faceless killer. If anything happened to her . . . what? What would he do?

His thoughts circled around something. He could see it, lying there in his mind, waiting for him to turn it over. But if he did, his life would change forever. He didn't know how or why he knew it, but it was true. He had to do it, though. He owed her that. She'd left for him, so what, he turned coward now? He couldn't do that. She deserved better than that, better than him.

He . . . loved her? Was that it? Was it possible? Would he recognize love if he felt it? He rubbed his chest. It felt as if his heart had been ripped out by the roots. There was only a hollow where . . . love had been. And peace, peace like he hadn't known in years.

He rubbed his face. He hadn't been playacting. How could he have pretended when she was so real, so dear? She'd tried to save his life. She probably thought he was dead. She would have heard the shots. He felt gut-kicked. He almost staggered with it. He had to find her. He had to tell her the truth. She needed to know he was alive and that he loved her. He owed her that. Surely someone had seen something?

To hell with his feud with Titus. He needed him and any resources he could pull together. At least he'd be motivated to find her. He pulled out his phone and started dialing his number. He didn't know how much time they had, but his gut told him it wasn't much.

Dorothy clawed at the hands cutting off her air. The world started to go dark when suddenly the pressure eased, though his hands still circled her throat. Darius leaned close to her again and whispered in her ear, "You thought you loved Mistral enough to die with him and now you know that's not true. That's your first step toward the kind of clarity you're going to need to survive."

The darkness receded, leaving her in the painful, and perilous, present. Each breath was agonizing, so desperately necessary and yet awful to take with him close enough to feel each one. She felt his pleasure at her struggle against unconsciousness. At the moment, it was the only thing she feared more than Darius. At least with tongue and wit, she might be able to keep him at bay.

"Clarity?" The word came out as a sad croak of a sound.

"The clarity of expedience. It's the only kind that really matters."

There was a flaw in there; she struggled toward it and produced, "I'm not expedient."

He actually looked mildly pleased. He drew back, giving her much needed space.

"True, you are expendable. But even the most expedient of lives needs some . . . pleasure." Again his gaze raked her body with that odd, clinical thoroughness. He seemed unable to produce even the warmth of passion.

"You won't get away with this. Someone may have seen me leave. And your driver walked me to this car." As soon as she mentioned him, she knew it was a mistake, though she had a feeling he'd already considered the problem.

"True, but he won't be able to tell anyone." From a bag, he produced two sets of handcuffs.

Dorothy pressed harder against the door, instinctively putting her hands behind her back and pulling her feet in. Darius arched his brows, as if surprised.

"Do you really think you can fight me on this?" He waited a moment. "Do we need another breathing lesson? Once you're unconscious, you know I can do whatever I want to you."

Her body contracted with horror at the thought.

"What if I promise I won't touch you, except as needed for assistance, until we get where we're going?"

"Would that be like the promise you wouldn't harm Remy if I got in this car?"

His expression hardened slightly. "You don't really have a choice in this. I was trying to give you the illusion of one. Fine, we'll dispense with that. Your hands. Now." He waited for a count of ten, and then added, "You won't like it if I have to punish you, Dorothy. You won't like what I'll do."

As slowly as she could, she extended her hands, feeling the cold steel encircle them and then snap ominously shut. Her defeat felt final when her feet were secured. He pulled out some duct tape.

"Useful stuff, this," he said, studying her face, then measuring a length and cutting it off with a knife produced from the bag.

"Who will hear me in here?" Dorothy said. Words would be her only weapon against him now. She needed to be able to talk.

"It won't be for long, though maybe you won't want me to take it off when the time comes. It is rather painful."

There was nowhere for her to retreat to, no way to fight

him off. She twisted her head away from him, but when he put his arm across her already sore throat, she had to stop. She couldn't survive too many more assaults on her throat. She was a bit hazy on specifics, but she did know that if throat parts got crushed, she was finished. Darius pressed the tape in place, studied the effect of it, and then smoothed her hair back from her eyes.

"Emma's hair was longer. We'll have to let it grow out. I liked it long." He looked past her, as the car turned the corner, steadying her, and then letting her go. The road was a rough one and she had to brace herself as best she could while he turned away from her. When he turned back, he was holding a light blanket. "We just need to cover up, you know. We don't want Fred to get suspicious. I told him this was a romantic place for us. If he sees you like that, well . . ."

He tucked the blanket around her briskly and without intimacy, which was a relief, but only a small one. Her growing certainty of what was about to happen made it impossible for relief to linger.

Fred braked and then turned off the motor. Darius moved to the other seat and slid the panel back that separated the two compartments. Fred started to turn, perhaps in expectation of receiving instructions from his employer, but quick as a flash, Darius had his hands around Fred's throat, squeezing and squeezing.

Dorothy couldn't see that much, thankfully, just the thrashing of his feet as he tried to free himself from that iron grip. And she could hear the gurgling sounds he made as his life slowly slipped away. When all was silent, Darius sat back and looked at her.

"Problem solved." He stripped off the gloves she hadn't noticed him putting on and tossed them aside. He reached over and ripped the tape off her mouth, bringing tears of pain to her eyes.

"Men aren't as . . . satisfying to kill as women. I didn't know that, of course." He looked at her for a moment. "Not until Suzanne."

With the air conditioning off, the car was starting to heat up from the hot afternoon sun beating down on it. Under the blanket the effect was faster. Dorothy could feel sweat seeping out of all her pores. Of course, the sheer terror wasn't helping, either.

"You killed Suzanne Henry? Why?"

His brows went up. "She made me want her. I don't like that. I choose how I feel and when I feel."

"But I don't get to choose. It's not expedient."

For a moment, she wondered if she'd reached him. Perhaps there were some small threads of sanity left inside his head?

"Now you're being petty. And disingenuous. You have a simple and clear choice. Submit or die."

He turned and opened his door, then the driver's door, and pulled Fred out of the driver's seat. He fell facedown on the ground. Darius reached down and heaved him once, then again, until his body tumbled into a small depression. Darius brushed his clothes down and came around to her side.

Any relief she might have felt at being alone in the back of the car while he drove was quickly dispersed.

"Get out."

"Why?" Dorothy didn't move.

Darius pulled the blanket off, grabbed her arm and pulled. If she hadn't brought her feet out, she'd have fallen on her face. He pulled her around to the rear of the car and opened the trunk.

"Get in."

"There?" When he didn't answer, she added, "People suffocate in trunks of cars."

"You won't in this one."

"Why?" She held up her cuffed hands. "Hello?"

"You're intelligent and desperate. I don't think it would be smart of me to leave you alone back there. And," he moved forward suddenly, sweeping her off her feet and dumping her in the trunk, "it's your second lesson in clarity."

Before she could attempt a response or another question, he slammed the lid down, shutting her in the heated darkness. She heard his footsteps heading back to the driver's side and after a short interval the car's engine fired. When the car jerked forward, she realized that she was about to experience a new level of suffering.

The interior was capacious, but it was also indented and that indention wasn't as long as she was. It was designed for suitcases, not people. After some wiggling around, not easy with the cuffs hindering movement, she managed to get her body mostly curled into the space. But each bump on the road vibrated the length of her body. It was a relief when the main road was reached again.

Of course, that brought a new set of problems. Out on the highway, there was no protection from the sun. The temperature rose rapidly and soon she was completely soaked in sweat. She could feel it running in rivulets down her face, back, arms and legs. She had to close her eyes to keep the stinging stuff out.

And then Darius upped the stakes another notch, when she heard his voice come out of a speaker near her head.

"It's not very comfortable, I know, but very necessary. Have you heard of Stockholm syndrome? This is just a small taste of the mental and physical conditioning you're going to experience. Now you can stop it at any moment, by simply submitting to the inevitable. There's no dishonor in choosing to submit, you know. It's the expedient thing to do. Anyone would understand. And wouldn't you rather submit of your own free will instead of being broken and unable to stop yourself? After a month, you'll rob a bank for me if I ask you. Or perform in pornographic movies, or even have sex with anyone I order you to. You'll even kill for me. Your power of self-determination will be completely gone if I have to break you."

There was an awful inevitability to the flat, emotionless voice. It was the only cool thing in the trunk. The words were horrifying, but the tone was so reasonable, the words tangled in her head as the heat sapped her strength.

"But if you choose to accept your fate, you can self-determine to be my partner instead of my slave." He was quiet for a moment, before he said, "You can speak. I'll hear you."

"If I die back here from heat exhaustion, you'll never know what I would have chosen," Dorothy managed to gasp out.

He actually chuckled. "We're almost home. In fact, here's the turn now."

Home. If only it were true. She felt the motion of the turn, though her ability to protect herself from it had degraded seriously. Fortunately the pain of compression was relatively brief.

"We're driving down the lane now. I wish you could see it. I think you'd like it. It's a much more impressive residence than Oz."

Dorothy wasn't sure she could remain conscious. The air she inhaled was thick with heat and thin on oxygen and it felt as if she lay in a pool of water, as even more of the life-giving stuff flowed off her. Her clothes were completely stuck to her body and her hair felt matted to her head.

When the car lurched to a stop, she fought to hold on to the thin thread of awareness she had left. The lid finally opened. Even the hot afternoon air felt cool as it rushed into the trunk. Darius grabbed her legs and undid the handcuffs around her ankles, then helped her out of the trunk.

When her weight went on her legs, she almost fell. He looped an arm around her waist, but she pushed him away. Amazingly, he let her. She leaned against the car for a moment, fighting to bring her body back under her control.

"It's cooler inside. And there's water," he said, his voice that same, tempting calm one that had assailed her inside the trunk.

She managed to stay upright and follow him inside the wide, double doors.

"There's no staff, of course. That will come later, when we've worked things out."

Just inside the entry was a wide mirror, nearly two stories high. In it, she saw a scarecrow of a woman, with matted, stringy, wet hair and filthy clothes clinging intimately and revealingly to her body. The transition from hot to cold was a painful one. The cold air slammed into her head and pain throbbed behind both eyes. It was hard to believe that this was the same person who'd looked in her mirror at Oz this morning and wondered if Remy would be pleased with how she looked.

Stockholm syndrome. She knew what that was. Hostages begin to identify with their captors, who alternately abuse them and then are kind to them. This was a kind period, but the abuse was waiting for her on the other side of it. She could have no illusions. He'd told her exactly what he was going to do.

He handed her a bottle of water with the cap loosened. It was a good thing. She probably couldn't have opened it herself. She took the bottle, almost too weak to lift it to her mouth. She wanted to gulp it down, but she forced herself to sip it slowly. He needed to know she was still in control of herself.

He couldn't be reading a lot of emotion from her right now. She was too exhausted to feel anything. In an odd, ironic way, that gave her an edge, too. She braced herself for the next round as she slowly downed the life-restoring water. When the bottle was empty, she lowered it and looked at him. There was probably no chance he'd give her another.

"I need to use the bathroom."

"Of course." He indicated the stairs with a short wave of his hand.

Dorothy looked up. They seemed to go on forever. Didn't he have anything closer? One step at a time, just take it one step at a time. She managed the first one. The second wasn't as bad. When she got to the stairs, it got hard again. She had to lift one foot up, and then lift the other, before attempting the next.

"Do you want me to carry you up?" Darius asked behind her.

She ignored him. There was only the next step. And the next. After a small eternity, the steps ended. She was on a landing facing a row of closed doors. Now Darius stepped ahead of her and pushed one open, indicating she should enter.

Still waiting for the next blow to fall, she stepped into a room that was almost lovely. It was too sterile, too store display, to be warm or welcoming, but it was better than the trunk of a car.

"The bathroom is through there."

It was a relief to be free of him, even briefly, to not feel him watching her. There was no lock on the door, but she was in too much distress to worry about it. She relieved herself, then washed her hands and face in the sink. It wasn't easy with the cuffs still on, but she managed it. She set the towel down, and combed through her hair with her hands. It helped a little. She couldn't bring herself to move.

"You know I can come in and bring you out," he said through the door.

In the mirror, she saw herself straighten her shoulders, one vertebra at a time. You wanted to know who you were, Dorothy, she thought, now you get to find out. She turned and opened the door. He was waiting right outside.

"You're feeling better." It wasn't a question, so she didn't bother to answer it.

She was dying to sit down. Her legs trembled with the effort of supporting her weight. She noticed a tray of sandwiches covered with plastic and more water on a table by the window. He noticed the direction she looked.

"You can sit down and eat it right now, if—" he stopped, one brow slightly arched.

"You told me I had twenty-four hours." It was easy to keep her voice flat now. She didn't have the energy for inflection.

"You do, but you can choose not to wait." He put his hands in the pockets of his slacks, studying her in that impersonal way that would have unnerved her had she been less hammered.

"If I had a real choice, I'd go home," she said.

"None of us have real choices. We just think we do." He turned and walked toward the bed, stopped and looked at her. "This is the bed where your mother and I made love. If you get in it right now, if you choose to submit, you can eat after, drink all the water you're craving, shower and then sleep undisturbed for as long as you want."

"Or?" She knew there was an "or."

"Or you can spend the night in less comfortable accommodations. Trust me when I say you won't like them."

She did.

"It's the expedient thing to do. If Mistral were still alive, he'd understand. He'd probably even forgive. It's not as if your romance weren't expedient for both of you. Or did you think he really loved you?"

Dorothy looked at him. "No, I never thought he really loved me. But he would never do this. He would never, ever be what you are."

"And what is that?" He looked mildly amused.

"A dirty old man who wants something he hasn't earned the right to have."

That stung, she could tell.

"My mother came to you willingly, for whatever insane reason she may have had, that I'm sure she regrets now. What really sticks in your craw is that she left and never came back. So I'm guessing it wasn't that good for her. Not exactly incentive for me to crawl in that bed and give it a whirl, now is it?"

For just a moment, something flickered in his eyes. She'd hit home with something she said and it gave her a surge of strength and resolution that she desperately needed.

"I'll take that as a no, then," he said, his voice still even, but not as perfectly as before. "You have more stairs to climb."

He directed her out the door, down the hall and up another flight of stairs, and then another. She went passively, because she didn't want him touching her.

"We're here," he said, stopping at a door at the end of a narrow, somewhat shabby hall. "This is the attic." He unlocked the door and a wave of heat poured out on to them. "I'm afraid the air conditioning doesn't extend to up here."

It was late afternoon. Outside, as they passed windows, she'd noticed the shadows lengthening and the light turning gold. It meant the heat had had all day to build up under the rafters. But that wasn't the worst he had in mind.

He steered her toward a long, narrow box, held closed with a padlock. He took out a key and undid the lock, letting the side down to reveal an oddly lumpy floor surface.

"This is where you'll be spending your time until you make your decision. There is an air supply, but as I mentioned, no cooling. You can communicate with me, if at any time you wish to come to a new agreement. There is also surveillance inside, in case you had any thoughts of trying to get out."

He stood there looking at her with his dead gaze. Already she could feel the sweat starting again, minimally fueled by the bottle of water. As she stared into the narrow opening, it seemed to grow smaller and tighter and hotter.

He's trying to break you, she told herself. He knows if you sleep with him, he knows if you give in, that you can never go back to who you were. He knows you'll have lost your soul. He's clever, but you're strong. You can do this. You can take anything he can throw at you. Even death.

She stepped toward the dark square and started to stoop down, when he stopped her with a touch. She froze. What now?

"Two things." He studied her for a moment. "I believe you have recently come into some information about your father's death?"

Dorothy didn't have to pretend to be surprised. "What?"

His gaze narrowed slightly. "You're an excellent actress, but you see, I know the truth."

"And what truth would that be?"

"There were three conspirators. Bubba Joe Henry, myself, and . . . you."

Dorothy didn't have time to process anything but the part about her. She'd suspected it anyway. "Me? Why would I have wanted Magus dead?"

"He abandoned you as a child, then used you for his political purposes. No one had a better reason than you, my dear. I need to know where the evidence is. Does your mother have it?"

Dorothy shook her head wearily. "You can believe what you want. Clearly you will, no matter what I say."

She bent to climb in the box.

"I said there were two matters."

"Right. I was never that good with math."

His lips thinned. "Your dress."

"What about it?" Dorothy drew slightly away from him, her cuffed hands drawn up to her chest. The movement chafed the already reddened skin some more and her sweat burned into the sore areas.

"Take it off."

Her throat dried out. "Why?"

"Because I told you to. I won't make you take anything else off . . . yet. But if you don't take it off now, I'll cut all your clothes off. It's your choice."

"Your choices suck."

His expression didn't change. He did reach behind and pull a knife out of the back of his slacks.

She reached up and unbuttoned the front of her dress. "I can't get it off with my hands tied."

278

He studied the problem, then slid the blade of the knife up the sleeve, the steel wonderfully, awfully cold against her skin, and sliced the dress. He repeated it on the other sleeve and the dress fell into a soggy pile at her feet. All she had on now was a bra and panties. She covered her breasts with her hands, but kept her chin up. He could only demean her as much as she let him.

"Seen enough?" she asked him. When he nodded, she bent and crawled inside the box.

That's when she realized what a complete and utter psychopath he was. The floor was hard and lumpy, making it impossible for her to be comfortable in any position. The box was too low for her to sit up, forcing her down to the floor. The material he'd used was also abrasive to her exposed skin. And her sweating aggravated the abrasion and the pain as salt went into her scrapes.

And when he lifted the door back in place, the darkness inside was absolute. She couldn't even see her hands in front of her face. Sensory deprivation. Sleep deprivation. Dehydration. And the camera, Peeping Tom aspect.

He'd brought out the big guns.

All she had in her arsenal was a healthy dose of stubborn from both her parents. And the knowledge she only had to survive until noon tomorrow. Then she'd be dead. Because there was no way in hell she was ever giving into that horror of a man.

Unless . . . what if he didn't intend to kill her?

She managed to not whimper out loud, but she did curl into as much of a fetal position as the box would allow. Almost against her will, she found herself drifting into the blessed peace of sleep. But before sleep could completely claim her, bright lights flashed on, stabbing painfully deep into her eyes.

"I'm afraid I can't let you sleep yet, Dorothy. Let's talk some more about clarity and expediency. Because I think you've realized I can't let you choose death. I let your mother go, but I won't let you go. You'll never be able to leave. You can fight me for a while, but someday you're going to crawl out of the box and into that bed. You're going to share it with me when I want. How I want. Until I don't want you anymore. And then, only then, will you die."

He paused, as if to give her a chance to comment. When she couldn't, he went on, "Your only chance is to submit by choice. You need to embrace what's expedient and make me need you. Keep me wanting you. It's your only hope."

"Go to hell," she said.

The light shut off again. Darkness closed in around her, outside and in. Even though she couldn't afford to lose the moisture, she felt silent tears join the stream of sweat pouring down her face.

Chapter Eighteen

Titus got there so fast, Remy knew he hadn't left like he was supposed to, but it didn't matter right now. Nothing mattered but finding Dorothy. Whoever had written that note had been cruel and malignant, and he hadn't kept his word. He had tried to kill Remy anyway. There was something going on, some hidden agenda he couldn't see, but could sense.

When he'd filled Titus in on what had happened, he went to work. He needed to get hold of Kate, he realized. She needed to know. Titus had her cell phone number, thank goodness.

He filled her in, heard her inhale sharply. "You don't know who it might be, do you?" Remy asked, when she didn't say anything.

"No, of course not," she said.

So why don't I believe her, Remy wondered. "If you know something, Kate . . ."

"If I did, what could the police do without any evidence? What I know is just what I feel. Let me check something out."

"Let me come with you!"

"If you did, I wouldn't find anything. I need to do this alone. If I'm wrong . . ." She choked back a sob.

"I'll pray you're not," Remy said. "Please let me be your backup at least! Whoever did this is dangerous!"

But she'd already hung up. He considered telling Titus, but the bodyguard was shutting him out, too. He needed to get his head clear and think. *Think*. He knew the players. If it was one of them, he could figure out who was likely to do something like this. He could.

Darius kept up his campaign of dark, then light, then dark again for what seemed like an eternity. But the worst part was the campaign of words. The more exhausted she got, the more reasonable he sounded.

The heat eased some, so she figured it must be dark or close to it. Maybe long past it. She had no way to tell the passage of time. There were times, in the dark, when she couldn't tell up from down. There was only light, dark, his voice, and pain, so much pain.

After a while, she realized she needed to empty her bladder again. It seemed amazing that there was any fluid in her to discharge. The rough covering on the bottom of the box was slippery with her sweat and blood. Once, during a period of darkness, she tried to scrape her wrists against the surface, hoping to bleed to death, but she only managed to mangle them to a new level of pain.

As the time passed, the pain in her bladder built and built. Was he going to make her wet herself? When she couldn't stand it any longer, she broke the silence for the first time since she'd told him where to go.

"I need to use the bathroom."

There was silence. She didn't know why the thought of adding her urine to the mess she was lying in was somehow worse than anything else she'd experienced, but it was. It just was. And if he knew it, he'd just leave her.

Just when she thought she was going to have to let go, she heard him fumbling with the lock. The end slowly lowered, letting in the softer light from the overhead. So it was night.

"You can come out, Dorothy, but I should warn you, I'm now armed."

She pushed up, and backed her way out, humiliatingly aware now of her scanty attire. Her panties were transparent with sweat, except where stained by blood. She managed to turn around where she could see him, because she needed to rest before trying to stand up.

He was standing a short distance away, a pistol pointed at her.

"Go ahead and shoot," she said, wearily pushing her wet hair off her face.

"There's a bathroom one floor down."

She wasn't sure she would make it, but she still refused the hand he held out to her. She managed to get upright, down the stairs and into the bathroom before it was too late. He wouldn't let her close the door this time.

When she'd finished, he handed her half a bottle of water. Just enough to keep her alive. She wanted to throw it at him, but she couldn't. That shamed her, too.

He propped a shoulder against the doorjamb. His gaze seemed to hammer into her, leaving her no place to hide, even inside her own head.

He's not really in there, she reminded herself. He just wants you to feel that way. You can change how you feel. And amazingly, he was pushed back. Even that small victory heartened her.

"Your mother is coming to see me," he looked at his watch, "soon. I really can't let her live, you know. She's the only person who might figure out what I'm doing. Shall I bring her up to say good-bye? Or would you rather she doesn't see you like this?"

She wanted to lunge at him, but he could brush her off like a fly. She was out of the box for the moment. He'd be taking her back as soon as he finished tormenting her. She had to outthink him. She could do this.

"Why should I care what you do to her? She abandoned me and now I'm stuck here because she couldn't keep her legs together."

His thin lips curved into a slight, pleased smile. "That's expedient thinking. We're actually making progress. I'm very pleased. Perhaps when I've killed your mother, I'll give you a break from the box."

He curved his hand under her jaw and lifted her face up for scrutiny. She didn't have to work too hard to keep her expression dead and dispirited. She was far too close to collapse. This might be her only chance to stave off the inevitable.

His hand trailed down the side of her jaw to the strap of her bra. He pushed it down her arm as far as it could fall, exposing the top curve of her breast, all while his gaze bored into hers.

She just stared at him.

He reached across and pushed the other strap down.

Still she stared. Right at this moment, she could do what she had to. She hoped. In a deep, hidden place, she hoped and held on.

His gaze narrowed slightly. Now he hooked one finger on the inside of her panties and ran his finger around one side, then back around to the other.

She was such a mass of pain, she barely felt it.

He stepped back. "Very good. You've come a lot closer to clarity in such a short time. Do you know you've only been in there two hours? I'll confess, I thought you'd last longer than this. But I think you'll be ready by the time I'm through with your mother."

He indicated he would precede her to the stairs. She'd

hoped he would. Her shoulders rounded in defeat, she did the slow-step thing. As she reached the top landing, he asked her, "Do you suppose she'll sleep with me one last time, for old times' sake? Do you think she'd like to go out as she lived?"

Dorothy turned slowly, her face as dead as she could make it. He was standing on the step below her, putting them at eye level for the first time.

"When you're choking her to death, tell her thanks for nothing." Dorothy deliberately licked her lips. His gaze locked on her mouth like some sick homing beacon. She lifted her cuffed hands and brushed them against his chin. She stepped closer, as if she were going to kiss him. He shuddered at her touch, his eyes glazing in anticipation, his mouth parting for her. It was his first moment of inattention to clarity.

Time to get really expedient. She gathered up the sides of his shirt, while still tracing the outline of her lips with her tongue. When she had a good grip, she jerked her knee up into his groin. She had a feeling it would hurt a lot worse when aroused. She hoped it would.

First indications were that she was right. It looked like it hurt. A lot. Air woofed out of his lungs. He wasn't down yet, though. Which made him still dangerous.

She did the next expedient thing, jerking her cuffed hands up. They connected with his chin, throwing him backwards.

He might still have recovered, if he hadn't been standing on the stairs. He was, so he didn't. Being a tall man, he had a long way to fall. He also had enough momentum to do one tail over head to the landing.

She hoped each contact with stairs and walls was as painful as it looked.

"How's that for expedience?" She was panting from the effort it had cost her fragile, remaining resources. She sagged against the wall, studying him cautiously. He didn't move. She eased down the stairs, pausing on each one for signs of movement. He'd dropped the gun, so she picked it up.

She prodded him with a toe, then cautiously reached down and touched his throat. He still had a pulse. A pity. She patted his pockets until she found the key to the cuffs and got them off. Feeling more in control, she eased past him, and tried a couple of doors before she found a bedroom. There was a throw at the foot of the bed. She put the gun down, grabbed it and wrapped it around her like a sarong. She picked the gun back up and turned around.

Darius was standing in the doorway. He was using the doorjamb to steady himself, but he was upright again.

She pointed the gun at him. She needed both hands to keep it up and steady.

He smiled. "Killing is easy, Dorothy. But it changes you. Once you've tried it, it's hard to stop. You should pull the trigger, though. It's the expedient thing to do. So even if you kill me, I win."

"I don't have to listen to you anymore. I have the gun now."

"The gun is only the instrument. What you have now is the power, Dorothy. The power of life and death. I told you I could get you to kill for me. Didn't I?"

She drew breath, but it broke on a sob. "If you touch me, I'll kill you!"

"You'll have to kill me then, because I am going to touch you. You started it on the stairs and now we'll finish it. For today."

He started toward her. She stepped back. "I will shoot you."

286

"I don't think you will."

"She might not, but I will," Emma said from the doorway. The gun she held didn't shake or wobble. Her eyes were fierce and determined. "He's lying to you, Dorothy. Yes, killing does change you, but not into him."

Darius half-turned to assess this new threat. "And how would you know, Emma? Who have you killed lately?"

"Bubba Joe Henry, actually. For pretty much the same reason I'm going to kill you now."

For the first time, Darius's calm showed a crack.

He didn't think I'd do it, Dorothy realized. He felt safe, but now he doesn't. She could tell he was considering how to neutralize Emma. If he got his hands on her, he might succeed, she thought, remembering their strength.

He clearly didn't consider her a real threat. She padded forward, raising the gun as she went. Saw his muscles bunch to pounce and brought the gun down on the base of his skull with all the strength she had left in her body.

He went down like a felled tree. Dorothy grabbed the bedpost.

"There are handcuffs in the hall."

Emma nodded, disappeared briefly. When she'd secured him, she stood up, facing Dorothy across the body of their fallen enemy.

"There's so much I need to explain to you—" Emma began.

Dorothy shook her head, as tears welled up in her eyes again. She was amazed she had any left. "Mom?"

Emma ran to her, her arms closing around Dorothy just as her knees finally gave out. They both sank to the ground. Dorothy laid her head on Emma's shoulder and sighed with relief.

"There, there, baby. It's going to be all right."

Chapter Nineteen

Dorothy knew she needed to move, but it was the first time in a long time she'd felt at home. She probably should be angry with Emma, but she couldn't summon the energy or the inclination. Whatever had happened in the past, neither of them were the same people they'd been. It wasn't, she thought wryly, expedient.

Emma stirred slightly.

"Not yet," Dorothy murmured, inhaling her mother's scent.

"I'm just getting my cell phone. We need to call Remy and the police."

Dorothy froze, and then slowly pushed back from Emma. "Remy? Isn't he dead?"

"It was a near thing, but no, baby, he's not dead."

Dorothy couldn't speak. It was too much to absorb after everything that had happened. It hadn't even been twenty-four hours, but everything felt different. She was different. How different, she'd have to find out. Distantly she heard Emma talking to him. Remy. Alive. Coming here. Seeing her like this? Okay, it was shallow, but she'd been deep, very deep. Shallow looked pretty good right now.

"I need to get cleaned up. I don't want him to see me like this."

Emma smiled tenderly. "Now I know you are going to be all right. But, baby, you can't. You're evidence." She hesitated. "Dorothy, did he rape you?"

Dorothy shook her head. "He was going to, but it wasn't

expedient yet." She was quiet a moment. "He was going to kill you."

"He was going to try." She squeezed Dorothy's hand and stroked her hair. "I knew he had you. As soon as I heard, I knew it was him."

"He knew you knew. I had to pretend like I didn't care. I had to pretend I was giving in." Dorothy shuddered, as the enormity of what had just happened swept over her. Then she couldn't stop shuddering.

Emma started to pull away.

"Don't leave." Dorothy looked at her mother, her teeth chattering.

"You're in shock, baby. I'm just getting a blanket." She stared at her directly. "I'm not going to leave you right now." She hesitated. "I'm so sorry."

Dorothy managed a shaky smile. "Families forgive each other, Mom."

She snuggled into the blanket, Emma wrapped around her. "Can we get away from him?"

"Of course!"

Emma helped her to stand, and with her arm around Dorothy's waist, they made their way downstairs. Dorothy didn't want to go into any of his rooms, so they sat huddled together on the stairs with the front door open, listening to the wail of approaching sirens.

Remy got there first. He stopped in the doorway when he saw them, unable to hide his shock.

Dorothy gave him a crooked smile. She felt more self-conscious at him seeing her like this than Darius. "Sorry about the rally."

Remy said something rude and to the point about the rally, then gathered her up in his arms, and just held her. She couldn't talk. He didn't seem able to, either. There was so much she wanted to say, but it would violate their deal. Of course he was shocked. Who wouldn't be? It didn't mean anything, other than that he was a nice man. With her cheek against his heart, she smiled at her mom.

"There's something you need to know," Dorothy said.

"It can wait," Remy said.

"No, it can't," Dorothy said. "You need to know that Kate isn't my aunt."

She felt Remy look at Emma. "You're not."

"No, I'm her mother, Emma Merlinn. Obviously I have a lot to explain, but now isn't the time."

That got his attention. Dorothy could feel the change in his body as he processed this.

"What do you want me to tell the police, Dorothy?"

Dorothy looked at Remy. "What do you think?"

He was quiet a moment, as the siren sounds drew closer. "What you tell people is your call, Emma, but in my opinion, secrets always come out. The truth is always the best policy."

"The truth isn't pretty," Emma said. "It may impact your run for governor."

"I'd rather lose on the truth than win with a lie," he said firmly.

"Good for you," Emma said. "I can see why Magus liked you."

That was all they had time for. The police arrived, sweeping into the house and pulling them apart. After finding out the main facts, they headed upstairs with their guns drawn. They came down again rather quickly.

"He's not up there," the older cop said.

"All we found were these," his partner said, holding up the cuffs.

Dorothy looked at Emma, who came quickly to her side

290

and grabbed her hand.

"He's not going to come after you, baby. It's not expedient. Because if he does, he'll go to jail."

"We need to get your statement," the older cop said.

"She's going to give you a bare outline," Remy said, "and then she's going to the emergency room."

Dorothy shook her head. "I want to go home. I'm all right."

The cop looked at her kindly. "I'm afraid you'll need to have a forensic examination, miss, but we'll try to get through this as easily as we can. Let's start with what we don't know. We know you got a note during the rally . . ."

Dorothy took it from there, outlining the basics of what Darius did. Remy had hold of one hand, her mother the other. They communicated their horror by painful squeezes of hands. She didn't mind. It helped keep her grounded in the present, not sucked back into the horror.

"He told me he killed Suzanne Henry," Dorothy said.

The two cops exchanged looks. "Did he say why?"

"He said she made him want her. He couldn't allow that."

"Did he mention her husband?"

Dorothy felt Emma's grip get tense. "He said men weren't as interesting to kill, but no, he didn't say he killed Bubba Joe Henry. I can see him doing it, though. He'd think it was the expedient thing to do. He liked to break things to me in pieces, not all at once. And I didn't ask. He wasn't exactly at the forefront of my mind at the time."

Maybe that wasn't the whole truth, but she was not going to point the cops toward her mother when she didn't *know* Emma had killed Bubba Joe. And after what had just happened to her, if Emma had killed him, well, it was justice too long delayed.

When she finished with the bare outlines of her experience, both men went upstairs to examine the box she'd been held captive in. The crime scene people also arrived and were directed upstairs. An ambulance arrived. When the blanket was peeled back to expose her raw, scraped skin, Remy's hands curled into lethal-looking fists.

"I'm riding in the ambulance with her," he told Emma, his tone not allowing for argument as he handed her his keys.

Truth be told, she was glad. She felt safer with Remy, knowing that Darius was still out there somewhere. When she was more rested, she'd have to deal with how to manage her life again, but for now, she just wanted to hide. She'd been awake for so many hours. With Remy watching over her, she could finally sleep . . . She closed her eyes and found Darius waiting inside her head. She tried to pull out, but was pulled back into the nightmare . . .

Remy looked across the stretcher Dorothy lay on, to Emma. He needed to absorb her new identity, but there wasn't time right now.

"Take care of her, Remy," Emma said.

He nodded, waited for them to load her in the back of the ambulance, before climbing in and taking a seat out of the way of the technician. The other climbed into the driver's seat. Dorothy's eyes fluttered open.

"My first ambulance ride," she murmured sleepily.

"Mine, too." Remy said, taking her hand. She seemed smaller and more fragile than before. There were scrapes on her face from her captivity and her wrists were raw and scored from the handcuffs. She was going to bear the physical scars of what happened for a while, but what worried him more were the emotional scars. Just the bare recital of facts was horrifying beyond comprehension, but the devil was in the details that would emerge later. To give fuel to his worry, she began to shift restlessly, as if her sleep weren't peaceful. He could just imagine what face was troubling it.

He took her hand. "Dorothy." His voice pulled her out of her restless sleep, thank goodness.

When they decided to kick the anthill of the past, he sure as hell hadn't counted on this. Guilt engulfed him in a bitter tide. He should never have let her do this. He'd convinced himself they could manage events. His arrogance, his lust for political power had resulted in this.

He was tortured with thoughts of how she'd looked the first time he saw her, and unable to look away from how she looked now. Battered and exhausted, and rescued by her mother, not by the man who claimed to love her. The man who'd conspired to send her bodyguard away.

He had no right to even think it. He'd let her down in every way he could. He didn't deserve her and he sure didn't deserve to be governor of anything. Both the state and this woman deserved better.

Even as the bitter thoughts assailed him, he held on to her hand. He couldn't let go. It felt so right clutching his. Amazingly, a small smile curved her chapped lips. He lifted her hand to his lips and whispered against them, "I'm so sorry."

Her lashes lifted. "No guilt trips allowed in this vehicle, Remy Mistral."

Her voice was still raspy, the bruises on her slender throat mute testimony to why.

"If only . . ." He stopped, because there were too many of them to list.

"I'm tired of them. That's all I thought about earlier." She sighed. "I thought you were dead. I'm glad you're not.

Talk about a guilt trip." She smiled at him and it turned into a yawn. "I didn't know you could be this tired."

"Try to rest," Remy said gruffly. He couldn't stop himself from kissing her hand.

Her head turned slightly away from him. "Yeah, sure."

"Dorothy?" Remy waited until she looked at him. "Look at me. Put my face in your head. Or your mom's. Don't give him the power. Take it back."

"I think I'm too tired."

"Right now is when you need to do it the most. He wanted to steal your peace, your rest, your willpower. Right now, you have to dig deep and push him out. It's the first step in getting your life back." He didn't know how he knew it, but in his gut he knew it was true. "Remember Scarlet O'Hara? Deal with it tomorrow. In Oz."

She smiled slightly. "You're mixing your novels."

He leaned over and smoothed her hair back from her face. It wasn't soft and silky, it was stiff with sweat and possibly blood and she'd never been more beautiful. He'd never loved her more than at the moment. He couldn't tell her. All he could do was try to shore up her strength enough to get her past this first hurdle. It was pitifully little, but it was something.

"Please don't tell me it's expedient," she whispered.

"I'll try to never use that word in conversation with you."

She stared up at him for a long time, before slowly nodding. She sighed, but the sound was stronger. She slowly closed her eyes. When her breathing evened out, he could tell her sleep was finally peaceful.

With his feet braced against the ambulance's movement, he rested his forehead on her hand, for the moment letting himself just be grateful she was back.

* * * * *

Emma watched the ambulance leave, then turned and went back inside the house. Her heart, her soul wanted to follow her daughter, but Remy's words about truth were echoing in her head. She wished so much that she could talk to Henry. Everything had seemed so clear when she went to Bubba Joe's house that night. He was a threat to Dorothy now. He'd raped her and gotten away with it.

She sank onto the stairs as crime scene activity went on around her. Darius was right. It was very easy to kill. Too easy. If Dorothy hadn't knocked Darius out, he'd be dead right now. The world would be better for it. She was the only one who truly knew what Dorothy had gone through here. Even the telling wouldn't communicate the full horror she'd experienced.

So why was she so relieved she hadn't killed him? He was still out there, might still be a threat to them both. He might be able to convince himself he only acted out of expediency, but she knew how easy it was to convince yourself that what you wanted was expedient.

She'd felt only satisfaction when she'd looked down at Bubba Joe's body. Today, she felt shame. She didn't want to leave Dorothy just when they'd found each other, but she was no mastermind criminal. There was a chance the police would find evidence linking her to the crime. She wouldn't put it past Darius to tip them off anonymously. He wouldn't like the expediency with which he'd been taken out of the game.

If she'd killed Bubba Joe twenty-nine years ago, they'd call it self-defense, but now it would be first-degree murder. She wouldn't be able to escape jail time.

And still she wanted to tell the truth.

Truth. It had been missing in her life for so long. She

wanted to be cleansed of her past, finally and completely cleansed. She was weary of carrying the burden of all her secrets, of all her mistakes, of all her sins of omission and commission.

And she wanted to see Henry one more time, but if she did, she wouldn't have the courage to do it. Truth was hard, at least in the beginning. Lies were harder in the long haul.

Dorothy had forgiven her so freely. It was astounding. Out of the violence of the day, there'd been no room for it, she supposed. If only she could forgive herself now. She almost wished Darius had succeeded in killing her. She had a feeling that she'd never been destined to live in peace, well, except during periods of amnesia. She smiled wryly.

She sighed and stood up, turning into Darius's library. It was probably the only empty room in the house at the moment. She sat at the desk, found paper and pen and wrote the truth as she knew it, one to each person who needed to know it. She addressed each separately, but put them in one envelope that she sealed and addressed to Dorothy. She looked at her cell phone. She wanted to hear Henry's voice so bad, it was a physical ache around her heart. But in that direction lay weakness. She needed to be strong for once in her life. She laid the cell phone on top of the letter and left both in the center of the desk. She was sure someone would find them eventually.

She stood up and went outside. "I'm going to the hospital now," she told the uniformed cop standing guard outside. "Mr. Mistral gave me his keys so I could bring his car, but I need to take my car. Could you have someone drive it over there for him?"

The cop nodded, accepted the keys and let her go.

She unlocked her rental car and climbed in, started the

engine and pulled away from the house, turning in the opposite direction of the hospital. She'd told the truth. Now she would find peace.

A stop sign forced her to stop. As she started to release the brake, the cool barrel of a pistol pressed against her temple.

"Where are you going, Emma?" Titus whispered, with his lips against her ear.

Chapter Twenty

Remy stayed with Dorothy all the way to her room. She'd drifted in and out of wakefulness, depending on what they needed from her. She was exhausted and dehydrated, but would recover, was the general consensus. Following the forensic exam, she was finally allowed to clean up, then collapse in the hospital bed with a sedative to ensure she got some rest.

As he sat in the chair by her bed, he found his own lack of sleep trying to catch up with him. Because Darius was still at large, there were cops all over this floor of the hospital, but Remy still fought sleep. It was illogical, but he still felt like he should stay alert. To ensure it, he chose the chair instead of the recliner in the corner, but when his head fell forward for the third time, he realized he needed some help.

He opened the door. The cop outside turned immediately. He was young and eager, Remy noted.

"Could you sit with Miss Merlinn while I track down some coffee? I'll bring some for you, too."

With the aid of his radio, he consulted with other members of the detail, and then nodded briskly.

"No one gets in this room, but me or hospital staff," Remy said. "Is that clear? She's not to be disturbed for any reason."

The cop nodded sharply, but changed places with him. Remy was partway down the hall when the elevator ahead of him opened, disgorging staff and Higgins, the detective, who'd been at the house.

"I need to speak with her," he said apologetically.

Remy shook his head. "It's not possible. She's been sedated. Can't it wait until tomorrow?"

He shook his head. "I found this back at Smith's house."

He held out an envelope with Dorothy's name written on the front.

"And this." In his other hand was a cell phone. "Isn't this her mother's cell phone?"

Remy looked at it, and then shrugged tiredly. "It could be, I suppose." He was too tired to figure this out. "Let's find some coffee. I can't think clearly anymore."

Downstairs in the cafeteria, with coffee and food in front of them, Remy took the envelope, turning it over in his hand. "Do you think this is urgent, detective?"

Higgins hesitated, before nodding slowly. "I'll be frank with you, Mistral. It's my belief that Mrs. Needham killed Bubba Joe Henry, though it's only a gut belief. I have no proof yet. Do you know where she is?"

Remy shook his head. Now that he thought about it, it was odd she hadn't turned up at the hospital yet. He'd been so focused on Dorothy, he hadn't noticed. He looked at the letter.

"I'll tell you what, I'll open it and if there's anything of interest to you, we'll wake up Dorothy and get her permission to give it to you. Fair?"

Higgins hesitated. "Fair enough."

Remy ran his finger along the flap and pulled out the contents. There were three folded sheets inside, each taped shut. One was addressed to Dorothy, one to Titus and the other to . . .

Remy looked up. "This one is addressed to you, Higgins." He handed it to him. Dorothy's letter he returned to the envelope. The note to Titus was puzzling. Why would Emma be writing to Titus?

Higgins looked up. "This is a confession to the murder of Bubba Joe Henry." He stood up. "I'm going to have to get on this." He hesitated again. "Did she seem like the kind of person to commit suicide?"

Remy shook his head. "I don't know. She told us she'd had some kind of breakdown ten years ago and suffered some memory loss at the time. That's why she didn't come to see Dorothy before."

"Did you believe her?"

"More now than I did at first," Remy said. "Why do you think she confessed now? If you had no proof—"

"She says it was something you said about the truth that made her realize it had to be done. Do you know what she meant by that?"

Remy nodded. "She assumed her sister's identity almost thirty years ago. Before you arrived . . . we talked about not disclosing that she was really Emma Merlinn. She was concerned that her past might affect my campaign."

"And you went with the truth." Higgins nodded his approval. "You've got my vote, Mistral."

Remy smiled crookedly. "Thanks. Right now, I'm more concerned about my fiancée and how this will affect her recovery."

"I understand." He looked awkward. "I'll leave her phone with you. She mentions someone telling her husband?"

Remy nodded, but when he was left alone, he found himself looking at the note to Titus. Where was Titus? Why hadn't he come to the hospital to see Dorothy yet? This might not be his finest hour of the day, but what the hell. He carefully lifted the tape and unfolded the letter.

Dear Titus,

There's so much to say and no time to say it. You were my friend and my lover and I know I let you down. I'm so sorry. Remy said something today about the truth. I don't know who said it first, but I've been thinking about that phrase, you shall know the truth and the truth shall set you free. I need to be free, so here's the truth. I hope it will set you free of the past, too.

I always cared about you, but I never loved you. I wasn't capable of it back then and now I love my husband. I slept with you the other night to keep you quiet. Because I felt I owed you something for the pain I'd caused. I betrayed my husband, myself and you when I did that. I convinced myself I was doing it for Dorothy, but it was for me, so I could get to know her. I didn't want her to hate me.

And I lied to you about Dorothy. She isn't your daughter. She is Magus's flesh and blood. There is no doubt about that. I made sure I protected myself when I strayed. The only reason Magus had doubts about her paternity is because I wanted to hurt him.

I've done so much damage to so many people, I don't expect to be forgiven, but I wanted you to know the truth so that you could move on with your life. I wrote to Henry before I went to see Darius, because I knew things might not go well. I'm weary of the burden of lies and mistakes I've carried for so long. You won't see me again. I don't want Dorothy to have to visit me in prison. She's suffered enough for my mistakes.

I have a last request that you don't have to honor, but I hope you will for old times' sake. Please let Dorothy go. I think she needed you, but now she needs Remy more.

Your old friend, Emma

Remy sat back. Titus and Emma. And Titus had believed that Dorothy was his *daughter*. Well, that explained the overly protective attitude that had so annoyed Remy. He needed to be told. For some reason it felt important that Titus know right away. He thought for a moment, then opened the letter to Dorothy and read it, too. He downed his coffee, then dragged himself out of the chair and went upstairs. Dorothy was still sleeping deeply. While he was gone, they'd assigned a policewoman to sit in her room with her.

Now that she'd had a chance to clean up, each bruise and scrape stood out in sharp relief against her unnaturally pale skin. He stared down at her, noting each wound inflicted on her by that bastard. He'd failed to protect her. That ate at him like acid. He'd been so focused on what he wanted, on his grand ideals, and this was the result.

Hadn't she dealt with enough? Emma may have believed she was freeing her from the past, but the truth was, she was just running out on her daughter again, leaving her more crap to deal with. And is that what he was going to do, too, he wondered? All his feelings about letting her down and how he shouldn't have used her, weren't they just rationalizations because he was afraid of how he felt about her? If he had any guts, he'd tell her he loved her, and that he wanted their engagement to be real and honest. He should tell her that he'd give up his political career for her if she wanted. If he had half her courage, he'd risk rejection. If he really loved her, he should give it to her as a gift, with no strings attached.

He wanted to be with her when she read the letter, but he also didn't want to keep it from her. After a moment, he laid it on the table by the bed.

He gave the officer his cell number. "Call me if she

wakes up. And tell her I'll be back. I need to see someone."

He hated like hell to leave her, but he needed to clear the decks with Titus first. He didn't like him, but he needed to know about Emma. He kissed her forehead gently and made himself leave. When she woke, she'd want answers. Maybe he could at least have some for her.

Exhaustion dragged at him as he drove to Oz. He took it slow and was surprised when he made it safely. Inside, he found the house oddly deserted. Where was all the staff? He made his way to the security room and found it shut down. He sat down and turned the cameras on, scanning room after room. It made no sense, but he was tired, so maybe nothing could.

He went back to the living room and sat down to wait. At some point, he drifted into sleep.

Dorothy came awake suddenly and completely, with her head full of questions needing answers. She hurt all over and she was ravenously hungry, but she felt like herself again. That awful, breakable feeling was gone. She struggled into a sitting position and found herself facing a policewoman.

"Where's Remy Mistral?" Okay, admit that she expected to find him still here.

"He had something urgent to do, someone to see, he said. He wants you to call when you wake," she said. "And he left that letter for you. He said you'd understand when you read it."

Dorothy picked up the indicated item and opened it, but it wasn't from Remy. It was from her mom.

My dear girl,
   I am humbled and amazed at your kindness to me,

considering the great wrongs I have done you in the past. What your Remy said about truth, it keeps echoing in my head, that and that saying about the truth setting you free. All I've done, all the mistakes I've made and the wrong things I've done, they press on me like a mountain. I've hurt the people I finally learned to care about, pretending I was doing it for them, when it was just about my own fear.

You guessed that I killed Bubba Joe. I could tell. You don't need the burden of that knowledge on your shoulders. Believe me, it isn't worth it. I've written a letter to that detective, confessing to the crime.

There's more you need to know. Titus has believed for all these years that he was really your father. He isn't, but I let him believe it so he wouldn't expose me to you as the fraud I am. I've wounded him, too. The only thing I ever did right was make sure Magus was your father. And then I took you away from him.

I am so sorry for what I've done. Magus and I both let you down. I know you think you've forgiven me back at Darius's house, but you didn't know all of it then. If you can't forgive me, that's all right. I can't forgive myself. Someday I hope that you'll meet my Henry. He's a wonderful man. I was lucky to have someone like him in my life. He's the one who taught me how to love someone other than myself. I've written him a separate letter, but please let him know that I'm gone. He'll need comfort when he knows the truth as well.

I'm glad you have your Remy to rely on right now. He's a good man and one day he may be a great man, if he keeps clinging to the truth in his life.

I wish I could tell you that I always loved you, but that would be a lie. I didn't know how to love for so many years. I do love you now, it is the greatest pain of all to leave you again. But I don't deserve to associate with you when I tell you my last, awful truth. I didn't conspire in Magus's death, but I did know it was going to happen and I did nothing to stop it. I was angry with him when he wouldn't give me money or let me talk to you. When you were hurt, too, that's what sent me over the edge. The guilt was awful. Verrol Vance gave me the proof that Bubba Joe was involved. I don't know how he knew about what Bubba Joe did to me, but he did. The only person I ever told was Helene, Magus's housekeeper. She was my only friend during that awful time. I promised him I wouldn't use it until he was out of jail. I didn't know Darius was also involved, though I did wonder.

I hope that in some way, you can be set free of the past and move on to have a wonderful, happy life. I'm sorry for what I've done and for my failure to eliminate Darius. I'm so proud of the person you've become. Kate did a wonderful job of being your mother. She deserves the title, not me, though it was sweet to my ears. Be happy, my darling girl.

Dorothy realized tears were streaming down her face.

"Should I call a nurse or your fiancé?" the officer asked her, worriedly.

Dorothy looked at her. "I need to get home. Now."

Everyone told her why she shouldn't go, but it was as if she was possessed by the spirit of Magus and erased objections as they arose. In less than half an hour, she was in a patrol car heading toward Oz. At the gate, no one responded. She climbed out of the car.

"What are you going to do?" the officer asked, alarmed.

"I'm going over the wall," she said with a grin. "No one

keeps Dorothy out of Oz. I'll open the gate for you when I'm inside."

"I'm not supposed to let you out of my sight!"

But she was already reaching up for the iron crossbar of the gate.

Remy woke with a start and looked at his watch. He'd been asleep all night.

"Damn." He rubbed his face and then looked around. That's when he saw Titus sitting across from him, watching him expressionlessly. After a long exchange of looks, Remy said, "Good morning."

"Emma's dead," Titus said flatly.

Remy looked down for a moment, then back up. He stood up and produced the letter. "She left you this."

Titus took the letter, but didn't open it.

"I tried to see Dorothy. They wouldn't let me."

"No one can see her. They gave her something to help her sleep, but she's fine. I expect they'll release her today or tomorrow."

His pale lashes lifted. "If I'd been here, this wouldn't have happened."

Remy met his gaze squarely. "No, I don't think it would have. But he wouldn't have given up, either. He'd have waited for a moment of distraction."

Titus looked down at the letter. "I'd like to be alone."

"I know you don't like me, but you shouldn't be alone right now." He had a feeling he was forgetting something important . . . Helene Terry! She was coming over today to talk to them. Titus still didn't move. Fine. He'd tried. "I'm going to go shower. I've got an appointment this morning. Could you let her in? Everyone seems to be AWOL."

"I sent them home," Titus said.

"Well, could you let her in or do I need to do it?"

There was a long pause, during which Remy wondered if Titus had even heard him, and then he slowly nodded.

Remy raced through his shower, anxious, but not sure why. He made a quick call to the hospital, but the line was busy. Downstairs, he found Helene had just arrived. She and Titus were awkwardly facing each other in the hall. Remy hurried the rest of the way down the stairs to join them, feeling unaccountably anxious.

Helene was a tall, gray-haired woman with a lot of presence and an air of quiet charm. He noticed that she clutched her purse to her chest, as if it were of immense importance. Despite his worries, he felt a shiver of excitement.

"Thanks for coming over, Mrs. Tierry," Remy said. "I supposed you've heard about Dorothy? She hasn't been released from the hospital yet."

"I can come back another day," she said, composed, but still uneasy.

"I think Dorothy would prefer to have the situation resolved, if at all possible, ma'am, if you would consent to talk to me as her representative."

She studied him for a long moment, and then slowly nodded. He indicated the living room, followed her through the double doors, then slowly, but deliberately, closed them in Titus's face.

"Please have a seat. Can I get you anything to drink?"

She shook her head, but seemed to relax a bit. After a moment, she straightened her back and looked at him, her chin up. "You know, don't you?"

"That Verrol Vance was your son? Yes, we do," he said gently. He sat down opposite her, trying to keep his expression neutral.

She looked away. "I should have come sooner, but he

307

was . . . my son. I made him a promise, even though it shamed me."

"He gave you his evidence against the men who hired him, didn't he?"

She nodded. "He told me if I gave it to anyone, Vonda would be killed. When she was murdered, I knew I had to send it to the police. He asked me to wait a week. He never said why."

"May I see it?" Remy asked.

She nodded again and slowly opened her purse. Inside was a packet of papers, which she handed to him.

"May I look?" Remy asked. Another nod gave him permission to look at them. He unsealed the package and pulled out the cover letter, rapidly scanning the words. They knew Bubba Joe had been involved and suspected Darius Smith. Interestingly, Bozo wasn't. The third man wasn't named. He looked up. "He mentions a third man . . ."

The door opened. Titus stood there, holding a gun. It was pointing at them.

"I'll take that," he said.

Chapter Twenty-one

"Why don't we let Helene go and we'll talk about this," Remy said, cursing himself for not suspecting something like this, once he knew Titus had been involved with Emma as well.

"Put it on the table, then both of you back off," Titus repeated. There was a look in his eyes, a blankness to them, as if Remy and Helene were barely visible to him. He seemed to be focused somewhere else, somewhere deeper, and very dark. When Remy didn't move immediately, Titus turned the gun toward Helene.

Cursing himself silently, Remy complied, helping Helene to the corner and standing in front of her. It wasn't much, but for now it was all he could do for her. Titus took the packet and retreated to the farthest table from them. He started reading it, pausing often to keep them at bay.

Finally he set the papers down, a look of disbelief on his face. "He didn't name me." He looked at Remy. "He didn't mention me at all. I did it all for nothing."

"All?" Remy asked, with some idea of keeping him talking.

"Verrol. That lawyer, Barnes." His voice changed slightly. "Vonda. And her friend. I can't remember her name. The neighbor."

"Leda Tasker," Remy said. And they'd just handed her over to him. They told her she'd be safe with them and then handed her over to a killer. He felt Helene's hand on his arm, as if she sensed how hard it was to not hurl himself at

Titus. "It was you in the library. You hit me. Your bugs and tracking device. You've been listening to everything we've said and done."

"Not everything," he said, "or I'd have known about her—"

". . . and killed her already?" Remy looked at him in disgust. "Is there anyone you wouldn't kill?"

"I had to keep Dorothy from finding out . . ." he trailed off.

". . . that you were involved in Magus's death. Why did you do it? You were his bodyguard. It was your job to protect him."

"It was my job to protect *Dorothy*. She was my daughter, not his! And he was doing the same thing to her that he did to Emma. *Emma*." His body drooped and he shuddered. "I loved her, you know."

There was such grief in the way he said it that the words just popped out. "You killed her, too, didn't you?"

His head came up slowly, his gaze distant. He nodded. "She lied to me. She said . . ."

". . . that Dorothy wasn't your daughter?"

Titus nodded. "She wanted to die anyway. She killed Bubba Joe, you know. We don't need her, Dorothy and I. We have each other."

"She'll hate you when she finds out what you've done," Remy said.

"She's not going to find out. Everyone will think Darius killed both of you and Emma, too."

Remy noticed he avoided looking directly at Helene. It was going to be a difficult kill for him. But how to use that information? There had to be a way to distract him and at least get Helene safely away.

"Helene doesn't deserve to die," Remy said. "She's done

nothing to you and you killed her son."

Titus shifted nervously, but said stubbornly, "What's got to be will be."

"Dorothy loves me and I love her," Remy said. "This will break her heart." He wished it were true.

"She'll get over you, just like she got over Magus. She'll have her answer with these papers and we'll put the past behind us, move forward again."

"And you'll have the money," Remy said. "Isn't that really what this was all about? You wanted the money so you could compete with Magus for Dorothy's affection. You've felt her pulling away from you, growing away from you and not needing you as much. Then she sent you away, but if we're all dead, you think she'll need you again."

Titus looked at him, his eyes burning with rage. He may have pushed him too far. The barrel of his automatic pointed at him. His finger started to tighten on the pull.

"But she won't, Titus. Now that I know the truth, it's over. I'll never need you again." Dorothy stood in the doorway to the room, her face white and shocked, her eyes filled with grief and disbelief.

"You forgave Emma. You even forgave Magus. Why not me?" Titus turned partway toward Dorothy. Now the gun pointed at her.

"Because you aren't sorry for what you've done," Dorothy said, shifting slightly so that Titus had to turn more toward her and away from Remy and Helene.

Remy looked at Helene, nodding for her to slip out one of the long, narrow windows. She nodded, and started edging toward the window.

"And now you're planning to kill the man I love and a dear, dear friend."

Remy waited until Helene was out of sight, before taking

a couple of steps toward Titus. He swung the gun back his way.

"Don't move. I'll shoot."

"I'll never, ever forgive you, Titus," Dorothy said, pulling his attention her way again. "If you cared about me at all, you wouldn't even think about doing something like this."

"Do you think I wanted to? Why did you have to go digging into the past? Why couldn't you leave it alone? Magus is dead. All you did was stir things up! Make me do . . . things. Awful things."

He rubbed his face with his free hand, but he was still too alert, too deadly. Remy used the moment to move a few steps closer. He nodded for Dorothy to get into the hall. She shook her head.

"You took my father and my mother from me."

"She was going to kill herself anyway and he wasn't your father! I am! I'm your father! Me! Emma loved me! She never loved him."

"But she didn't," Remy said, deciding it was time to get his attention again. "She wrote you a letter. That's why I came here last night, to give it to you. She wanted you to be free of the past, not bound by it. She wanted the lies to end."

"No. She's lying. She lied back then and she's lying now. Lying *bitch!*" He was moving, stepping from one foot to the other, making the gun waver between them, his hands clenching dangerously as he cursed her.

Dorothy took a step toward Titus. "Don't you understand, Titus? If you were . . . are my father, then you took yourself away from me by what you've done. You know me, probably better than anyone. Do you really think I would condone *murder?*"

He stared at her, his features twisted, his eyes tortured with doubt and rage.

"You didn't do it for me. You did it for yourself. All of it. If you really believed it was the right thing to do, you wouldn't have hidden it from me." Dorothy looked at him for one, desperate moment, then she said, "If you care about me at all, Titus, you'll leave now. I can't even bear to look at you."

For a moment, it seemed like sanity might return, but he shook it away, staring at her as if he couldn't believe what he was hearing. "You forgave Emma and she abandoned you! But you've got nothing for me, your own father?"

Dorothy frowned. "How could you know about that? You weren't there."

But Remy knew how.

"He had you bugged," Remy said. "Or Emma. Or both of you. How long were you going to let Dorothy suffer in that monster's hands, Titus? How long were you going to let him torture her, if you really believed she was your daughter?"

"I didn't . . . I wasn't . . ." But Remy noticed he couldn't look at her. He pointed the gun at Remy. "Shut up! Just shut up! I need to think!"

Tears were streaming down Dorothy's face now. "How could you listen to what he did to me and do nothing?"

Titus took a step toward her. "I didn't want to! But he was right. You needed to learn. You needed to understand that sometimes people have to do things. In case . . ."

". . . I found out? And then you were going to sweep in and rescue me? Accept my gratitude? Be the big hero so I'd like you *best* again? What kind of monster are you? I thought you were . . . kind and good and decent." Dorothy stared at him through her tears. "You *bastard!* If you really were my

313

father, you'd never have done that to me. *You're not my father.* I can prove you're not my father. Now get out of my house and out of my life! Get out!"

Remy saw the shift of focus in his eyes. He'd ceased to exist for Titus, but so had Dorothy. He pointed the gun at her heart, as Remy dove at him.

"You're an ungrateful bitch, just like your mother!"

The gun went off as Remy caught him midsection. They both crashed to the ground, rolling back and forth, a tangle of kicking legs and punching fists. He was smaller than Remy, but well-trained and desperate. Remy was desperate, too, for them to survive, for a chance to tell Dorothy he loved her.

Titus got his hands around Remy's throat, his thumbs driving for his backbone. Remy tried to pry his hands loose, as stars started spinning across his view. He dug his thumb into Titus's eye, and heaved his back up, flipping Titus over the top of his head. He rolled over and sprang to his feet, but Titus was already up. They both saw the gun and dived for it at the same time. Remy was a fraction of a second behind. Titus pulled clear, the gun in his hand, but the sound of a siren broke through his rage, turning it to panic.

"How did they know?"

"They brought me here," Dorothy said. "I opened the gate for them. I was worried when it wouldn't work. It's over. Give me the gun, Titus. At least you can be at peace."

Remy stepped in front of Dorothy, trying the human shield thing again as he felt an odd rush of cold air brush past him. Titus wasn't looking at them anymore. He was staring at a point beyond to their right, his eyes widening in horror.

"I was a better father to her than you were," he shrieked, then lifted the gun to his head and pulled the trigger.

Remy flinched away from the sight, trying to block it for Dorothy. He grabbed her and pushed them both around the corner into the hall.

"Are you all right?" he asked, clinging to her because he couldn't stop himself. He pushed her back, looking for wounds, feeling down her arms, and then grabbing her close again. He felt her nod. "Look, this isn't the time or the place. But the cops will be here in seconds and I don't know when we'll be alone again, so here it is. I love you. I know it breaks the deal, but I do. With all that's happened, I just thought you ought to know."

Dorothy lifted her head from his shoulder and looked at him, her eyes wide with wonder, but then she sort of flinched. "There's . . . stuff . . . on your face."

"Damn it, Dorothy—"

She put her hand over his mouth. "I'll just close my eyes." She did. "I love you, too."

He bent his head to kiss her, even achieved contact briefly, before the front door burst open.

Several hours later, Remy had washed the "stuff" off his face and the cops had been over this new crime scene with the magnifying glass and tweezers. All the evidence was in custody and silence was settling over the house again. They were sitting side by side on the couch in the sitting room that Helene said had been Emma's. Remy had his arm around her and Dorothy was happy to have it there.

"Is that jet of yours anywhere near?" Remy asked.

"Probably. Why?"

"Let's get on it, go to Vegas and get married by Elvis. I've always wanted to get married by Elvis."

Dorothy looked at him. "Always?"

"Well, at least for the last half-hour."

She relaxed against him again. "Okay."

Remy twisted around so he could see her face. "Really?"

"What's the point of having a jet at your beck and call if you can't use it to fly to Vegas and get married by Elvis?"

He chuckled. "True. You do realize he'll be a fake Elvis, don't you?"

Dorothy smiled at him. "Are you sure about that?"

"If you keep looking at me like that, I'm going to have to kiss you again and we have a jet to catch." He stood up. "Let's do this right." He grabbed her hands and pulled her up, holding her for a moment before stepping back. So much had been wrong in their lives, he wanted this to be right.

As they passed the room where Titus had killed himself, Dorothy paused by the crime scene tape, still blocking the doorway. "What do you think he saw, just before . . ."

Remy remembered that cold wind. Had Magus stepped in to save his daughter? Or had Titus's fevered mind just conjured him up? "I don't know."

Dorothy lifted her face, as if testing the atmosphere. "I used to feel him near me here, but I don't anymore. Oz is at peace, maybe for the first time. I think my parents are at peace with each other, too."

"For the first time?" Remy asked, with a half-teasing smile.

"Well, maybe the second. We know of at least one other time they got together effectively." She grinned at him.

Remy grinned back. "I was kind of hoping for some of that effective interaction myself, post Elvis, of course."

Her grin faded. "I love you, Remy Mistral."

He lightly touched her cheek, his heart contracting in his chest. "Are you ever going to call me plain Remy?"

She smiled the way she had his first day back in Oz. "I'd like to see how *effective* you are first."

About the Author

Award-winning novelist and screenwriter Pauline Baird Jones was born and raised in Wyoming, but currently calls Texas home—after an eighteen-year sojourn in Louisiana. Pauline's been a fictional killer since the first Gulf war. She claims it helps her to stay mellow.

"It's very cathartic," she asserts. "If someone annoys me, I just smile, then make plans to kill them in my next book." While people in her life might wonder if they've ever been her fictional victims, Pauline plans to take that information with her to the grave. Not even her husband of twenty-eight years knows, though he suspects he's been her victim more than once.

You can find out more about Pauline and her books at www.paulinebjones.com or e-mail her at pauline@paulineb jones.com.